ESPRESSO FOR TWO

Leading her upstairs, Sam flipped off the lights. His heart pounded as he led Brandi toward the bed. His fingers shook with emotion as he unbuttoned her sweater and eased it over her shoulders. He looked at her body as if seeing it for the first time and studied every ridge and curve. His hands slowly caressed her skin and fingered her hair. His lips traced gentle kisses along her neck and shoulders, down to her breasts, and along the flat surface of her stomach.

BOOK YOUR PLACE ON OUR WEBSITE AND MAKE THE ARABESQUE ROMANCE CONNECTION!

We've created a customized website just for our very special Arabesque readers, where you can get the inside scoop on everything that's going on with Arabesque romance novels.

When you come online, you'll have the exciting opportunity to:

- View covers of upcoming books

- Learn about our future publishing schedule (listed by publication month and author)

- Find out when your favorite authors will be visiting a city near you

- Search for and order backlist books

- Check out author bios and background information

- Send e-mail to your favorite authors

- Join us in weekly chats with authors, readers and other guests

- Get writing guidelines

- AND MUCH MORE!

Visit our website at
http://www.arabesquebooks.com

Espresso for Two

Courtni Wright

BET Publications, LLC
http://www.bet.com
http://www.arabesquebooks.com

ARABESQUE BOOKS are published by

BET Publications, LLC
c/o BET BOOKS
One BET Plaza
1900 W Place NE
Washington, DC 20018-1211

All Kensington Titles, Imprints, and Distributed Lines are available at special quantity discounts for bulk purchases for sales promotions, premiums, fund-raising, and educational or institutional use. Special book excerpts or customized printings can also be created to fit specific needs. For details, write or phone the office of the Kensington special sales manager: Kensington Publishing Corp., 850 Third Avenue, New York, NY 10022, attn: Special Sales Department, Phone: 1-800-221-2647.

First Printing: October 2004
- 10 9 8 7 6 5 4 3 2 1

Printed in the United States of America

Chapter 1

"Excuse me," Brandi Owens said as she eased her slender body through the Friday night crowd at Over the Rainbow Bookstore. Her short medium brown hair, soft honey-colored skin, sparkling hazel eyes, trim body, and warm personality seemed to draw people to her and her bookstore.

"Brandi, do you have the latest Eloise Greenfield book? I don't see it on the shelf and Mary has her heart set on reading it this weekend," Debra Morton asked as she and her daughter turned in Brandi's direction.

"It just arrived today, and I haven't had time to shelve it yet. I'll bring you a copy," Brandi replied, balancing the pile of rolled maps on top of the stack of oversized do-it-yourself manuals.

"Thanks. And bring out a copy of the latest installment of Maya Angelou's autobiography when you return, too, please," Debra added with a smile.

"I will. And you tell Mary that I said she'll love it," Brandi added as she continued to weave her way through the crowd.

"Mary nothing. It's for me! My daughter won't get her hands on it until I've finished the last page."

Debra laughed with an air of familiarity that all of Brandi's customers seemed to share.

Brandi continued to press through the crowd, stopping occasionally to offer suggestions or to retrieve a book from the top shelf. She had a steadfast rule that customers were not allowed to climb the library ladders propped along the edges of the old-fashioned bookshelves. She or one of her staffers always did that. At five feet nine she was able to reach many of the higher shelves without having to stand on the top rung of the ladder.

Reaching her desk in the shop's back room, Brandi gently dropped the maps and books among the clutter that perpetually covered her work space. With shipments arriving almost daily, she was always in the process of either cataloging and pricing new arrivals or ordering new stock. Since her staff consisted of only two employees, she did most of the day-to-day work herself before opening the shop in the morning or after closing at night. She was hands-on and loved every minute of her work. Unlike owners who just managed their bookstores, Brandi knew every title that came through the door and followed its progress from shipping to shopping bag.

Every morning as she walked the few blocks to work, Brandi Owens counted her blessings. She had a thriving bookstore, a wonderful home, good friends, and a big, fat, happy cat. She loved her Takoma Park neighborhood, on the border of the Washington, DC, and Maryland line, and the people who lived and worked there. Over the Rainbow was a thriving independent bookstore and a favorite hangout of D.C.'s black literary set. Nestled in a neighborhood of varied architecture, Takoma Park residents were a mix of high-level government officials, executives, successful business owners, doctors, teachers, and other professionals. Most were pillars of Washington's black establishment who had shunned the "Gold Coast" and upper Northwest with their pretensions. Brandi's clients were comfortable within themselves and enjoyed the life they led without feeling the need to flaunt their success.

After giving Debra Morton her books, Brandi shelved the others and returned to the cash register at the front of the cheerfully decorated store. The orange and red leaf cutouts on every table and ribbons dangling from the high ceiling added a fall seasonal touch to the deep pine bookcases and gleaming oak floor. Brandi loved the feel and smell of her bookstore. Potpourri added a spicy fragrance that mingled with the scents of customers' perfume and coffee. Strategically placed overstuffed furniture encouraged customers to linger and chat. As long as they didn't spill anything on the books, Brandi didn't mind that her customers sipped coffee purchased next door while browsing for the right book. She'd discovered they lingered longer if they had a cup of their favorite brew in their hands. And the longer they stayed in her shop, the more they bought.

Brandi loved chatting with her customers as much as she enjoyed selling books and tutoring children in the special sessions she arranged at the bookstore. Even the *ka-ching* of the cash register didn't give her the same satisfaction. She enjoyed being surrounded by people. Her regular customers called her by her first name, and she wouldn't have it any other way. She was not just the owner of Over the Rainbow, she was their neighbor and friend.

"Hi, Sam," Brandi said, looking up at the tall, handsome man wearing an apron that bore the name and logo of the gourmet coffee shop next door, Where Worlds Meet. "Did you find everything you wanted?"

"Thanks, Brandi. I sure did. What do I owe you?" Sam Carlson replied, taking change out of his wallet to cover the newspaper.

"Same as always, Sam. Nothing has changed except the headlines," Brandi replied with a chuckle as she held out her hand to collect the money.

"Good. That's part of the charm. I can come in here, find what I want, and leave without wasting time. See you later," Sam said as he slipped the newspaper under his arm and headed for the door. As usual, he did not linger.

"Night," Brandi called after him as she smiled at the next customer. Sam Carlson's image lingered a moment and then vanished from her mind.

Brandi and Sam had worked next door to one another, sharing a dividing wall and some of the same customers, for six years. Despite their longtime friendship, their conversations usually remained benignly the same almost every night. Occasionally, they might talk about news events or the weather, but they had never talked about their personal lives, although both were single and very much unattached. Sam was always in a hurry to get back to his coffee shop and Brandi was always in a hurry to get back to her customers.

Lately, however, Brandi had sensed a change in their relationship. A strange awkwardness had developed between them. Brandi felt giggly when she saw Sam and found it difficult to gaze into his eyes without feeling her stomach do flips. Sam seemed to shuffle his feet a bit more, too, when he was in the store. Putting aside the thought and chalking it up to overwork, Brandi remained detached despite her growing curiosity about her handsome neighbor.

"He lingered a little longer tonight," Susan, one of Brandi's assistants, said softly.

"It's all in your imagination," Brandi countered.

"If it is, it's in mine, too," Brad added with a grin.

Brad Campbell and Susan Douglas were seniors at Howard University who worked at the bookstore more for the contacts they made than for the money. Both could have earned more than Brandi could afford to pay them, but they wouldn't have met the influential folks who regularly dropped by the bookstore. Both were planning to go to law school after graduation, and had already been promised jobs by one of D.C.'s most important judges who was also one of Brandi's regular customers. The Honorable Cheryl Johnson had been so impressed with Brad and Susan that when she learned they were planning on law school, she offered them positions as legal assistants in her office.

"Your imaginations are working overtime again. You're worse than Mia Fernwood, and you know she can make nothing into something without really trying," Brandi said, laughing.

"Just because you've been hiding yourself from the world in this shop doesn't mean that the world hasn't noticed you," Susan replied. "You've spent too much time cataloging books. It's about time you started noticing more than bar codes."

"I told you that I'm not interested in a special relationship. I've been there, done that. I don't want the heartache again. I date sometimes. That's all I need for now," Brandi said firmly.

"You were in college. Times have changed. You've changed. It's time to try again. You might find the right man this time. The store's a big success and it doesn't require all of your time and energy anymore. It's time you built a life," Brad interjected.

"My life is my store, and I feel blessed to have it. I don't have time for any complications even if the temptation does present itself now and again," Brandi declared.

"Your friend Mia says that you're just afraid of being hurt again. You can't let one misstep stop you from taking the leap again. Besides, you can't snuggle up with inventory order forms," Susan added, wiping fingerprints from the shiny wood counter.

"I'm not afraid. I'm just not ready. When the time comes and the right man enters my life, I'll know it and act on it," Brandi insisted.

"If you don't get your head out of these books, how will you know?" Susan argued. "Mia says that she can't even get you to come to her dinner parties anymore. She's all but given up trying to fix you up with anyone."

"Mia has been in my business, personal and professional, since college. As a matter of fact, she introduced me to one of her clients just last week. He was a nice guy and very handsome," Brandi commented as she reviewed the day's tally.

"What happened?" Brad demanded.

"Nothing. He wasn't my type," Brandi replied absently.

"What is your type?" Susan demanded. "I want to know so if he enters the shop, I can throw a head-lock on him and hold him for you."

"This is silly," Brandi replied, trying to dodge the subject.

"Come on. Tell us," Brad demanded, blocking her way as she tried to leave the counter area.

After a long sigh Brandi replied, "He's very tall, mature, well built but not so athletic that all he thinks about is sports. He's independent and dedicated to his job. When he laughs, his eyes crinkle at the corners. He doesn't have to be in business for himself, but it helps. I'd like a man who has seen a bit of the world and taken time off from it. Experienced, I guess that's what I mean, but not jaded. There, are you happy now?" Brandi said, wistfully.

"Completely," Susan replied, "You've just described Sam." Looking from one to the other, Susan and Brad barely suppressed their smiles.

"I did not!" Brandi said.

"Oh, but you did," Brad chimed in.

"That's ridiculous. Sam's simply the owner of the shop next door and nothing more. There's nothing romantic between us. Neither of us has the time or interest. Ridiculous," Brandi sputtered.

"The woman doth protest too much," Brad teased, switching off the lights.

Minutes later as they waited outside on the sidewalk for her to lock the door, Susan said, "He certainly fits the description. The only thing you didn't mention was his apron."

"Good night. I don't want to continue this conversation. I'll see you in the morning," Brandi replied as she waved good night and started toward her house.

"What? No hot chocolate tonight? Sam'll think you're angry with him," Brad called after her, amused by Brandi's nightly ritual that took her to Sam's shop for a cup of hot cocoa and company.

"No. Good night," Brandi replied, although she would have loved to stop by Sam's tonight.

"Good night," Susan and Brad said as they headed toward the subway.

Brandi could hear their clucking as she continued walking home to the house she shared with her cat, Midnight.

She loved the neighborhood of older, revitalized homes, and the people who inhabited them, almost as much as she loved her shop.

Standing on her front steps, Brandi smiled and surveyed the block of inviting homes. Even at that late hour, the porch lights were still on, invitingly. She knew that at any hour she could call on any of her neighbors. Susan and Brad were wrong. She did not need the complication of a relationship when she was already so richly blessed.

Brandi was very happy and could think of nothing more that she needed. Since opening the bookstore, she had pushed everything from her mind, even love. She simply had not enjoyed the time despite an overwhelming number of offers. The business had come first. Now that the ledgers showed a healthy profit, Brandi had discovered that she was beginning to see things differently and on occasion found herself wondering if she had missed something by being so engrossed in her work. The business was thriving. Maybe it was time for her to let her hair down a little and live.

Chapter 2

Sam Carlson, the owner of Where Worlds Meet, watched as Brandi, Susan, and Brad walked past his shop window. As he wiped the counter clean, he wondered why Brandi had not stopped in for her usual nightly cup of hot chocolate. He had become so accustomed to her visits that he always cleaned that pot last.

Shrugging, Sam poured a cup of hot chocolate and placed it in the refrigerator in case she changed her mind. Thinking about Brandi these days gave him a warm feeling, and he was not sure that he liked the intrusion into his life. His daily trip to her shop to purchase the newspaper added a little spark to his day if he saw her and a touch of disappointment if he did not.

"I've finished, Sam. I think I'll leave now," his assistant Fred said, interrupting Sam's thoughts of Brandi.

"Fine. I'll see you tomorrow evening." Sam smiled.

"Where's Brandi? Should I take a cup of hot chocolate to her?" Fred asked.

"No, she just left. I guess she's not stopping by tonight," Sam answered, feigning a lack of interest.

"That's strange. She always wants hot chocolate.

Oh well, that's women for you. You think you have them pegged, and they do something that throws you a curve," Fred added, grabbing his jacket.

"You're too young to be cynical," Sam advised the college junior and added, "Have you made up with your girlfriend yet?"

"That's yesterday's news! I've moved on. I'm like a rollin' stone that gathers no moss. It's time you picked up one of those keys that's always landing at your feet. You need a woman in your life," Fred replied from the door.

"I have one," Sam replied, spreading his arms wide to embrace his shop, "and she's a full-time job."

"Ya gotta make time for more. All work and no play . . ." Fred added with a grin as he left the shop.

Sam chuckled at his assistant. One day he would understand that work sometimes had to come before romance. Owning a business was very time-consuming, leaving him with little opportunity for romance.

Drying the chocolate urn, Sam thought about the many opportunities for relationships he had resisted over the years. From the way his female customers flirted with him, Sam could tell that they found his six-foot-three trim physique attractive. Despite the bewildering number of women who had tried to catch the eye of the medium-brown-skinned entrepreneur—he had dated a few of them over the years—there was nothing serious. He had married his college sweetheart immediately after graduation, divorced her five years later, and sworn that he would never marry again. Until the right woman came along, once would have to be enough.

Tossing yet another business card from an admiring female into the trash can, he looked at his reflection in the mirror behind him. Straightening his apron, Sam liked what he saw. Hard work and long hours had not caused him to slump as they did many tall men. The salt and pepper in his hair gave him an air of maturity that his female customers seemed to appreciate.

The jingling of the shop's doorbell pulled Sam from his thoughts. Waving, he tossed the chocolate-brown apron, on which his logo of a globe surrounded by W-W-M decorated the bib, onto the counter. Opening the door, he smiled and waved his friend Doug into the shop.

"What brings you out here so late?" Sam asked as Doug stepped inside.

"I forgot to give these to you this morning. Mia threatened to divorce me if I didn't hand-deliver it to you," Doug replied with a chuckle as he handed Sam an envelop containing advertising plans. Doug and his wife ran a successful consulting firm that focused on serving the needs of the small entrepreneur. Sam had been one of their first clients. A fast friendship had developed between the two men who played basketball together in an early Saturday morning league.

Sam laughed. "Mia's some woman. She has you on a short rope and doesn't plan to cut you any slack."

"I learned a long time ago that it's better to do than to argue. Besides, she's right. I should have gotten your signature on page three this morning," Doug replied, pointing to the signature line.

Skimming the plans quickly, Sam said, "I don't argue with her about business either. If it hadn't been for Mia, I wouldn't have this shop. She certainly pushed me in the right direction. I would have joined my dad's law firm if she hadn't encouraged me to start my own business. She said coffee shops would do big business. I'm glad I listened to her. I'm not cut out to be an attorney. Navy blue suits fit my brother better than they do me anyway. I'm a jeans kind of guy."

"Have you listened to Mia and bought that condo yet?" Doug asked, looking around the impeccably clean, old-style coffee shop. The dark brown wood floors and counters shone from recent waxing.

"I settled on it yesterday. If she's right, I'll be able to resell it in a year or two for a big profit. She thinks the price of real estate in downtown Silver Spring will soar," Sam replied, returning the signed copies.

"It pays to listen to my wife," Doug commented and added looking around the shop, "Hey, where's Brandi tonight? She always comes in here after work. I'll have to catch up with her early tomorrow."

Feeling a familiar flip in his stomach at the mention of her name, Sam replied, "You're right, it's not like her to miss a night. I guess she had something to do."

"You know, Sam, your business is sound. You've bought a new condo. Now all you need is a wife," Doug advised with a grin. "Mia can help you out there, too. She knows a lot of single women who'd love a chance to help decorate your place for you."

Walking his buddy to the door, Sam stated, "Mia's fixed me up plenty. No, thanks. That's one endeavor that won't need her handiwork."

Laughing, Doug said as he opened his car door, "I'll see you tomorrow. Cards on Saturday night?"

"I'll be there," Sam replied, flipping the sign on

the door from open to closed and locking it behind him.

Walking across the street to the subway, Sam stopped and looked over his shoulder. Mia had been right. The coffee shop was the best thing that could have happened to him. The strip of stores was centrally located on the line between two thriving neighborhoods.

Sam had opened Where Worlds Meet in the vacant space on the corner to the right of Brandi's shop. Brandi's bookstore had been the first one to open in a block of abandoned shops inhabited only by a mom-and-pop cleaner that barely turned a profit. Within six months of her grand opening, Tattered and Torn, an ethnocentric dress shop that carried one-of-a-kind items, had opened to the left of her. Drums and Bugles, a musical instrument store, had opened to the left of that. In time, a bank had restored the remaining space to the left of Sam. With so many thriving shops on the block, even the owner of the cleaners had renovated his shop and gotten a lot of new customers.

Chapter 3

Every morning long before the first customers arrived, Brandi cleaned the glass in the front door and display window. She took pride in the appearance of her shop and wanted as much natural light as possible to flood the dark wood paneling and floors that gave the bookstore an old-fashioned library appearance and charm. While Susan and Brad stocked the shelves, Brandi hummed as she welcomed the new day.

"You're in a good mood," Sam said as he stepped into the shop.

"And you're early. I usually finish this window before you arrive. What'll it be . . . the regular?" Brandi asked, handing Sam the newspaper that she always saved at the counter for him.

"Thanks," Sam replied, counting out his change and then added, "Where were you last night? I saved a cup of hot chocolate for you."

Feeling the color rush to her cheeks, Brandi said, "For once, I just wasn't in a chocolate mood. I went straight home and to bed."

"You? You never sleep. Besides, chocolate's your favorite food," Sam teased, lingering in the quiet shop while Susan and Brad pretended not to notice him.

"Unlike you folks from Ohio, it's sometimes too warm here to drink hot chocolate, even for me," Brandi said with a laugh.

"I'll have to remember that. Maybe I should start making milkshakes along with the frappes. See you tonight, or will it be too warm?" Sam asked with his hand on the doorknob.

"I'll be there. I can't go two nights without hot chocolate even if it's one hundred degrees," Brandi said.

For a long minute, Brandi watched the spot where Sam had stood and tried to make sense of the feelings that ran through her. Even their friendly sparring had taken on a new meaning. Something in the way Sam looked at her made Brandi want to reach out to him. With a shrug, she turned her attention back to opening up the store.

"What's up with Sam? He certainly stayed here a long time this morning, didn't he?" Susan said with a little wink.

"What's wrong with your eye?" Brandi asked jokingly. "You're too young to develop a twitch."

"Don't dodge the question. What's up with Sam? He never stays away from his store this long" Brad interjected.

"I hadn't noticed," Brandi replied, trying to avoid the subject.

"I think he has a crush on you," Susan teased.

Waving them away, Brandi said, "You're making too much of nothing. First, we're not kids anymore so we don't have crushes. Second, we've known each other for a long time and have a good working relationship. Maybe he just felt like hanging around before the shops fill up."

"Or maybe Susan's right," Brad said and vanished into the back of the shop.

Looking from Susan to Brad's vanishing back, Brandi sighed deeply and began arranging the display in the front window. With the shop open for the day, she did not have time to entertain flights of youthful fancy. Besides, Brandi did not know if she wanted to awaken thoughts of romance that had lain dormant for so long. She was happy with her life and saw no reason to change it.

Brandi had not set out to be an entrepreneur. On the contrary, she had studied education as an undergraduate and business administration in graduate school with the plans of opening a school. However, she had encountered so much red tape that she had decided she could help others and feed herself at the same time if she opened a bookstore and offered low-cost reading and writing courses to children and adults on weekdays.

Her best friend, Mia, had tried unsuccessfully to steer her into a modeling career instead of opening a bookstore. She thought that Brandi's short medium brown hair, soft honey-colored skin, sparkling hazel eyes, and trim body would guarantee that she would make a fortune. Brandi had other plans and only smiled and continued to order books that she hoped would soon line the shelves of her new store. She wanted the freedom of being her own boss and the responsibility of making the decisions.

"Is she here yet?" Mr. Nelson whispered as he paid for the how-to book on pipe repair.

"No, she hasn't arrived, but she'll be here. You know that she never misses a Friday night," Brandi replied in a matching whisper.

"She's never this late," Mr. Nelson stated in a worried tone. "Maybe something's happened. Maybe she fell and hurt herself."

"Don't worry. If she's not here in ten more minutes, I'll phone her home," Brandi said as she handed him his change.

Looking Brandi in the eye with a very serious face, the elderly widower advised, "It's not good to live alone. Something could happen and no one would know. You remember that, Brandi, and get yourself a husband."

Smiling indulgently, Brandi replied, "I'll remember. Look, here she comes now."

Mr. Nelson's face flushed deeply as a sprightly woman in her late seventies entered the bookstore. She wore a tailored gray pantsuit and bright red silk blouse. A rhinestone red rose sparkled on her lapel. Mrs. Wilson had pulled her curly gray hair into a carefully controlled bun on the back of her neck. Although she had been a widow for ten years, she had not forgotten how to dress to impress the gentlemen. Her eyes danced merrily as she searched the room, and a smile played at the corners of her mouth with the knowledge that she could still turn heads and stop hearts. As she looked at Mr. Nelson, her cheeks reddened attractively.

"What a beauty!" Mr. Nelson breathed softly.

"She sure is, and she's waiting for you," Brandi whispered, leaning across the counter to speak directly into his ear.

"I'm one lucky man," Mr. Nelson said with a wink.

"I think it's time you followed your own advice, Mr. Nelson. Tell her you love her, marry her, and live happily ever after. You two have been meeting here every Friday night for the last six years. It's time you took the next step," Brandi stated with encouragement.

Barely pulling his eyes away from Mrs. Wilson's face, Mr. Nelson replied, "You're right. I'll do it. Someone has to teach you young folks a few lessons."

Straightening his eighty-five-year-old body, Mr. Nelson suddenly looked less frail as he walked toward Mrs. Wilson; he was her knight, her prince, her suitor. He placed a kiss lightly on her cheek, and they walked toward the rear of the store and the seating arrangement that Brandi had created as a private reading area for customers to read and sip coffee if they wanted to linger. Mr. Nelson and Mrs. Wilson were always the only occupants on Friday nights. The regular customers knew that they would sit and talk until the shop closed, and then Mr. Nelson would walk Mrs. Wilson home. The neighborhood had already privately discussed the wedding reception it would host if Mr. Nelson ever got up the nerve to ask Mrs. Wilson to marry him. Maybe the time had finally arrived.

Smiling, Brandi turned her attention to the next customer. A little boy of six proudly held out a comic book and his money. His watchful mother peered over the crowd as she waited by the door in an effort to give her son the chance to feel like a big boy while remaining nearby in case he needed her help. Her face radiated a sense of pride that made Brandi's heart warm.

"That's a great comic book, Tommy. You'll really

like it. How many do you have in your collection now?" Brandi asked as she rang up the sale.

"This is my fifteenth," Tommy replied proudly. "My mommy just bought me the protective covers and the special box for them."

"Hey, that's great! I'll have a new shipment again next month," Brandi offered with a smile.

"I know. You always get them on the fifteenth of the month," Tommy said as he clutched the bag protectively to his chest.

"I'll put one aside for you. I do that for all my regular customers," Brandi said in a serious tone.

Standing tall, the little boy replied, "Thank you. I'll make sure my mommy brings me here on time."

Brandi watched him almost float toward the door with the comic book in his hand, and the pride of readership surrounding him. Despite her friend's words of advice against carrying children's books and comic books in the shop, Brandi had decided that she wanted to encourage children to be responsible readers by offering them a range of quality selections. From the first, she had been glad that she did. The kids shopped with their parents and were an important part of her business. The combination of offering tutoring sessions and supplying children's reading material had made Over the Rainbow a favorite hangout for everyone.

As the grandfather clock struck nine, the last of the customers carried purchases to the counter. Smiling, Brandi and Susan rang up the sales and wished everyone a good night. By 9:15, the store was empty. Brad turned out the front display window lights, locked the door, and flipped the sign to CLOSED. Another long but fulfilling day had ended.

"It was really crowded in here tonight," Brad said as he straightened the books on a nearby table.

"You say that every Friday," Susan reminded him.

"I know, but tonight seemed different somehow," Brad insisted.

"Maybe it was all that hot air coming from the philosophy and politics sections," Susan offered with a laugh.

"That's it. Congressman Philban really was on his soapbox tonight. I was afraid he'd alienate the other customers," Brad said, stretching the fatigue from his young body.

"Never happen," Susan replied. "They come in here so that they can argue with him. He's quite an attraction."

"Did Mrs. Wilson and Mr. Nelson leave together tonight? He was really worried when she arrived so late," Brandi said as she counted the day's receipts with Susan's help.

"They certainly did," Brad said as he tidied the books. "They were having a heavy conversation in the reading section every time I walked by."

Sighing, Susan said, "Maybe that little scare will give him the courage to ask her to marry him. It must be terrible to be alone at that age."

"It's not too great at any age," Brad called from the religion section. "What's happening in your love life, Brandi? You need to get hooked up. People aren't meant to go through life alone. What'll you do when you don't have us to cluck over like a mother hen?"

Smiling indulgently, Brandi replied, "I'll do just fine, thank you. And I am married . . . to this business. I don't have time for anything else."

"That means that she hasn't left this little cocoon of hers since the last time we asked about her love life. I don't know what to do with you, Brandi. Mr. Nelson and Mrs. Wilson should be a lesson to you. There's a hunk next door who would make an ideal companion," Susan said, taking the stack of currency, checks, and charge slips from Brandi to recount.

"When do I have time? Besides, I'm completely happy with my life as it is. If I weren't, I'd do something about it. And stop making up stuff. Sam has never given the slightest indication that he's interested in me," Brandi replied as she made out the deposit slip.

"Yeah, right. You haven't so much as looked at a man since I've worked here. If you had, you'd see the sparkle in Sam's eyes when he buys his morning paper," Susan quipped.

"There you go again, making up stuff. He's probably just happy to be away from his shop for a few minutes. Besides, Mia has introduced me to many suitable gentlemen," Brandi said.

Joining them at the front of the store, Brad declared, "Finding you a life partner will be my project from now until graduation."

"Mine too. We'll work on it together. It's the least we can do to thank you for all you've done for us," Susan said happily.

Looking skeptically at the eager faces, Brandi said, "I'd rather you two thought of another way to thank me. You could dust all of the books, clean up the back room, organize my desk, or wash the windows."

"We'll do all of that and find you a partner," Susan pronounced with youthful confidence.

"For the time being, I'd be more than happy if you'd simply wait there for me until I lock this bag in the safe," Brandi stated, walking toward the office.

"No problem," they replied in unison.

Laughing, Brandi entered the office and approached the wall safe. After spinning the dial, she opened the door and laid the deposit bag inside. After Susan and Brad arrived in the morning, she would slip around the corner to the bank and make the deposit. Although the bank offered both a drop box and an ATM, she did not trust the streets enough at night. The neighborhood was as safe as any big city street could be, but she saw no reason to tempt fate. Becoming a crime statistic was not on Brandi's list of activities to try before her next birthday.

As Brandi set the alarm and pulled down the metal security door, Susan asked, "What kind of man do you like? We don't want to make the same mistakes that Mia did."

Defending her friend, Brandi said, "She introduced me to many perfectly lovely men who simply were not right for me."

Kissing both of them lightly on the cheek, Brandi said, "Look, guys, I appreciate the thought, but this is too big a task for anyone to take on. Besides, like the song says, 'I'll know when my love comes along. I'll know by the touch of his hand.' You won't have to arrange a thing. It'll just happen."

"Not if you don't leave the shop," Susan moaned.

Laughing, Brandi gave them a playful shove on their way and said, "That's enough for one night. Good night. I'll see you tomorrow."

Waving good-bye, Susan and Brad linked arms and walked toward the metro station. Brandi had long suspected that a fondness had developed between the two members of her staff who had not known each other, despite attending the same college, until they started to work at her shop. Now they seemed quite devoted to one another, although neither one had ever hinted at it.

Smiling, Brandi entered Sam's shop for her usual cup of hot chocolate. Several customers still lingered at the tables and engaged in low, intimate conversation over cups of coffee that had cooled unnoticed. It was 9:45, just time enough for her to order a cup of hot chocolate before Sam closed his shop for the evening. Brandi took her usual seat near the cash register and waited for the proprietor to notice her.

Placing her customary order on the counter in front of her, Sam said, "I saw you and the kids talking on the sidewalk. They looked as if they were trying to involve you in something important."

"They're young. I remember thinking that I could solve all the problems of the world, too, when I was twenty-one," Brandi replied as she stirred the thick, rich chocolate.

"Yeah, well, that thought changes quickly. The first rent check, the first car payment, and the first sick kid make people grow up real fast. Are they still going to law school?" Sam asked. Like everyone else on the block and in the neighborhood, he knew everything about everyone.

"Uh-huh. I'll miss them," Brandi said as she sipped the delicious hot chocolate. The warmth flowed all the way down to her toes and pushed away life's little cares.

Ever the realist, Sam commented, "You'll find other help."

"Yeah, but it won't be the same," Brandi responded, watching as Sam carefully washed and waxed the rich mahogany counter trimmed in a brass rail and rich leather. The slowly revolving ceiling fans gently moved the exotically scented air and the leaves of the tall palms that softened the corners.

Brandi often thought that the décor and ambiance of Where Worlds Meet complemented her shop perfectly. Both exuded the classic charm of days gone by. Sam's shop invited people to sit for a while and let the brew wash away their troubles. Her shop encouraged customers to lose themselves in the pages of a book.

The mantel clock chimed ten o'clock as Brandi finished the last drop of her hot chocolate. The last couple, wrapped in each other's arms, lingered at the cash register as Sam filled their order. They were so engrossed in each other that the man did not even count his change but only shoved it into his pocket. They left after a muttered good night.

Breathing deeply of the delicious aromas, Brandi watched as Sam prepared his shop for closing. Susan was definitely right about his physical attributes and his sex appeal. Brandi could not deny that Sam had a certain something. His appeal was deeper than just his hot chocolate.

Feeling her eyes on him, Sam looked at Brandi and smiled. Their eyes met for a long moment during which Brandi felt as if he wanted to say something to her. However, the time passed and nothing happened. Feeling strangely disappointed, almost as if an opportunity for something exciting had slipped through her fingers, Brandi only smiled and looked away.

Slipping the change into her pocket, Brandi walked toward the door. "Night, Sam," she called as she opened it. The fragrance of the night mixed gently with the aroma of coffee and chocolate.

"Night, Brandi," Sam replied, holding the uncounted receipts in his hands.

Hands deep in her pockets, Brandi walked home along a path that was well illuminated with streetlights and the glow of the lamps from her neighbors' homes. The memory of the unspoken words lingered. Shrugging, Brandi reminded herself that she was not a hopeless romantic like Susan. She had known Sam too long to think that anything akin to unrequited love existed behind the incredible depths of his eyes. She had simply allowed Susan and Brad to put ridiculous thoughts in her head.

Squaring her shoulders, Brandi walked a little faster. She loved this time of night when the neighborhood had slowed from its activities and was relaxing from the week's hard work. She especially relished the sight of the lights in the windows of her house as they welcomed her home. Her black cat, Midnight, sat silhouetted in the living room window's lamplight. Turning the key in the lock, Brandi entered and closed the door. She was home.

Chapter 4

The sun felt good on her back as Brandi strolled from the bank the next morning. She loved all aspects of the seasonal changes, except maybe the summer's humidity, but was especially fond of the fall as the touch of chill filled the air. She liked to wear sweaters and feel the slight coolness of the approaching fall as it mingled with the remains of the usually hot summer in D.C. Something about fall and winter put her in the mood to curl up with a good book and a cup of cocoa. Her customers must have felt the same way because sales soared as the temperatures dropped.

Buttoning her red cardigan a little higher and stuffing her hands deep inside the pockets of the matching trousers, Brandi surveyed the neighborhood that she loved so dearly. The leaves had changed to a splendid assortment of oranges and fiery reds and would soon blanket the sidewalks in a stunning carpet of color. All of the shopkeepers had planted mums and pansies in boxes that flanked their shop doors and along the curb. The mixture of yellows, oranges, reds, and purples added even more color to the storefronts.

Walking past Sam's shop, Brandi inhaled deeply of

the exotic and intoxicating aromas that wafted from Where Worlds Meet. Although she needed to return to her store to help Susan and Brad with the crush of customers that would soon fill the shop on that Saturday morning, Brandi felt her willpower melt away. She was not sure which compelled her to return . . . Sam or the beverages.

Customers standing in clusters, sitting at tables, and occupying stools at the bar packed the aromatic shop. The line for carryout orders reached almost to the door. Although she craved a cup of hot chocolate to warm her hands and insides after the short, brisk walk from the bank, Brandi almost changed her mind and left the shop. Besides, she had an unexplainable need to see Sam.

Smiling, Brandi watched Sam's efficiency of movement as he ground, brewed, poured, and capped cup after cup of his prized beverages. He ordered the beans from a highly acclaimed organic farm on the West Coast, ground them as he needed them to maintain their freshness, and used only the finest filtered bottled water. He wanted to be absolutely certain that nothing would mar the taste of his black, strong coffee, the base for all of the exotic concoctions on the menu.

Sam's operation had an assembly-line quality that worked efficiently but did not allow him to socialize with the customers. Two of his assistants placed the customers' orders and accepted their payment while Sam and two others filled the orders. Sam, however, was the only one who could grind the beans and brew the coffee. Since he had never missed a day of work in the six years that Brandi had known him, she did not know if he had trained any of his staff to run the massive coffee grinder.

Inching along the line, Brandi remembered that she had not taken a day off either since opening Over the Rainbow. Three years ago, she had dragged herself into the shop for a week while suffering from the flu, and had stayed away from customers as much as possible to avoid infecting them. Working in her office, she had coughed and sniffed while Susan and Brad ran the shop in the evenings and on the weekend that she had felt the full kick of the illness. Her mother, long retired from teaching, had filled in for her in the front of the store during the day.

Since then, every holiday season, Brandi's mother had joined her in the store as an extra assistant. She loved being able to help her daughter on a temporary basis and enjoyed the opportunity to chat with the customers who shared wonderful anecdotes of Brandi's impact on their lives. Mrs. Owens was very proud of her daughter, as was her father, who never failed to brag to his golf buddies about her successes. However, he preferred not to work in the shop, claiming that he would be like a bull in a china shop if he tried to help her. He was the same way about making repairs, so Brandi did not press the point.

"Hi, Brandi. What'll you have?" Mark, one of Sam's assistants, asked with his fingers hovering over the cash register's touch screen.

"Good morning, Mark," Brandi replied cheerfully. "Give me two blacks with cream and double sugars on the side and one hot chocolate."

"Got it. That'll be six dollars," Mark said as he held out his hand.

"Thanks, and have a good day," Brandi said, placing the crisp bills in his palm and then adding, "That crossword puzzle you ordered arrived yesterday. You can come in any time to pick it up."

"Great! Is Susan working today?" Mark asked as his cheeks colored slightly. He was a handsome graduate student of twenty-three who had fallen for Susan the first time he walked into Over the Rainbow. Although Susan was very friendly to him, Brandi knew that her heart would belong to Brad if he would finally get around to asking for it.

Teasing him, Brandi responded, "And I thought it was your love of good books that brought you into my shop. Yeah, she's there. I guess I'll see you later."

"The books are an added bonus." Mark laughed as he handed Brandi her claim ticket.

Stepping down the length of the bar to the pickup sign, Brandi waited only a few minutes before Sam handed her the little brown box bearing his logo. She accepted it with a touch of regret at having to leave the wonderful aromas of the shop. Pulling her sweater a little closer, she prepared to walk the short distance around the corner to her shop.

"I'm surprised to see you here today," Sam said as he paused a minute from filling orders to speak with her.

"I couldn't help myself," Brandi replied with a laugh. "The aroma prevented me from returning to my shop. It's all your fault. If your shop didn't lie between me and the bank, this wouldn't have happened."

Smiling broadly, Sam said, "I'll take full responsibility, since the result is having you grace my humble shop two days in a row."

"You charmer, you," Brandi joked. "You keep that up and I'll have to return for another cup. You'll have my bankruptcy on your conscience."

"Far be it from me to interfere with your business. However, I would be able to expand my shop if that happened." Sam laughed as he lingered over the un-filled orders.

"Monster! Just for that, I'll take my business else-where," Brandi declared, jerking her chin and holding the sturdy box closely.

"Hardly," Sam said, laughing. "You know that no one makes hot chocolate that tastes as good as mine. You'll be back."

"Alas, betrayed by a few cocoa beans," Brandi quipped as she placed her hand on the knob and opened the door to the sound of Sam's deep chuckle.

Brandi barely noticed the cool air that added to the rosy pink of her cheeks. Something had changed, but she could not put her finger on it or remember when it happened. Not wanting to ana-lyze a good thing, she decided to enjoy the moment.

Entering her own shop, Brandi smiled at the sight of the press of people, many with steaming cups of coffee from Sam's shop in their hands. Everywhere she looked, Brandi saw customers carrying newspa-pers, books, and magazines as they searched for even more reading material. She could not have been more thrilled.

Brandi handed the cups of coffee to her assis-tants, who stopped long enough for a sip before returning to their checkout duties. Surveying the room and seeing that everything was in order, she decided to mingle with her customers before vanishing into her office to do the day's paperwork. Liking that part of her job the least, Brandi always put it off as long as possible.

"Susan," Brandi said teasingly as she slowly eased from the counter, "I told Mark that his order had arrived. He'll come over as soon as he has the chance. It's on the second shelf behind you."

Before Susan could answer, Brad snarled under his breath, "I'm surprised that he didn't beat you over here. It must be really busy next door."

"Behave!" Susan said without looking from the pile of books she was entering for the customer at the front of her line. The blush in her cheeks deepened noticeably.

"What's this? Do I hear jealousy?" Brandi asked.

Glaring at her, Brad replied, "No. The guy's a big jerk. He follows Susan around like a sick puppy. It's disgusting."

"He does not. His attentions are charming. He makes me feel special. A woman likes to know that she's admired," Susan quipped.

"That's not admiration, that's subservience. I admire you, but you don't see me acting like that," Brad argued.

"Maybe you should try modeling your behavior after Mark's. A little honey would go a long way toward catching this bee," Susan retorted as she rang up another customer.

"Children! Such bickering! You sound just like Mia and me," Brandi scolded, and wandered away chuckling.

Thinking of Mia caused Brandi to wonder at her friend's conspicuous absence. On Saturday morning, Mia always stopped by the shop with gossip or information on a new man she wanted Brandi to meet, while her husband, Doug, did the yard work or played handball with one of his friends. If she had not arrived by noon, Brandi would have to phone her at home.

Brandi and Mia had been best buddies all of their lives. As kids, they had lived within a few doors of each other and had spent their free time with each other's family. They had played together as children and shared makeup and clothes as teenagers. When it was time to select a college, they had decided to attend the same one and room together so that nothing could break up their friendship.

When Mia fell in love with Doug, she had encouraged Brandi to date his roommate, hoping that they would one day plan their weddings together. However, Brandi and Frank had not hit it off despite Mia's best efforts. They had quickly parted company. After graduation, Brandi had helped Mia with the details of her wedding and had then gone to graduate school, while Mia and Doug had opened their consulting firm.

Mia worked long hours in their business, but she always had time to try to arrange relationships for Brandi, her workaholic friend, despite her husband's admonition against matchmaking. Since Brandi was the last of their single friends, Mia made Brandi her cause celebre, wanting her to join the ranks of happily married women despite Brandi's insistence that she needed to give her full attention to running the shop. Knowing that her husband and Sam were best friends, she even tried to engineer a relationship between Brandi and Sam, but neither showed any interest in the other.

Reaching her office, Brandi entered and pressed the play button on the answering machine. She was not surprised to hear Mia's voice announce that she was bringing out-of-town guests to visit the shop. Smiling, Brandi acknowledged that Mia was very good for business, having introduced more people to the shop than any single customer. Mia, despite her many matchmaking fiascos, was a true friend.

Chapter 5

Brandi was so engrossed in her work that she did not hear the door being opened unceremoniously. Dressed in a winter-white wool sweater and slacks set with a touch of red in the scarf at her neck, Mia filled the room with her statuesque presence. Although only five-eight, Mia carried herself as if she were much taller and looked wonderful in everything she wore. Not many women could dress in all white without looking out of season despite the fashion industry's claim that white was equally suitable for fall and summer.

"Where've you been? I thought you'd given up on me," Brandi said as she continued to bubble the marks that would generate paychecks for Susan and Brad.

Sighing with great fatigue, Mia replied, "You remember my cousin Myriam and her husband, Calvin? Well, they're here for a few days on their way to visit her paternal grandmother. I promised to show them around town, but they're so slow that it's killing me. There simply weren't enough hours in the day to transport them everywhere at a snail's pace."

"You'll survive." Brandi smiled.

"Barely. I left a message on your machine. Didn't you listen to it?" Mia asked.

"Sure I did, but it was a bit vague," Brandi replied, grinning at Mia's dramatic hand gestures of frustration.

"I couldn't say more than that. Myriam sticks to me like glue," Mia moaned, speaking in a subdued tone and leaning closer.

"Where is she now?" Brandi asked.

"I left both of them at the front door to do a little shopping. Actually, they're looking for celebrities. I told her about the sports figures that shop here. I hope someone special is in the store today. Myriam pouts so much when she's disappointed. She can be so unattractive," Mia replied, opening the door for a peek.

"How'd you get away from her?"

"I told her that I needed to use the little girl's room and ducked through the crowd in this direction. I didn't exactly lie, you know. You do have a bathroom back here." Mia quickly shut the door.

"Yes, but it's not for customers. She'll catch you in a lie when she reaches the philosophy section and sees the restroom door," Brandi said.

"She might not be exactly the philosophical type. With luck, she won't get that far." Mia laughed.

Leaning back in her chair, Brandi scolded lightly, "You should be ashamed of yourself. It wasn't nice to ditch Myriam like that."

"Do you want me to get her?" Mia asked as she stood up ever so slightly from her perch in the chair next to the desk.

"No, thanks," Brandi replied quickly. "I remember the way she acted when we were kids. It doesn't sound as if she has changed very much. The constant chatter was too much then, and I'm sure it'll grate on my nerves even more now. Besides, you can't tell me all the latest gossip with her around."

"You're so right about that," Mia agreed and added, "I heard the juiciest tidbit yesterday at the beauty shop. Maude, my nail lady, told me that she heard that Philip Lee and his wife broke up. You remember him from college, don't you? He was tall and skinny with bad skin but lots of money, especially after he opened that ob-gyn practice. The women chased him as if he were Denzel Washington and Luther Van Dross rolled together."

"He married a girl from Richmond?" Brandi said.

Nodding, Mia continued, "That's right. Her name was Sheila Thomas. Anyway, Philip came home early one day to find Sheila in bed with another man. He packed up her stuff and kicked her to the curb without asking any questions or waiting for any excuses. According to Maude, that same afternoon Philip visited his attorney, who drew up separation papers. It's over and done."

"Poor guy. He must be devastated," Brandi said sympathetically.

"You'd think it, wouldn't you? However, Maude says that he had been dating up a storm. He's been free for two weeks and has been seen with fourteen different women." Mia laughed.

"That must be an exaggeration. He has his practice to run," Brandi stated in disbelief.

"I'm sure it is, but the point is that he's happy to be free of Sheila. Would you like to meet him?" Mia asked, getting to the purpose for her information.

"No. I don't need the complications," Brandi said

firmly. Knowing Mia's favorite pastime, she did not want to leave her reaction open to interpretation.

"I didn't think you would. You never do."

"And it doesn't stop you from trying."

"Whatever. How's business?" Mia asked, changing the subject in a way that made Brandi very suspicious.

"It couldn't be better. You see that crowd? It's like this from Friday night until closing on Sunday, as you know. Why'd you ask?" Brandi asked warily.

"I was thinking that a block party would bring the neighborhood together and bolster sales. But if you don't need the extra revenue, forget it," Mia said with a shrug.

"I didn't say that. Tell me more," Brandi demanded as she finished the last payroll sheet and gave Mia her undivided attention.

"Here's my idea. If you don't like it, just tell me and we'll scrap it." Mia leaned closer to Brandi for effect. "My agency would contact the *Post* to tell them the date and time for inclusion in the weekend section. We'll involve all of the shops and charge the customers fifty cents each for the hot dogs and sodas. We can even have an apple-bobbing contest if you'd like or maybe a pie eating contest. I know where we can rent a cotton candy machine and one of those popular funnel cake stands. If the police department will cooperate by closing the block to traffic, we could even position a carousel at one end. What do you think?"

"It sounds great, but when do you plan to pull off this mini festival? The air's already feeling a little nippy," Brandi said with a touch of skepticism, but not wanting to put a pall on the plans.

"Let's do it in two weeks. The beginning of November would be the perfect time. The excitement and sugar high of Halloween will have ended and Thanksgiving will not have arrived. It'll be a fall festival," Mia stated without looking at the calendar.

"You've already done a lot of work on this, haven't you? How'd you know I'd agree?" Brandi studied her buddy's face.

"Easy, you never miss a party or a chance to make money," Mia replied with a chuckle.

"What do I have to do?" Brandi asked as she laughed heartily.

"Nothing. I'll talk it up to the others, mentioning that you and Sam are already involved. It's as good as done," Mia replied with a confident smile.

"You've already discussed this with Sam? When? I thought I was your first touch." Brandi feigned hurt feelings that her friend had proposed the idea to someone else first.

Ignoring Brandi's pout, Mia stated, "Hey, he's one of our clients, too, you know, and Doug's best friend. We thought that both of you would go for it. Besides, we needed his support just in case you weren't interested."

"Nothing like being second string," Brandi teased as she stood and prepared to return to the bookstore's main section.

"Do we have to go out there? Myriam's probably looking everywhere for me, and I'd rather be lost," Mia whined uncharacteristically.

"You can stay here if you'd like, but I really need to give Susan and Brad a little help. They've held down the shop long enough," Brandi replied as she slowly opened the door.

"Your mom can help them. She came into the shop the same time I did. Please, don't make me go out there," Mia pleaded.

Before Brandi could answer, a loud voice filled the shop's back room as Myriam burst through the crack in the door. Her red and black cape floated over her ample frame and filled out like a sail behind her. Immediately, she grabbed Brandi and hugged her, almost crushing a few ribs in the process.

"Brandi, it's so nice to see you again. Your shop is just darling. Your mom's been showing me around the place," Myriam gushed before turning her attention to Mia and adding, "I've been looking everywhere for you. I thought I'd lost you. You're missing all the commotion. One of those really famous basketball players just entered the store. The kids and men are going crazy!"

Seeing Mia at a loss for words, Brandi chimed in saying, "We were discussing a little promotion idea of Mia's, but we've finished. It's about time I rejoined the others."

Linking her arm through Mia's, Myriam burbled happily, "Yes, you must see this man. I've never seen anyone this tall in person. He had to bend over to enter the shop and all those cute ribbons and decorations hanging from the ceiling keep hitting him on the head. It's just too funny."

Trying not to laugh as Mia cut her eyes in agony, Brandi brought up the rear and securely locked the back room. Slipping the key inside her sweater pocket, she followed them into the shop in which a famous basketball player and regular customer stood encircled by admiring children. Their parents, only a little less starstruck, gawked from the periphery as he signed autographs for all of the kids, even the ones who had not bugged their parents to purchase a copy of his book.

Myriam, too, stood spellbound. For the first time in their long acquaintance, she was too impressed to speak. Brandi wished she had a video camera to capture the moment that might never come again.

Easing through the crowd, Brandi finally reached the cash register at the front of the store. The more she thought about Mia's idea, the more she liked it. The shopping block, so vital to the community's financial health, had not hosted an activity for the neighborhood since the summer of her second year in business. It was time to pull everyone together again.

"Mia shared her idea with me, and I think it's wonderful," Mrs. Owens, Brandi's mother, commented as her daughter joined them at the counter.

Nodding, Brandi replied, "I do too, and it'll give me a chance to chat with all of my neighbors. I don't ever see anyone except Sam. I hardly ever see Ally Marks, who owns Tattered and Torn, or Kevin Town, the proprietor of Drums and Bugles. I open early to catch the rush hour traffic and close after the tutoring sessions in the evening. Both of them open their shops at ten and close at six. Neither of them maintains Sunday hours."

"They don't know what they're missing," Mrs. Owens said. "Your store is packed on Sunday and so is Sam's. They're just letting revenue slip through their fingers."

Leaning closer, Susan quipped, "Not to be disrespectful, Mrs. Owens, but maybe they want a life.

Brandi only lives for this shop. She needs to get out more often before she becomes as dusty as the collector-item volumes in that cabinet."

Sighing, Brandi rebutted, "This is one of Susan's constant complaints. I go out plenty, thank you."

Looking from Brandi to Susan, Mrs. Owens said, "I'm not one to interfere, but if I were, I'd agree with Susan. I'm not saying that you should close the shop on Sundays, but it wouldn't hurt you to turn over the running of the shop to your trusted assistants once in a while. You work every day from morning until late at night and so does Sam. None of the other shop owners put in such long hours. You're not getting any younger."

"Ah, Mom!" Brandi exclaimed.

"At the rate you're going, your father and I will be too old to dance at your wedding," Mrs. Owens said with upturned hands of exasperation.

"Mom, you're right. I have to open the shop on Sundays; it's one of my busiest days. I don't know what I'd do with my time if I didn't come to work. I love being here. I love the smell of new books. Owning this shop isn't work at all. Most of my customers are my friends," Brandi explained.

"You'd find something to do. You'd have time to date. You'd learn a new language. You'd find a way to have a life," Susan interjected as she exchanged glances with Mrs. Owens.

"I feel as if I'm being double-teamed. Did you two rehearse this conversation while I was in the office?" Brandi chuckled, seeing the sly looks.

"Us? We wouldn't do that." Mrs. Owens grinned.

"I think I'll go for coffee now." Susan laughed and slipped away.

"Good idea," Brandi agreed as she turned her attention to one of her youngest customers.

"Hey, Johnny, I see you got Mr. Cables's autograph, too," Brandi said as she rang up the purchase of a young customer.

"Yeah! He's cool! I'm gonna show all my friends," Johnny replied proudly, clutching the carefully wrapped book to his chest.

"You should bring them," Brandi suggested. "That way, you could enjoy seeing him again and sharing the experience with your friends."

"That's a great idea! Can I, Mom?" Johnny asked with glowing eyes.

"Sure, honey," his mother replied and then added to Brandi, "I guess you'll have a store full of little people next week. Do you think he'll come in again? I'd hate to disappoint them."

"He's here every Saturday at exactly the same time, but I'll ask him to make sure. I'll phone you if he's not coming," Brandi said as she handed Johnny's mother change for the three books she had purchased.

"Thanks," the mother responded, steering her son toward the door.

"Bye, Brandi," Johnny called as he skipped out the door and down the sidewalk.

Smiling, Brandi knew the reason that she kept her shop open such long hours and worked so hard. Johnny and kids like him needed a place in which they could learn the thrill of reading about the real-life celebrities who were their heroes. Over the Rainbow gave them the opportunity to purchase books and meet the stars who shared her dedication to reading. Unlike other presents that kids received throughout the year, Brandi knew that these special books would not spend their time under the bed covered in dust.

Chapter 6

Moon glow shined through the window as Brandi finished the last of the evening closing tasks. She had sent Susan and Brad away early after seeing them studying their watches in a less than subtle manner. It was clear that they both had dates, which the romantic in Brandi hoped would be with each other.

With only the night-lights burning, Brandi had tidied the last stack of books when she heard a light tapping at the front door. She could not imagine who would come to her shop that late. Everyone in the neighborhood and all of her customers knew her store hours and never pressed her to make an exception in consideration of the long hours that she worked. No one had ever asked her to open after hours, even for the purchase of gifts for forgotten birthdays.

The man on the other side of the door knocked again and shouted, "Brandi, it's Sam. I need to talk with you."

Turning the key and ushering him inside, Brandi asked with a tease in her voice, "Sam, what brings you here so late? You should be in your shop getting my hot cocoa ready."

"I brought it with me," Sam replied as he handed

her the cup of steaming brew. Immediately, the fragrance of the cocoa mixed with the aroma of the potpourri and the books to create a smell akin to perfection.

"Thanks," Brandi said as she motioned to two stools behind the counter. Her heart fluttered strangely as she perched next to him and said, "What's so important that it couldn't wait until I stopped by for my evening libation?"

Sipping the cup of coffee that he had brought for himself, Sam said, "Mia's idea for a block party. That's what's up. She's spreading the word that we've agreed to do it. It's a good idea, but we haven't discussed it yet. I think she's a little premature."

"You know that Mia gets charged up and rolls over everyone in her enthusiasm," Brandi said, laughing. "I've never known her to wait for anything. She has an idea, and she translates it into action."

"Well, I still think she should have given all of us the chance to discuss it before she made it a done deed," Sam said with a touch of irritation in his voice.

Warming her hands on the hot cup, Brandi said, "The way she explained it to me, we don't really have a lot of time to think about it. The advertising needs to hit the paper now. Are you for it or against it?"

Perching on the stool beside Brandi, Sam replied, "I'm for it, but I would have liked a little time to reflect. I'm not the kind who jumps into things. Doug had to learn that about me when we worked on the preliminary advertising for the shop. I'm slow and steady, not a quick starter. Mia knows that, too. I just felt that Mia was steamrolling the idea into reality too quickly."

"I'm sure she wasn't trying to do that. She just had a thought and ran with it. Since she and Doug will do everything and the festival won't cost us anything, I'm for it. What do the others think?" Brandi asked as she studied Sam in the soft lights of the silent shop. He was indeed handsome even with a deep frown on his forehead.

Sam replied, "They're all for it, but they're for anything that doesn't carry a big price tag. You and I are the only ones who stand back and assess a situation prior to jumping into it. We're more conservative than they are. I don't remember either of us ever running extreme ads like some of the way-out stuff that Ally likes or even slightly radical ones like Kevin's. But I remember that they jumped on another idea of hers that made us the butt of jokes all over town. Something about a talk show moderator and a series of interviews focusing on the successful black businesses of Washington. It was a good idea, too, but it set us up for criticism. Our colleagues in the board of trade talked about the size of our heads for weeks. Anyway, it was very embarrassing."

Coming to her friend's defense, Brandi stated calmly, "The interview idea was Doug's. He's the one who thought that we'd benefit from the Round Table folks interviewing us. You're right. It was a little less than comfortable to have to answer all of those questions about it. I think our advertising is more conservative than the others' due to the nature of our shops. Our merchandise isn't radical like some of those outfits that Ally stocks, and we don't attract the over-the-top crowd the way Kevin does in his music shop. Even our shops echo our traditional nature. I purposefully wanted to evoke memories of the slower bygone days with the décor of this shop. I'd bet you did, too. Slow and gentle is good for our businesses. This block party sounds about right for our clientele."

"I stand corrected," Sam acquiesced with pride in his voice. "That's what I've always liked about you, Brandi. You know just the right approach to tame the charging tiger. I remember your ability to calm the angry crowd at the last block meeting when the District government wanted to install those ghastly streetlights in this neighborhood. They were far too modern for us."

"Ah, Sam, you weren't so much charging as purring loudly." Brandi laughed as she accepted the compliment. Sam looked particularly handsome in the shop's low light.

For a few minutes they sat in the comfortable silence that came from having known someone for years. Neither felt the need to offer small talk. Only the soft ticking of the grandfather clock and the cooling of their beverages reminded them of the passage of time. Although they had known each other professionally for six years, they had never dated. Their conversation was almost always professional in nature with only the rudimentary questions about health and family. On the rare occasion, they might discuss the wistful dream of expanding or combining their shops. Brandi and Sam had long ago learned that they were very compatible and always sought each other's opinion in business matters.

Rising to leave, Sam turned and stated with a sincerity that stunned Brandi, "It's a shame we've never spent time together socially. I like you, Brandi Owens. Maybe one day we'll have time for a life outside of work and can get to know each other better."

"I'd like that, Sam," Brandi said, thankful that he could not see the color rise to her cheeks.

Studying her face in the low light, Sam said, "Let's try to free up our calendars after the fall festival. We could go to dinner and a movie."

"That would be great, unless, of course, Mia's little idea makes us even busier than we are now," Brandi replied as the moonlight flickered in her eyes like candlelight.

Not wanting to leave but needing to return to his shop, Sam said softly, "We'll find a way."

Silently, Brandi walked him to the door. Not knowing the response to make or if one was even necessary, she said nothing. Locking the door behind him and pulling down the shade, Brandi felt an uncustomary confusion. For the first time since opening the shop years ago, she did not remember which task needed to be done next. Sam's arrival had interrupted her routine, and his last statement had disturbed the tranquility of her thoughts.

Tossing their discarded cups into the trash, Brandi surveyed the shop. Not finding anything more to do, she shrugged and chucked softly at her adolescent reaction to a man's offhand comment. Moonlight could certainly do strange things. Since everything looked in order for the next day, she grabbed her coat from the rack behind the counter, turned out the light, and left the shop.

Locking the door securely, Brandi walked down

the street and past Sam's shop. He was inside tidying up as usual. From his attention to the details of closing his shop, she could see that their conversation had not rattled him. For once, she would not stop for her customary cup of cocoa. Instead, Brandi crossed the street and headed home.

The night air was cool against her cheek as Brandi briskly walked the short distance to her house. Having forgotten her gloves, she thrust her hands deeply into her jacket pockets. Despite the wind that whirled around her ears, she could not stop thinking about Sam. He had shoved their professional relationship into the realm of the personal with his casual comment, and Brandi did not know how to react to the change.

Brandi liked her life as it was without complications or confusions. Her conversations with people were very straightforward, without any of the innuendos of flirtation. Even while in Sam's company, tall and handsome as he was, she had not reacted to him the way she had seen other women respond to him. She had not giggled, smiled cutely, pressed her hands tightly to her chest, or offered any of the other mating signals that girls and women display to transmit their interest in a man. Despite Susan's and Brad's encouragement, she had not considered Sam a romantic interest until lately. Now, however, he had changed their purely business association into a more personal one.

Actually, Brandi was always so busy with work that she did not think of any man in a romantic way. Many handsome professional men entered the store daily. More than a handful of the most eligible bachelors in D.C. bought their reading material from her shop. To her mind, they were customers just like everyone else who helped to make Over the Rainbow a successful enterprise.

Mia, on more than one occasion, had tried to introduce her to likely romantic candidates. However, Brandi had not been interested. Brandi did not want to divert her energy from the shop to the cultivation of a romance. She had enough on her plate already.

Stepping inside her blissfully warm house, Brandi tossed her coat onto the sofa uncharacteristically. Sam's comments and gaze had completely disrupted her routine. The silence that greeted her was heavenly after a busy day in the shop, but it, too, seemed different and perhaps empty. Usually, the solitude of her home was comforting after a busy day. However, Sam's eyes, the closeness of his lips, and the smell of cocoa and coffee on his skin had changed all that.

As her cat rubbed against her ankles, Brandi decided that she would try to ignore Sam's comment. Besides, he had probably not meant it the way it sounded anyway. The moonlight was probably playing tricks on her. From what she could tell, he was content with his life. Undoubtedly, Sam was only making small talk. Perhaps the magic of the late night had affected him, too. Unless he pressed her to change the relationship, Brandi would let the discussion pass into the recesses of her mind.

Inhaling the fragrances of her home, Brandi collapsed onto the sofa with the cat at her side. She was sleepy and needed to go to bed but felt too tired to walk up the stairs. Slipping off her shoes and pulling the afghan her mother had knitted over her tired body, she yawned and closed her eyes. Thoughts of

Sam, Over the Rainbow, and the block party would have to wait until the next day.

In the weeks that followed, the plans for the block party unfolded without any help from the proprietors along the row of shops that comprised the economic center for the Takoma Park neighborhood. Mia and Doug handled all of the arrangements, with the shop proprietors going about their business as usual. With the exception of having to decide which wares to emphasize for the day's festivities, Brandi and the other shop owners experienced little change to their routines.

Brandi was too busy logging in astounding sales volumes to think about the block party. The fall shopping season was generating more revenue than she had expected and boosting her reordering activities considerably. Between sending orders to the book distributors and unpacking boxes of books from them, she was inundated with work. She had no time to think about anything other than the need to order replacements for the stock that flew from the store.

Sam, however, appeared in the shop more often than usual. In addition to purchasing his morning paper, he had started bringing over afternoon cups of coffee and cocoa. Something in the way he walked looked different, too. Even Brandi noticed the change and wondered about the cause.

"I thought you might like a little libation," Sam said, placing the cups on the counter. "It's getting rather chilly out these days."

"Thanks, Sam. You must have read out minds. We were thinking of taking a coffee break," Brandi said.

"I'll bring some over every day if you'd like," Sam suggested, studying Brandi's face as if they had just met.

"Oh, no, don't bother. We'll make the run," Brandi said, wondering if the cool weather had put the touch of color in his cheeks.

"No problem. I'll see you tonight," Sam replied, and hastily left the shop.

Susan and Brad could hardly contain their reactions until the door closed. They were like children who had made a great discovery and wanted to share it with others. In this case, Sam's reaction to Brandi was the source of their excitement.

"I told you he was interested," Susan whispered after Sam had made his delivery.

"Don't be silly," Brandi chided as her cheeks reddened. "He's merely being neighborly."

"He's been your neighbor for years, but he's never come to the shop more than once a day," Brad said.

"I see a budding relationship," Susan interjected.

"Nothing of the kind. He's just touching base to make sure that all's well with the festival preparations," Brandi said.

Brad laughed. "He didn't even mention the festival."

"And the festival didn't make him blush, or you either," Susan joked.

Huffing, Brandi replied, "If my cheeks are red, it's because you're getting on my nerves with this silly business. We're both too busy for infatuations. I'll be in the office if you need me."

"You can run, but you can't hide," Brad called.

Ignoring him, Brandi took refuge in her office. She needed time to think but would not find it with tons of reorders on her desk. She promised herself that she would take time to think about Sam once the shopping crush ended.

Chapter 7

The next day promised to be cool, clear, and sunny—perfect for the coming together of neighbors and friends. Mia and Doug Fernwood appeared early to supervise the setup. By the time the first customers arrived, the hot dogs were grilling on the barbecue, the apples for bobbing were floating in several massive tubs of water, the cotton candy machine had churned out colorful cones, and the candied apples covered with nuts sat ready for purchase. Colorful banners flew from the street lamps, banners crisscrossed the street, and police cruisers prevented traffic from traveling the length of the block. The carousel at the other end blocked the exit. Each shop had its front window decorated in a fall scene that pulled the outside into the store and helped to create the proper mood.

"Isn't it wonderful?" Mia asked rhetorically as she bounded into the shop. "Everything looks so festive."

"You've done a great job," Brandi complimented her friend. "I saw the ad in the paper this morning. How much is that setting me back?"

"Nothing," Mia replied quickly. "It's our gift to all of you for being such good clients."

"That certainly is novel . . . a consulting firm that gives as well as receives." Brandi chuckled as she rubbed furniture polish into the top of the counter.

"Have you seen Sam?" Mia asked in an offhand manner.

"I saw him last night when I bought my usual hot chocolate. Why?" Brandi replied, without looking up and concentrating on adding additional cream into a particularly stubborn scratch.

"Oh, I just wondered. I think he looks unusually handsome this morning," Mia commented, studying her recently manicured nails.

Brandi responded with an indulgent smile, "It must be the cool air and the increased coffee sales. We're all looking rather perky these days. I saw Ally this morning as she opened her shop. She was humming at eight o'clock . . . highly unusual for her since she never comes to work early. I guess her shop is showing record sales, too."

"Is your mind always on work? Isn't it possible that Sam is simply an attractive man?" Mia groaned.

"I'm not trying to take anything away from Sam," Brandi explained with difficulty. "He's a nice-looking guy, I guess, not that I've really paid much attention to his appearance."

"Well, you should. You could be working next door to the perfect man and not ever see him," Mia countered with exasperation in her voice.

"That's true, but it's just as possible that Mr. Right will one day enter my shop. Isn't that what you tell me . . . repeatedly?"

"If I were still single—" Mia began in earnest.

"Here we go again," Brandi interrupted, holding up her hand. "Mia, save it for a rainy day. It's too pretty outside for a lecture today. Besides, shouldn't you be out there helping to push the customers in here? I thought the idea of the weekend festivities was to encourage not discourage spending. The shop's empty! I can see my regular customers milling around out there rather than in here where their presence will do me some good. A few minutes ago, I could hardly catch my breath, now I'm alone."

"Oh my gosh! You're right," Mia exclaimed, looking around the silent shop. "I'll talk to you about the dearth of male companionship in your life later."

Brandi laughed out loud as Mia rushed from the store. Although the shop was empty of customers, she was not really worried. She knew that they would all soon return, carrying their hot dogs, cotton candy, and sodas. At the moment, they were enjoying the beautiful sunny day and the festivities that Mia had so carefully orchestrated.

"Did I just hear Mia's voice?" Mrs. Owens asked as she appeared from the office. She had come to help with the anticipated crush of customers and to enjoy the festivities.

Brandi laughed. "She's flying high today. Why are you in here and not out there?"

"I'm leaving right now, and if you have any sense, you'll join me. The day's too beautiful to spend it in here."

"I'll be there in a few minutes. Where's Daddy?"

"You know your father and golf. He'll try to make it, but I wouldn't cross my fingers if I were you," Mrs. Owens explained as she exited the shop.

Gazing through the front window, Brandi smiled at the sight of her neighbors and regular customers mingling with the newcomers drawn by the announcement in the newspaper. Everyone appeared to be having a great time. Even her assistants, lingering in the cool air rather than entering the store, stood in line for a chance to participate in the apple-bobbing contest. The prize was a ten-dollar gift certificate that was good at any of the stores in the block.

Smiling, Brandi thoughtfully fingered the keys that hung on the chain around her neck. Since she had no customers, she could lock the shop and join the festivities. The sun would feel good on her face and back. Besides, winter would keep her locked inside soon enough; this might be one of the few remaining good weekends. She could always post a sign on the door telling customers where to find her.

However, as she slipped into her jacket, a customer entered. Mr. Bird's glasses fogged immediately, throwing him into blindness. Wiping them on his jacket sleeve, he smiled a greeting and headed on instinct toward the newspaper section with a steaming cup of coffee in his hand. Brandi's window of opportunity had closed.

Removing the jacket, Brandi perched on the stool behind the counter. Hugging herself against the draft that Mr. Bird's entry had created, she once again turned her attention to the revelers. With a little shrug, she acknowledged that she was not meant to be among them.

However, Sam had managed to liberate himself from Where Worlds Meet but not from the duties of a shopkeeper. He stood behind a long table on which sat urns containing coffee, tea, and hot chocolate as well as an equally large one of mulled cider, all supplied by Mia and Doug's firm. He appeared to be having a good time, especially when a little girl of maybe four, dressed from head to toe in red, held up her tiny hands for a cup of hot chocolate. Her precious little brown face glowed with healthy happiness. Brandi thought that his smile looked particularly handsome in the fall sunshine.

Pink-cheeked and laughing, Susan and Brad entered, bringing yet another burst of very cool air into the delightfully cozy shop. Although they had not yet acknowledged the relationship that existed between them, their smiles indicated that their bond had increased considerably. Pulling herself into a tighter ball, Brandi moved away from the sweet-smelling cool air that clung to their coats.

"You have to go outside. It's too lovely a day to stay in here," Susan stated as she tossed Brandi her jacket.

"It's too chilly out there for me. Besides, the customers will soon start coming in, and you'll need help," Brandi replied, waving off the jacket.

"One of us will come for you if things become hectic. Go!" Brad insisted as he pushed Brandi toward the door.

Brandi laughed. "All right, but I won't go far. If you need me, just shout."

Pulling the collar tightly around her ears, Brandi braced herself against the chilly air. The day would have been stunningly beautiful if the stiff northwest wind would only die down. However, the forecast called for the windy trend to continue throughout the weekend. The late fall sun had a difficult time competing against the first blast of winter.

"How's it going, Sam?" Brandi called as she approached his table.

Looking up from the Styrofoam cup that he was in the process of filling with thick, hot chocolate, Sam replied, "Hi, Brandi. It's going pretty well. The crowd has thickened in the last hour. Everyone seems to be having a good time. As much as I hate to admit it, this was a good idea."

In defense of her friend, Brandi said, "Don't be so tough on Mia. She usually comes up with good ideas if given enough time."

"Yeah, but she can dream up some real winners, too," Sam said as he handed a cup of coffee to a waiting parent.

Chuckling, Brandi replied, "Well, at least this is a good one. I see a number of new faces in the crowd. Maybe they'll like what they see and become regular customers."

"Looks like we're being observed," Sam said, indicating the direction of the seemingly casual customer.

"Who do you mean?" Brandi asked, scanning the crowd.

Handing her a cup of hot chocolate, Sam responded, "That guy in the black leather jacket is one of the vice presidents for Nailor Industries. They own Cuppa Cuppa Coffee and Pages Galore. He has already surveyed my shop and has been keeping a pretty good head count. He's giving your shop the once-over now."

"I don't think we need to worry. There aren't any empty shops on the block," Brandi stated, trying to assuage any fears that might be bothering him.

"True, but the hardly used parking lot around the

corner's for sale," Sam added with a quick glance in Brandi's direction.

"I hadn't heard about that," Brandi admitted. "I guess we'd all better keep our eyes open. That lot's big enough for a mall."

"If I had any extra money, I might want to purchase it just to keep anyone else from muscling in on our neighborhood," Sam said absently.

"That's a good idea, but it probably wouldn't stop them. They'd just find another location. That row of houses would make a good spot." Brandi pointed across the street.

"But they're occupied."

"Yes, but by older people who might be interested in selling and moving to a warmer climate. If a mall developer offered just the right incentive, they might sell."

Shaking his head, Sam said, "Let's hope that no one else has thought about that. Not only would we find ourselves surrounded by trouble, but the neighborhood would change drastically. Our stores offer just enough commerce. This quaint little refuge wouldn't be able to handle any more. In no time it would start to look like 'M' Street in Georgetown."

Bursting into their duo, Ally Marks asked, "Is this a private conversation or can anyone join? Smile. You two look too serious for a day like this."

Ally was the owner of the ethnocentric dress shop on the block and a major flirt. She collected men and tossed them away at will. In her mid-thirties, Ally maintained a figure that would make Hollywood stars envious. She lived in a condo in Bethesda that rivaled those of celebrities, too. Her choice of vibrant colors in the styles she carried in her shop accentuated the sheen of her blue-black shoulder-length hair. Her signature red nail polish drew attention to her long, graceful fingers. Adding to her initial appeal was a sweetness that lured people to her until they discovered that underneath the brilliant smile and behind the sparkling brown eyes was a woman who loved to create messes. Once people were aware of her habits, they shied away as much as possible, knowing that behind her ready smile was a less than pure heart.

Forcing a smile as Sam glumly returned to filling cups, Brandi replied, "By all means, join us. We were only speculating on the future of our businesses if a mall opens in the old parking lot around the corner."

"I just heard about that from the guy in the leather jacket. It seems that he works for a large, well-diversified company and has interest in this area," Ally said as she sipped the cup of rich brew that Sam had placed in her hands.

"You see?" Sam said grumpily.

Waving away the thought, Ally said, "You won't have to worry, Sam. Your business is going great, and you're probably safe, too, Brandi. Actually, we'll all be okay. He'd be silly to compete against us. We have such wonderful customers. They'd never leave us. They could go to the stores in downtown Silver Spring now if they wanted to, but they don't. They like our personal service."

"They might like deep discounts even better," Brandi offered.

"If I owned an independent bookstore, I'd be worried, too, Brandi," Ally purred sympathetically. "A store like Pages Galore would probably put you right out of business. However, Sam's different. There's always room for another coffee shop."

Coming to her defense, Sam retorted, "That would never happen to Brandi, Ally. Her shop makes numerous contributions to the neighborhood . . . more than either one of us. The tutoring service alone would keep her customers loyal to her."

Laying her hand apologetically on Brandi's arm, Ally said, "I didn't mean to step on your toes, Brandi, I was just saying that everyone knows the plight of independent bookstores. It's common knowledge. Hollywood even made a movie about it. I'm sure Sam is right. Your dear little shop is invaluable to the neighborhood."

"That's okay, Ally. You're right, that is common knowledge. I've held off the invasion of volume discounters before, and I'll do it again. Let's just hope that guy doesn't have plans for a women's discount dress shop." Brandi smiled sweetly.

Tossing her empty cup into the trash can, Ally replied with disdain, "I only stock specialty dresses in my shop. Its uniqueness will keep it open regardless of the competition from discount, mass-produced, common, ordinary women's clothing. I can't imagine that a mall would offer any competition for me."

"We'll be okay as long as we watch each other's back," Sam added as he studied the tension between the two women.

With a huff, Ally stated, "I can assure you that I won't be the one whose back needs watching."

"I guess she told me," Brandi said as she drained the last drop of hot chocolate from her cup.

"Ignore her, she's usually harmless," Sam advised.

"On a beautiful day like this, I think I'll take that advice," Brandi replied and added, "I'll see you later."

"Wait, Brandi," Sam called.

"What?"

"I hope you haven't forgotten our tentative date. Maybe we could have dinner next weekend?" he asked with a touch of hesitation in his voice.

"That sounds good as long as nothing comes up. With that guy roaming around, you never know what next week will bring," she replied, smiling at the nervousness that tugged at the corners of Sam's mouth.

"Don't let him bother you. I'll try to find us a good movie," Sam said with a big smile on his usually serious face.

"Great!" Brandi said and moved past the revelers toward her shop.

Before she could return to Over the Rainbow, Kevin Town, the proprietor of Drums and Bugles, advanced toward her, wearing a baseball cap turned backward and covering his sandy brown hair. Brandi smiled at the tall, trim, handsome man who rushed toward her. Kevin always looked as if he was in a hurry with his shirttail waving beneath the thick wool sweater that accentuated his broad shoulders. He hooked his sunglasses in the V of the sweater as he approached, revealing eyes that danced merrily. His long slender fingers clutched the flute that he had recently played as a member of a group providing Renaissance music for the festivities.

Kevin had opened his music shop a few months after Brandi opened her bookstore. They had shared the shame SBA counselor, the same worries about being able to make a living, and the same euphoria at the success of their businesses. Since his first meeting with Brandi, Kevin had dreamed of singing a sweet tune to her, but she had never noticed the infatuation that illuminated his rugged features and made his eyes sparkle whenever he was near her. They had simply remained friends despite his dreams and hints.

Feeling her cheeks burn from more than simply the weather, Brandi returned to the bustling store. Sam's renewed invitation had done wonders to push Ally's comments to the back of her mind. So, too, had the expression of pride on Sam's face in discussing Brandi's contributions to the neighborhood. She had not realized that he had noticed.

Like all independent bookstore owners, Brandi occasionally worried about the impact of a large chain on the continued success of her store. However, she hoped that her contributions to the neighborhood would be enough to keep her in business regardless of the competition. Her customers had an alternative within an easy walk now and chose to remain faithful to her.

Filling yet another shopping bag to the brim with books, Brandi forgot about Ally and her negative vibes. The day had been every bit as profitable as Mia had anticipated. Many new people had made purchases and promised to return, saying that they liked the intimacy and charm of the smaller bookstore.

As the afternoon turned to evening, Mia reappeared. Although she was tired, she was also thrilled with the turnout. For a modest outlay, the day had lured many new customers.

Mia beamed. "Wasn't the festival wonderful? The

weather cooperated completely, and people came from everywhere to enjoy the festivities. Your cash register must be about ready to burst. We'll have to do it again next year."

"It was indeed a success," Brandi replied with a smile, "but did you see that guy in the leather jacket? He was really checking us out."

Nodding, Mia responded, "His name's Frank Henderson, and he's a vice president for Nailor Industries. Sam already asked me about him. Don't worry about Nailor. This area is too small for them. Even if they were to purchase the lot around the corner, this area doesn't offer enough foot traffic or parking access for the financial success of a large company. Your neighborhood watch and parking restrictions have taken care of that."

"How do you know all of this?" Brandi asked.

"Nailor's one of my corporate accounts. You don't think that I keep the bill collectors away from my door by only doing business with you and Sam, do you?" Mia laughed.

"Then, why was he here?" Brandi asked as she handed a customer a book from the will-call rack.

"You're going to get mad at me when I tell you," Mia stated with a shrug.

"No, I won't. Tell me."

"Well, when you said that you weren't interested in Sam, I invited Frank. He's looking for a significant other or a wife and wanted my help. He was here on personal business and just happened to throw in a little professional work."

Placing her hands on her hips, Brandi turned to face Mia and said, "I know you're not telling me that while I was worrying about my future, you were playing matchmaker."

"Sorry," Mia said with an engaging smile.

Shaking her head, Brandi exclaimed, "I can't believe it. One minute you're trying to hook me up with Sam and the next you've found a new guy. If I really needed your help in sorting out my life, you'd really have me confused. Which one of these guys is right for me? Never mind. Don't answer that. I don't want to know."

"Some people solicit my help," Mia stated. "Not everyone turns his or her back on my suggestions."

"If you value our friendship, don't ever try to arrange a relationship for me again for any reason or at any time. Is that clear?" Brandi asked angrily.

"Crystal. However, there's one small problem," Mia muttered.

"What?" Brandi asked with exasperation.

"I've invited Frank to the little gathering at my house tonight. Don't worry. He doesn't expect you to spend any time with him. He just liked what he saw today and wanted to meet you," Mia explained.

Breathing deeply, Brandi said, "This is the last time, Mia. I'm not kidding. No more. I'm happy as I am. Don't do this again. As my oldest and dearest friend, you've overstepped your bounds this time."

"I won't matchmake ever again," Mia promised as she crossed her heart.

"Okay. As long as you understand, I'll come tonight. Just make sure this guy knows that I'm not interested in a relationship, arranged or otherwise, right now," Brandi said as her blood pressure started returning to normal.

"I'll take care of everything. Still angry?" Mia asked hesitantly.

"No, we've been through too much for something like this to come between us. But don't do it again. That guy really gave Sam and me a scare. The only one who didn't react was Ally, who can be an issue unto herself sometimes," Brandi managed to say with a smile.

"See you tonight." Mia waved gleefully as she headed to the door.

Brandi watched her friend walk past the front window. Stopping for a minute, Mia waved again and then vanished around the corner. Brandi knew that Mia would break her promise; she had in the past and would again in the future. Her dependability on this and all issues was part of her charm as was her big and generous heart.

For a moment, thoughts of Sam ran through Brandi's mind. She could hardly wait until the evening when she would see him again. The gathering at Mia's would give them a chance to socialize without the pressure of their jobs hanging over them.

Turning her attention to the crush of customers that filled the store, Brandi managed to push Mia, Ally, and the evening's gathering from her mind. She was once again so busy that she could think of nothing but the operation of Over the Rainbow. From the number of Where Worlds Meet cups in the hands of her customers, she could tell that Sam was up to his ears in business, also. The fall festival had indeed been a big success.

Chapter 8

By the time Brandi closed the shop and arrived at Mia and Doug's home in the upper northwest section of D.C., the place was jam-packed and jamming. Not only had they invited all of their clients on the Takoma Park block, but they had included everyone with whom they did business. Some of the faces looked familiar but most were people that Brandi had never met before that night.

Mia had decorated her spacious home with an abundance of little white lights that twinkled in every tree and shrub outside and adorned all the live plants on the interior of the house. She had also interspersed the greenery of living plants with the seasonal browns and golds of fall. Mirrors and crystal reflected the sparkling lights and added to the festivities. Although many weeks from Christmas, the adults-only party had the feel of a Christmas–New Year's bash. The only thing missing was the mistletoe and eggnog. Instead, cider flowed from the fountain in the dining room and cornucopias decked the hall table.

Arriving late, Brandi stood on the stairs in an effort to find Mia in the crowd of people. Tiptoeing, she managed to see Mia dressed in a harvest-gold silk pants outfit, standing near the fireplace. Pressing through the crowd, Brandi started the arduous trip from the foyer to the living room. Although she could not see over the shoulders of the taller guests despite her own height, she followed the increasing warmth of the room until she found Mia.

"You finally got here! I was beginning to give up on you and Sam, too. The Nailor rep who you saw at the festival, you know, Frank Henderson, couldn't wait any longer. He left. You blew that one," Mia gushed as she hugged her friend. Looking over Brandi's shoulder, she asked, "Where is Sam?"

"I don't know. He isn't with me. He was still closing his shop when I went home to change, but he said that he planned to come," Brandi replied, accepting the glass of spicy mulled cider that Doug pressed into her hand.

"You two work too hard," he said. "I've been trying for years to get him to lighten up. You're always the last to arrive because you have to close the shop and the first to leave because you need to reopen it in the morning. Hire more help. Give yourself a life."

Brandi smiled. "More help would cost more money. I have a life. My shop is my life. I'm happy. Don't bug me."

"Fine." Doug held his hands up in surrender. "If that's what you call living, have it that way. For me, I'll keep my nine-to-five job."

"If I remember correctly, you used to put in more than eight hours in your business, too," she rebutted sweetly.

"That's right. I did until the doctor diagnosed me as having hypertension. That did it. I stopped eating fast food and working late. I'm home every night on time, and I bring nothing with me except my empty hands. Life's too short."

"As long as I'm healthy, I'll keep doing what I'm doing, thank you," Brandi stated with a beguiling smile.

"Your physical health is sound, but your love life's on a permanent life-support system. You'll wake up one day and find that you're old, wrinkled, and alone."

Brandi's brows rose. "How long have you two been married now? You sound just like Mia."

"Fine, blow me off if you want, but I hope you'll see the light before it's too late. I did. The same goes for our buddy. He needs a life, too." Doug sipped his cider.

"Who needs a life?" Sam asked with a big smile as he joined the group. "Are you talking about me?"

"Hey, buddy!" Doug patted Sam on the back. "Indeed we were talking about you. You and Brandi need to get a life outside of your shops. I had to learn to separate work from play and to force myself to stop working. It's hard when you're self-employed, but you have to do it."

Sam nodded and said, "I know, but as you said, it's hard. I tried hiring someone to clean up at closing so that I wouldn't have to balance the till and do the menial tasks, but it didn't work out. The girl only half cleaned the hoppers. You can't make good coffee in dirty equipment. The next morning before I could start the coffee I had to scrub the pots. Cleanup's easier at night. I learned that I can't trust other people to do my work. It's probably the same way for Brandi, too."

Agreeing, Brandi added, "I tried not to double-

check the day's receipts, thinking that I could cut
down on time and give that job to one of my assistants, but I got too many calls from the bank the
next day. The kids made careless errors. They're
great assistants, but when they're in a hurry they get
sloppy. To save the frustration, I returned to my old
practice of double-checking the receipts with them.
I could be doing something else; they could be
straightening the shop. It's unnecessary lost time."

"You two are hopeless," Mia said with frustration.
"How will either of you meet the right person if you
never leave your shop? You can't leave all of your life
to chance . . . the chance that Mr. or Ms. Right will
walk in at closing, sweep you off your feet or buckle
your knees, and then stick around until you finish
cleaning the pots and checking the register."

Turning his attention from Mia and Doug to
Brandi, Sam said, "I think we're upsetting our hosts.
The music sounds great. Let's dance."

Placing her hand in his, Brandi replied, "That
sounds like a perfect solution to me."

Leaving Mia and Doug to contemplate ways to interfere in their lives, Brandi and Sam walked toward
the makeshift dance floor in the living room. The
caterer had moved the heavy pieces of furniture to
the perimeter and the lighter ones to another room
in order to create a small but workable dance floor
on which two couples swayed to the mellow jazz
sounds.

Joining them, Brandi and Sam discovered that
they moved to the soulful rhythm as if they had
danced together all of their lives. With their faces
close but not touching, they glided in tandem in
their little corner of the dance floor, even affecting

an occasional turn in the cramped space. Sam was just the right height not to brush Brandi's hair with his arm as he spun her. Her body fit his perfectly.

"You're a good dancer," Sam said, twirling Brandi again.

"You're not so bad yourself." Brandi smiled into his eyes as her heart fluttered.

"We should do this again sometime. Maybe go dancing instead of to a movie?" he suggested, holding her close.

"I haven't danced since the last wedding I attended three years ago. If you don't mind the inevitable crushed toe, I'd love to go," Brandi agreed as Sam executed a jazzy step.

"I'm game if you are. It's been years for me, too. But somehow, with you in my arms, it feels natural." Sam wondered at the crazy thumping of his heart.

"For me, too, Sam," Brandi said honestly, finding no need to hide her feelings.

As Brandi settled into his arms again, she allowed the lateness of the hour, the warmth of the room, and the stability of Sam's arms to encircle her. She was tired from the long day and should have been in bed rather than at a party, but she felt comfortable in his arms and did not want to go home. Sam was strong and sturdy, a man of substance and maturity. Brandi relaxed and sighed. Sam smelled so good, a combination of coffee, chocolate, vanilla, and sugar. Although he had changed from his customary jeans, he still bore the aroma of his shop. Brandi found it a comfortable fragrance. She felt strangely sorrowful when the music stopped.

Sam, too, had enjoyed the closeness of Brandi. She was not a fragile, little woman but a woman who could stand a little squeezing without breaking, manage a store without compromise, and supervise employees without prejudice. She had changed clothes and sprayed a spicy perfume behind her ears and on her neck that made him want to bury his face in her flesh and hold her tight forever. His sigh matched hers as he held her a little closer and breathed deeply of her warmth. He had to force himself to release her at the end of their dance.

"Would you like a drink or something to eat?" Sam steered Brandi toward the dining room and the incredible spread. Her hand fit his like a glove.

"No, I'm not hungry." Brandi was aware of the warmth of his hand and the closeness of his lips. "I'm too tired to eat. This idea of getting all of us together was great, but I'm too exhausted to enjoy it. I have to get up early tomorrow morning, unlike their other clients who can sleep late. I'd better go home before I won't be able to drive."

"I'll walk you to your car. It's time for me to leave, too," Sam said, finding it difficult to breathe in the warm house yet knowing that this had nothing to do with the heat from the fireplace.

"No, you stay," Brandi insisted, as they reached the front door. "You arrived later than I did. Have something to eat. I'll see you tomorrow."

"No, I—" Sam began only to be cut off by a voice from the depths of the crowded room.

"Sam, you're not leaving without giving me a dance, are you?" Ally asked, pushing herself between them. The black velvet jumpsuit clung to her every curve and revealed the fullness of her bosom.

"Good night, Sam." Brandi chuckled as she eased her hand from his.

"Wait, Brandi," he called.

Waving good night, Brandi stepped through the door and into the night air. A strange little stabbing pain came over her at the sight of Ally pouring herself against Sam's body that almost made Brandi change her mind about leaving. She did not understand her reaction and was too tired to analyze it. Maybe she should feel sorry for Sam being trapped by Ally. He certainly looked unhappy at the nearness of her. Whatever the cause of her feelings, Brandi would deal with the reaction when she was not so tired. For the moment, her main concern was making the drive home and getting enough sleep so that she could get up early and start her day at the shop.

From the living room window, Sam watched Brandi drive away despite Ally's attempts to drag him back to the dance floor. Strangely, he missed her already despite the voluptuous woman pressed seductively against him. Looking down at Ally's carefully made up face and clingy black velvet outfit, he thought she looked overdone rather than fashionably attired. He preferred Brandi's simplicity and the light dusting of powder that highlighted her features rather than modified them. Ally's perfume was too cloying, not at all subtle like Brandi's. Her lipstick and nail polish were too red. Her hair was too stiffly sprayed, and her lips were too pouting. She looked like an advertisement for her shop rather than a colleague at a social function. Sam thought that other men probably would have found Ally to be very sexy, but he thought she was too over-the-top for his taste.

"Come on, Sam, dance with me," Ally purred, tugging on his hand.

"Okay, one dance and then I have to go home," Sam agreed reluctantly to keep Ally from making a scene.

Oozing carefully planned sex appeal, Ally replied confidently, "It'll only take one dance, Sam."

As Ally pressed against him on the dance floor, Sam thought about the women like her that he had known. They had all been determined business-women who had put as much effort into luring partners as into running their business. They had looked at him with the same half-closed lids and slightly parted hungry lips. They had wanted to combine more than just their product lines. When he was a young divorced man in his late twenties, he had found them alluring and had yielded willingly to them. Now he was not impressed by the glitz and glimmer that faded too quickly; he wanted a woman of substance and sincerity. He wanted a woman like Brandi.

Despite the heat emanating from Ally's body, Sam could think of only one person. This was not the first time that Brandi had consumed his thoughts. He had often marveled at her ability to manage her business and appear cheerful despite the fatigue that accompanied the long hours. He had said as much to her only a short time ago, only to see her look shocked at the admission. He wondered if she ever thought of him as a man not a business colleague. Brandi never let him know if she did.

However, while holding her in his arms, Sam had sensed something more. He would have liked more time to uncover the change. Brandi left too soon to be replaced by Ally's blatant seduction efforts. He would have to find a way to take her in his arms again when she was more willing to let him into her life. The trouble was finding a time when work did not occupy every thought and drain all energy.

In the meantime, Ally's attention was flattering to Sam's ego. A beautiful woman had not thrown herself at him with such abandon in a long time. At least, he had been too busy to notice if she had until now. Ally made no pretext of her desire to seduce him, and he was too tired to resist her gyrations as one dance led to two.

"Sam, you're a handsome man. Why hasn't someone snapped you up?" Ally cooed, stroking the back of Sam's neck.

"I've had a number of offers, Ally, but I just haven't met the right one," Sam replied, separating her almost pulsating body from his.

"Maybe you've met one tonight." Ally smiled and winked.

"You might be right," Sam said, not thinking of Ally.

"It only takes a few dances to know for sure," Ally purred, pressing against him again.

Sam's body danced with Ally while his mind raced to catch up with Brandi. He should have left with her despite her insistence that he remain. He had missed her warmth from the moment she left his arms. Next time, he would not let her get away.

On the drive home, Sam could think of no one but Brandi. Ally's blatant attempts at seduction only served to cement Brandi's charms more firmly in his mind. She was not as flashy as Ally, but flash soon dies. Brandi's beauty and warmth would last forever. By the time he reached his front door, Sam was determined to continue the dance that the evening had only started.

Chapter 9

The next morning as Brandi and Susan unlocked the door to Over the Rainbow, Ally, who never opened her shop early, greeted her with a cup of coffee from Where Worlds Meet. She was very energetic after the long day and longer evening. Looking at her skeptically, Brandi could not at first understand the nature of Ally's early visit. Susan quickly vanished into the rear of the shop.

Ally, dressed in a native-print pants outfit, perched on the stool behind the counter and watched as Brandi switched on the lights, opened the shades, and turned up the heat. She had arrived at her own shop early so that she would not miss the opportunity to be the first one to greet Brandi that morning. Sipping her coffee, she alternated between observing Brandi's morning ritual and studying the brilliant red of her nails.

"Thanks for the coffee. You're up early," Brandi remarked as she sipped the coffee and booted the cash register's software. "What's up? Are you starting a new trend?"

"I wanted to be the first to tell you about something that happened last night. I didn't want you to hear about it from someone else," Ally replied sincerely and with contrition.

"What happened?" Brandi asked with alarm. "Are Mia and Doug all right?"

"They're fine. Nothing happened to them. It's about Sam and me," Ally said softly while fluttering her eyelids.

"What about you and Sam?" Brandi held the coffee cup with both hands. A strange feeling of foreboding had chilled the air and caused goose bumps to cover her arms.

Speaking through slightly trembling lips, Ally tried to explain, saying, "I don't know how it happened, but we found ourselves in each other's arms and one thing led to the next. Before we knew it, everyone was talking about us. It seems we've become an item. I'm awfully sorry. I could tell last night that you liked him. Sometimes things just happen. We can't always control our lives or actions."

At first Brandi could only stare at the pained expression on Ally's face. As that strange little pain stabbed behind her ribs, Brandi wondered when the relationship between Ally and Sam could have developed. Had it developed under her nose while she studied her cash flow? Ally had been in his arms on the dance floor only minutes after Brandi left. Surely Ally could not have seduced him and cultivated an affair in that short amount of time.

"I'm confused," Brandi confessed. "What relationship do you have with Sam, and why would it be of interest to me?"

"I saw the expression on your faces as you danced last night. It was clear to everyone in the house that you and Sam had the beginnings of a relationship.

Unfortunately, it just wasn't strong enough to stand the competition. I'm so sorry to have been the person to come between you two," Ally replied earnestly.

Willing her face to remain impassive, Brandi said, "I don't know what you and the others thought you saw last night between Sam and me, but there's nothing between us except that wall. We're neighbors, and that's all. Your apology is misdirected at me."

"Oh, I could have sworn that I saw more. Everyone misread the closeness between you two and the handholding as something more. I've so relieved." Ally sighed and smiled.

Trying to hold the rising anger in check, Brandi stated, "The closeness came from fatigue, and the handholding was so that we wouldn't lose each other in the crowd on the way to the buffet and front door. There's nothing between us."

"Great! That's good news. I felt awful about stealing from you, but now I understand that he was available for the plucking. I couldn't be happier. Well, I'll see you later," Ally gushed as she slid from the stool and headed toward the door. Her heels clicked victoriously on the wooden floor.

"Good. I'm glad you feel better. Have a good day," Brandi called as the pain in her ribs increased.

Ally waggled her fingers at Brandi as she pranced past the front window. Watching her, Brandi thought that Ally definitely looked relieved, although she herself felt awful. Until Ally's visit, Brandi had thought that she might be able to find time for Sam in her life. She had definitely felt a new closeness despite her contrary statement to Ally. The smell of his skin and his warmth, the feel of his hands on her back, and the sound of his breathing in her ear had made her feel that he had shared the same thoughts. Obviously, she had been incorrect. Sam was beyond her reach and tightly in Ally's grasp.

Pushing away the nagging pain, Brandi turned her attention to her morning's work. She forced herself not to brood over the loss of Sam. Besides, she could not lose something or someone that she did not have.

Love . . . Shaking herself, Branding wondered when that word had entered her mind. They had danced and passed a few wonderful moments, but that was not love. They had planned to have dinner and see a movie, but that was not love. Sam had brought her hot chocolate, but that was not love either.

Yet, the smell of Sam's skin still lingered in her memory. That tantalizing combination of coffee and chocolate teamed with his natural chemistry had been intoxicating, or at least in her fatigued state, she had been drawn to him because of it. The feel of his hands on her back and the sturdiness of his build had worked to create the image of security and stability.

"You're slipping, old girl," Brandi muttered to herself.

"Did you say something, Brandi?" Susan asked as she quickly joined Brandi.

"What do you make of that conversation?" Brandi asked.

Susan feigned innocence. "I didn't hear a word. You know I never eavesdrop."

"Right. What do you think that was all about?" Brandi demanded, flipping through index cards that she did not see.

Perching on the stool behind the counter, Susan replied, "Well, to tell you the truth, I'm not surprised. One of Ally's assistants moonlighted at Mia's party last night and saw the whole thing. Ally practically poured herself on Sam after you left. I understand they did some pretty steamy dancing . . . or at least Ally did. She insinuated herself like a question mark on that man."

Brandi shrugged. "What's the harm in that? They're both single."

"Everyone thought you two were becoming an item. Pasha said that things seemed to be going pretty good until Ally came between you," Susan commented.

"I certainly don't have ownership rights on Sam. It's silly for people to have imagined a budding relationship simply because we danced together," Brandi proclaimed.

"According to Pasha, you looked made for each other," Susan added. "Besides, he's really been hanging around here a lot lately. Maybe someone saw him leaving the shop and put two and two together."

"That was just friendship," Brandi explained. "We've known each other a long time. Mia's festival idea pushed us together more than usual, that's all. We do share the same friends, you know. People shouldn't make nothing into something."

"I guess it's only natural when two people seem so perfectly matched." Susan watched Brandi's face closely.

Restacking the already neat bookmarks, Brandi

said, "Do me a favor and tell Pasha that Sam asked me to dance as an escape from Doug and Mia, who were giving us a hard time. We're just friends. We're both free to date anyone we please with no strings attached. A few dances certainly do not constitute a relationship."

"Okay, I'll tell her," Susan agreed.

"Good. I don't want people jumping to embarrassing conclusions," Brandi stated firmly and added, "Now let's get to work."

As Susan raised a skeptical eyebrow, Brandi turned her attention to the contents of a box that had arrived during the height of the previous day's activity. She was so busy checking the invoice against the box's contents that she did not hear the door open.

Silently, Sam stood inside the quaint bookstore watching Brandi busily at work. He knew that by now someone had told Brandi about his evening in Ally's company, and he wanted to set the record straight. He regretted his ability to be seduced by a pretty woman and did not want to jeopardize his friendship with Brandi because of it. He was weak, but he was not a total fool. He had felt the change in Brandi as he held her in his arms. He could still smell her perfume as he lay in his sleepless bed that night. He knew that in some almost imperceptible way their relationship had changed. He had to set things right before he damaged it beyond repair. He wanted to continue from where they were after the dance, not from simply being business associates.

Clearing his throat and shifting his weight to make the floor creak, Sam waited until Brandi looked up from the sheets of paper. He marveled

at the swiftness of her slender fingers as they skillfully floated over the columns of titles and
transferred the information to the computer. He always felt so inept with the necessary but often
confounding technology that promised to make his
inventory job simpler but often added to the frustration of keeping track of supplies.

Smiling, Sam found that he enjoyed watching her
work almost as much as he had thrilled at holding
her in his arms. Everything about Brandi from the
conservative yet fashionable slacks and sweater to
the softness of her hair impressed him. He had
loved many women in his lifetime and even married
one of them, but he could not remember ever feeling so impressed by any of them. Brandi was clearly
in a league of her own.

When he could wait no longer, Sam softly called,
"Brandi, could I have a minute?"

Without looking up and seemingly without surprise at the sound of his voice, she replied, "Just give
me a second to enter this last column of numbers,
Sam."

Once again, Sam was struck by her confidence,
composure, and concentration. Brandi had known
that he was observing her and had been able to continue her tasks despite his presence. She could push
everything from her mind and dedicate herself to
the task at hand. She was a marvel. He did not know
that she had transferred the same data to the file
twice in error.

"Okay," she said with a smile as she looked from
the monitor into his eyes. "What can I do for you?"

Stepping behind the counter, Sam perched on
the stool next to hers. Something in the openness of

her expression compelled him to be near her when he began the discussion of Ally. He felt that being close to her would make it easier for him to handle the delicate situation.

Deciding on a neutral topic to open the conversation, Sam said, "The idea of the block party was certainly a good one. My store brought in fifty percent more revenue than usual."

"Mia and Doug outdid themselves," Brandi agreed. "Everyone seemed to have a great time. A number of the visitors to the neighborhood said that they'd return and bring their friends. The influx of new faces was good for my store, too."

Silence fell between them as Brandi waited for Sam to state the purpose of his visit, although she had guessed it as soon as he entered. Sam never made social calls, not even to comment on financial success. This time, he wanted to discuss something that he considered important enough to take him away from his shop when he should have been setting up for the morning rush. The nervous drumming of his fingers on the stool confirmed her suspicions.

Sam appeared in no hurry to break the silence. Feeling the tension tightening her shoulders, Brandi watched and waited. One of them had to speak or burst.

Taking charge of the situation, Brandi said, "The party at Mia and Doug's was really nice. It's just a shame that I couldn't stay longer. It's tough enough getting up early without staying up late."

"That's exactly what I wanted to discuss with you," Sam said, grabbing the stool for support.

"What? Staying up late?"

"No, the party."

Again, Sam stopped speaking even before he began. Brandi felt as if she were watching an old movie in which the hero and heroine were constantly at odds over insignificant events in their lives. She could feel herself leaning forward as if to coax the conversation from him. When the grandfather clock struck 8:45, Brandi knew that she had to take action. Customers would begin to flood the store in fifteen minutes. She had heard Ally's side of the story and Susan's gossip. Now she wanted to hear Sam's version.

"Ally dropped by to see me this morning. I heard that you two really looked good on the dance floor last night," Brandi said.

"She did? I don't know why she would. We only danced a few times," Sam said, stumbling over his words. "She got the wrong impression and is leading people to think that a relationship is forming between us."

"That's what she said . . . the part about the relationship. Ally seemed to think that she needed to apologize to me for sabotaging something between us. It seems that a few people saw us dancing and assumed that something had developed between us. She wanted to make it clear that she had not set out to break us up. I assured her that nothing had happened. We were simply two friends sharing a dance. Silly, isn't it, what people can make up?"

"But something has happened between us, or at least I think it has." Sam looked seriously into Brandi's eyes. "I think I'm falling in love with you."

"From a few dances? Sam, we're too old for this stuff, and we've known each other for too long. You were just tired. I know I was."

"I liked the way you felt in my arms and the way you smelled. I couldn't stop thinking about you all night," Sam said bluntly.

Feeling her temper flare, Brandi snapped, "You thought about me while giving another woman the impression that you had the hots for her? Should I feel flattered by that?"

"It's not like that at all," Sam began. "I had a . . . physical reaction to Ally and an emotional one to you."

Standing her full height, Brandi asked angrily, "Are you telling me that while you were trying to contain your physical hard-on for Ally, you were experiencing an emotional one for me? I thought I'd heard them all, but that's a new one."

Sam groaned. "This conversation isn't going as well as I expected. I was drawn to Ally, it's true, but only because of the outfit she was wearing. I was really tired, and my defenses were down. I would have had the same reaction to a lingerie catalogue. It's you who really touches me and makes me feel warm inside."

"That's heartburn, Sam, plain and simple. You must have eaten something last night that didn't agree with you. Take an antacid and call me in the morning." Brandi walked past him and headed toward her office at the back of the store.

Jumping to his feet, Sam laid his hand on Brandi's arm and said, "I don't want an antacid; I like this feeling. I want you. I love you."

When Brandi said nothing, Sam walked in front of her and looked into her eyes. Mingled with the anger and confusion, Sam could see something else burning there that gave him the impetus to continue.

Placing both hands on her shoulders, he pulled
Brandi toward him and gently kissed her.

At first, Brandi remained rigid in his arms, but
slowly the closeness of his body and the warmth of his
kiss pushed aside her anger. Easing her arms around
his neck, she allowed herself once again to experience
the emotions that had been awakened while dancing
with him at the party.

Suddenly, the door burst open and Ally entered,
bringing with her a cold wind that chilled Brandi to
the core despite the warmth of Sam's body against
hers. Although Ally had undoubtedly seen the embrace through the shop's big front window, she
pretended to be surprised at finding them together.
Her negative vibes bounced off the shop walls.

Waggling her fingers, Ally declared, "There you
are, Sam. I've been looking everywhere for you."

Pushing away from the tenderness of Sam's embrace, Brandi declared with pain in her voice at the
apparent betrayal, "You've found him. Sam's all
yours. He was just leaving."

"But, Brandi, I don't understand. I thought . . ."
Sam sputtered helplessly.

"After last night, I don't think Sam's free to think
such thoughts, do you, Brandi? Come with me, sweetheart. After what I've just seen, you have some
explaining to do," Ally stated as she pulled the confused Sam from the shop.

"You should keep your man on a shorter leash,
Ally," Brandi called.

"Oh, don't worry, I will, especially after I move my
shop in here," Ally replied.

"What do you mean?" Brandi demanded angrily.

"You didn't know? Well, I guess he hasn't arrived

here yet. An Internal Revenue Service auditor was looking for you and stopped in my shop by mistake. I gave him directions to your shop. Have you been playing little games with your tax return and SBA loan? It doesn't really matter. I'll help you pack. This shop is so much larger than mine. I can hardly wait to move in," Ally explained with an expression of concern mixed with elation on her face.

"Not hardly. I paid off the SBA years ago. As for the taxes, my accountant does everything by the book," Brandi rebutted.

"I guess you'll have to prove it to the auditor. An audit can be so time consuming," Ally gloated sweetly. "I guess we won't see much of you for a while. I'm sorry, Brandi, but it looks as if the pot of gold over your rainbow is empty."

Seeing Brandi's confused expression, Sam pulled away from Ally, stepped toward her, and said, "I'll help any way I can, Brandi. Just tell me what you need, and it's yours."

Holding her hands out to stop him, Brandi answered, "No, Sam, just leave. I have too much to do right now to have you around. This is all too confusing. Thanks for the offer, but I have to handle this alone."

"But I want to help you," Sam protested as Ally tugged on his arm.

Looking from one to the other, Brandi replied, "You've done enough, thanks. Now leave, please, both of you."

"Come on, Sam. We can tell when we're not wanted," Ally declared with a smirk.

Looking back one last time, Sam allowed Ally to drag him from the shop. The expression on his face spoke clearly of his confusion, pain, and heartbreak. Somehow, he had fallen into Ally's trap and lost any opportunity of winning Brandi's affection in a matter of minutes. To make the situation even worse, if Ally was correct, Brandi was in desperate financial trouble and might lose Over the Rainbow, the shop to which she gave her life.

Sam felt responsible for at least part of Brandi's pain and silently vowed to do something to right the situation. If he had not allowed Ally to seduce him, Brandi would not turn away from him now at her hour of need. As soon as he could, he would return to Brandi to make her understand. She needed to believe that he was in her corner and would support her in any way possible.

Brandi watched them leave without reaction. Her mind was spinning. She could not get a grasp on the chain of events that had brought Sam to her and taken him away while leaving behind the destruction of her shop and livelihood. She felt lost and very much alone.

The grandfather clock solemnly struck nine o'-clock. Walking as one in a dream, Brandi turned off the light that burned outside after hours, signaling that Over the Rainbow was open for business. Sinking onto the stool behind the counter, she surveyed the work she still had to do on the most recent order and contemplated the task that lay ahead of her. She had to save the shop at all cost. Nothing, not even Sam's entanglement with Ally or her own feelings for him, could stand in her way. Once the IRS agent stated his business, she would be able to apply herself to the task of defending herself. Until then, Brandi could only wait.

Chapter 10

The auditor must have been waiting for the official start of business, because he entered the shop with the appearance of the first customers. He was a short, squat man with a stubbly beard, unpolished shoes, and rumpled clothing. He looked as if he had either been caught in the rain or had slept in his suit. His squinting gaze at the store showed neither admiration for its tidiness and abundance of customers nor his disapproval. He stopped at the door only long enough to ask a teenager to identify Brandi from among the people gathered at the checkout register.

Walking toward her, the auditor extracted a surprisingly crisp business card from the pocket of his rumpled raincoat. He extended it to Brandi and said nothing, waiting instead for her to make the first move. When she nodded toward her office in the back of the shop, he followed her without hesitation as if this silent pattern were part of his normal behavior.

Walking past a wide-eyed Susan and closing her office door for privacy, Brandi stated, "I don't understand the reason for your visit. I keep very careful records, and I paid off the SBA loan some time ago."

As he sank into the offered seat, the rumpled man replied, "We've had a tip that you've been consistently underreporting your income with intent to defraud the government. I'm here to investigate your books."

"It's a lie! My accountant is one of the most reputable and honest people I know. Who would make such an allegation?" Brandi responded angrily.

The IRS agent replied, "It's against our policy to divulge the identity of the person making the accusation. I've made a detailed list of the information that you'll need to provide me over the next few days. I'm sure you'll be able to explain all of the charges. You might want to engage your CPA to help you."

"Of course, I'll cooperate completely, but it's really a waste of your time and mine. Give me the list, and I'll contact my accountant. We should be able to pull the information that you need if I don't have it here in my files," Brandi said as she extended her hand toward the man.

Smiling, the IRS agent handed Brandi a file folder containing three sheets of single-spaced information that covered the entire operational years of the store. Shaking her head as she scanned the information, she was at a loss to think of anyone who would make false statements against her. She would have to spend hours and considerable money responding to all of the questions. The effort would consume the little free time she had for several days.

"I'm sorry," the IRS agent said as he watched Brandi struggle with her emotions.

"It's not your fault," Brandi said as she tried to smile. "I've obviously angered someone. The really stupid part of this whole thing, aside from the cost and time, is that the SBA helped me file for part of the time. I'm squeaky clean. Oh well. There's no point in crying over it. Exactly when do you want the information?"

"I'll sit down with you and your CPA next Wednesday if you think you can get everything together by then. We can meet in the Rockville field office," the man replied.

"No problem," Brandi said with a heavy heart. "I have duplicate copies of the SBA information right here. The other stuff's on disk at home and with my CPA. What time on Wednesday?"

"Let's make it early . . . ten o'clock. I know it won't take us long. The list looks overwhelming, but the SBA connection simplifies it considerably. Call me if your CPA needs more time. I'll see you then." The IRS agent snapped his briefcase shut in preparation for his departure.

"We'll be ready," Brandi stated slowly.

Turning toward her, the man said sympathetically, "I know you're feeling betrayed, but, not that it makes you feel any better, this happens all the time. Someone wants to ruin another person, drive her out of business, or destroy her reputation. We'll settle it, and you'll keep running your business."

"Jealosy's an awful sickness, isn't it?" Brandi stated rhetorically.

"You'll survive. If you can make a go of an independent bookstore these days, you can do anything," he commented with a smile and added, "I can find my way to the door. Besides, I saw a book on fly fishing that I'd like to buy. None of the chain stores carry it."

Brandi watched as the IRS agent wove his way

through the crowded store. The top of his head barely cleared the shoulders of her tallest customers making their usual Saturday purchases. Several of the taller teenagers even towered over him.

Slowly, Brandi closed the door and returned to her desk. Dialing her CPA's number, she left the voice mail message about the audit and needing his help. She did not mind leaving a message, knowing that he worked as hard and long as she did and was probably busy with a client.

Sinking into her chair, Brandi reflected on the bizarre happenings. The time needed to pull together the information was not the only thing bothering Brandi. The fact that someone she knew had betrayed her hurt terribly. She would forget the lost time, but Brandi doubted that she would ever recover from the disloyalty.

Brandi sat with her hands folded across her knees looking at the floor. She wished that she could learn the identity of the person who had betrayed her, not for the purpose of staging an angry confrontation but so that she could learn the cause of the action. She must have done something without knowing it although she always tried to deal honestly with people. She tried hard to think of someone who would make up a baseless story and take it to the IRS rather than bringing the anger directly to her.

A soft knocking at the door interrupted the silence. Barely lifting her head, Brandi called, "I'm really busy. Come back later, please, or ask Susan to help you."

"Brandi, it's Susan. Can I come in?" the voice asked.

"It's open."

Susan entered slowly as if visiting the room of a hospital convalescent. She gazed at her boss with gentle, tear-filled eyes and placed her hand gently on Brandi's shoulder. For a moment, she could think of nothing to say that would ease her friend's pain.

"How did you know?" Brandi asked, breaking the silence that enveloped them.

"All of the shop owners and clerks on the whole block know," Susan explained. "It seems he asked Ally about the shop's hours. You know how she is, she told everyone that the IRS was looking for you. You know what that means these days . . . an audit. Will you be okay?"

"Yeah, sure. The audit's no big deal. I have all the information, most of it from the SBA filings," Brandi replied, trying to smile.

"Then why do you look so glum?" Susan asked.

"I feel violated in my own shop. I don't know who to trust anymore. Someone has deliberately set out to ruin me," Brandi responded sadly.

"I know you feel awful, but this'll pass. You can't stop being yourself just because of the actions of one hateful person," Susan advised.

"You're right, but I can't push the feeling of betrayal aside. I thought everyone here worked well together. I guess I was wrong," Brandi said as she rose slowly, blew her nose, and prepared to return to the crowded shop's main floor.

"Brad and I will help you find the person who did this to you. We'll snoop around on the quiet," Susan said loyally.

"No, stay out of it," Brandi insisted. "We don't

know what kind of person we're dealing with. You might get hurt. This'll blow over in time."

Stubbornly, Susan stated, "We'll see. Brad's already hatching a plan of investigation. We might as well get something for our prelaw money."

Smiling, Brandi replied, "Suit yourself, but be careful. And thanks for the support."

"Hey, we're with you a hundred percent," Susan responded, her eyes sparkling with unshed tears. "You're the bomb!"

"Thanks. I'll take that as a compliment, although I've never understood that expression. It's an age thing." Brandi smiled, giving Susan a pat on the shoulder.

Slowly, the warmth and normalcy of the store began to push aside the hostility of the act of betrayal. As Brandi worked beside her assistants or mingled with her customers, she felt her equilibrium return and along with it her good spirits. Although she had many hours ahead of her in the preparation of the information the IRS agent needed, she knew she would be able to accomplish the task and survive the mess someone had maliciously created.

As the grandfather clock chimed noon, Kevin, the owner of Drums and Bugles, entered the shop, carrying two steaming cups of hot chocolate. His gentle eyes searched her face as he extended the hand bearing the cup of chocolate. He could imagine the worry she felt.

Sinking into the sofa, Kevin said, "Hey, Brandi. How about taking a little break?"

"Thanks. Your timing is perfect," Brandi replied.

Smiling tiredly, Brandi accepted the cup. His quiet presence filled the office and made her feel better. At least, Brandi knew that Kevin had not betrayed her.

"I missed you at Mia and Doug's party," Kevin said as he adjusted his body in the too-soft sofa.

"I arrived late; you had already left. You know I can never leave here early. There's always one more thing to keep me busy," Brandi said.

"This isn't easy to discuss, so I'll get right to the point. Someone did you a dirty deal; we all want to know what we can do to help you," Kevin said angrily.

"So, it's true. Everyone knows. Thanks, but it's not as bad as it sounds," Brandi explained with a smile. "I have all the documentation the IRS could ever need, and most of it's SBA stuff that follows federal rules precisely. It's just the idea of betrayal that's so hard to take."

"Don't be brave, Brandi," Kevin insisted. "If you need money, just let me know. If you need a shoulder to cry on, I'm here for you. Ally made it sound as if the IRS could close you down almost immediately. She's already planning to move in."

Smiling sadly, Brandi said, "I suppose that could happen if I didn't have everything in order to respond to the accusations, but I do. As a matter of fact, I have copies here, at home, and in my CPA's office for safekeeping. I've asked him to join me for the Wednesday meeting. It shouldn't take long."

Grinning broadly with relief, Kevin replied, "That's good news, but remember, if you need anything just let me know. My business is doing well. I can lend you whatever you need."

"Thanks, but I'll be okay as soon as I shuck this

shadow of suspicion. That's the bad part. I don't want people thinking that I'm a crook," Brandi said.

"Did the agent say who gave the tip?" Kevin asked as he tossed his empty cup into the trash can beside the desk.

"No. Actually, he said that he couldn't tell me. I don't know who to suspect," Brandi said.

The two neighbors sat quietly for several minutes in the silence of the office. Both of them were deep in thought with one trying to deal with the pain of betrayal and the other struggling to formulate a plan to catch the culprit. They had known each other so long that they did not mind the lull in their conversation.

Kevin hated to see Brandi look so down. He had been secretly enamored with her for years but never been forceful in pressing the issue. She was always surrounded by either people or paperwork associated with Over the Rainbow. His opportunities passed before he could disclose his feelings.

Seizing the moment now, Kevin cleared his throat and said, "Brandi, this might not be the best time to say this, but since it's so hard to get you alone, I'm going to take a stab at it."

Jarred from her reverie and only half listening, Brandi inquired, "What was that, Kevin? I'm sorry, but I was so deep in thought that I didn't hear you."

Smiling uncertainly, Kevin said, "I'm on the verge of telling you—"

A heavy knock at the door interrupted his words. Sam entered almost immediately without waiting for a response. Closing the door behind him and leaning against it, he looked from one to the other.

"Am I interrupting anything?" Sam asked.

"No, nothing that hasn't been put on hold a thousand times already," Kevin replied, shaking his head.

Looking confused at Kevin's statement and Sam's appearance, Brandi demanded, "What's up? You didn't finish your sentence, and you never leave the shop at this time of day."

Folding his arms across his chest, Sam said, "I had to see you. Are you okay? I've heard from everyone on the block about the audit. Ally did a good job of passing the word."

Rising, Kevin said, "She would. I'd better get going. I'll finish that sentence some other time. See you later."

"No, don't go. Sam can wait. Finish what you were saying," Brandi urged.

"It'll keep," Kevin stated with a firm shake of his head. "I've been away from my store too long now anyway. My helpers will give away my inventory if I don't hurry back. I'll see you later. See ya, Sam."

Sam immediately sank into the sofa that Kevin had vacated. Staring at his hands, he sat silently for a while. He knew that he had to say something, but the words escaped him. The sight of Brandi's tortured expression had erased the speech that he had practiced all morning.

Usually, Brandi would make her guests feel at home in her office but not this time. Brandi sat with her hands folded in her lap as she watched Sam struggle with his thoughts. She could not imagine the purpose of his meeting since another woman so clearly occupied his heart. She willed the jabbing pain behind her ribs to subside, seeing no reason to pine for another woman's man.

Without looking up, Sam stated firmly, "There's

nothing between Ally and me. Despite the show she put on this morning, nothing happened at the party. We danced and maybe drank a little too much, but that was it."

"She doesn't seem to understand that," Brandi said calmly with a detachment in her voice that startled her. "From the way she all but dragged you out of the shop this morning, I'd say that she has a different opinion."

"I don't know why she was putting on that act," Sam continued. "I've had a talk with her, and I think she understands. We're colleagues, and that's it."

"Maybe she senses something that you're not ready to admit," Brandi offered, shifting slightly in her chair without unfolding her hands.

Growing irritated, Sam replied, looking Brandi in the eyes, "If I were going to admit something, it wouldn't be about Ally. It would be that I'm in love with you after all these years of buying newspapers from you and selling you hot cocoa. I finally understand why no other woman has interested me since I met you. It's not only that I'm working my butt off next door, it's that I love you."

Never had Brandi understood the term "pregnant pause" until that moment. The air hung heavily with Sam's declaration. She could sense that the next move lay in her lap, and she did not know the right steps to take to deal with it. She was hesitant to trust Sam after seeing him with Ally. She feared trusting anyone after the IRS betrayal. So, she did nothing although she wanted to melt into his arms and take refuge in his strength.

Sam watched the emotions play across Brandi's face and waited for her to say something. He had clumsily proclaimed his love and could think of nothing more to do. If only Brandi would say something or open her tightly clenched hands, he would take her into his arms. However, until then, he simply stared at her and remained silent.

Brandi was the first one to react. For the first time since she was a teenager, she covered her face in her hands and cried. She sobbed from the insult of the investigation and the hurt of betrayal. She cried for the loss of the secure world that she had so carefully constructed. And she cried because she was loved by a wonderful person but afraid to accept that love.

Sam's heart dissolved as he watched her thin shoulders shake from the intensity of her sobs. Rising, he crossed the short distance to Brandi's chair and placed his hands on her shoulders. When she did not resist, he pulled her to her feet and into his arms. At first, her body rested rigidly against his as if afraid to bend for fear of breaking, but slowly he could feel her muscles relax as the warmth of his body melted the cold within hers. Gently, he rubbed her back and shoulders until the sobbing ceased, and Brandi nestled quietly against him.

"Oh, Sam," Brandi cried into the handkerchief that he had pressed into her hands, "this is such a mess. I'm so unhappy."

"You know that I'll help any way that I can. I have money put aside for emergencies. It's yours if you need it. You don't have to go through this alone." Sam lightly massaged the tension from the back of her neck.

"That part's okay." Brandi shook her head and dabbed at her eyes and nose. "Kevin made the same offer. I don't need money. My books are in perfect condition. I'm just so upset that someone would do this to me. Who could hate me this much? Who would want to ruin my name and jeopardize my business? What if my customers find out about the audit and believe the worst about me? They might take their business elsewhere. This is a tightly knit little neighborhood. It's impossible to keep a secret here. And I live here. How will I hold my head up if there's a scandal? Who could want me out of the way that much?"

"We all saw that Nailor representative at the festival. Maybe his company's behind it," Sam offered as he lowered Brandi into her chair and perched on the desk beside her.

"They've made all kinds of offers over the years and never done anything like this. Besides, he's a client of Mia's. His visit was harmless," Brandi said with a sniff.

Sam held her hand tightly in his. "Maybe they're tired of waiting for you to agree to sell."

"I just can't imagine that they're resorting to this. They could always buy the parking lot, build a store, and starve me out," Brandi stated calmly as her composure returned.

"Yeah, but they'd have to wait. This way, they could spread the word among your customers and suppliers. The more people who hear the rumor of tax misbehavior and believe it, the sooner it becomes truth. They wouldn't have to wait the year to be rid of you."

"My suppliers?" Brandi repeated in horror. "I didn't even think about them. Do you really think that someone might have phoned them? That really could be devastating. Book wholesalers are squeamish about advancing merchandise or credit to independent booksellers anyway. They'd believe almost anything even though I never run a balance due on any account."

Patting her hand comfortingly, Sam said, "You should probably put your attorney on notice that you might need a well-written letter to quiet the noise. You don't know how much proof the person had to invent to get the IRS to agree to an audit. Hearsay might be enough these days."

"Okay. Let's assume it was the chain bookstore that set all of this in motion. What's their next move?" Brandi asked, still too upset to think clearly on her own.

"You might receive an offer that's substantially lower than the usual ones. They might think that you'll take anything as business starts to drop off."

"I'll have to make sure that business remains constant. I'll phone Mia and get her on the job. She'll think of something in the advertising line that'll put this scare to rest."

"Good idea. She called me earlier to say that she'd get here as soon as she could. She was shocked to hear about the IRS investigation. The idea that someone set out to get you really upset her, but she didn't want to bother you. She's feeling a little guilty about Ally coming between us. I told her it was my fault. Brandi, I could have stopped her, but my ego got in the way."

Shaking her head, Brandi stated, "Mia shouldn't feel guilty. She didn't do anything. We're both grown. You acted in a way that confused me, and I responded to what I thought I saw. Case closed on that one. The IRS business will end on Wednesday. Now, if I could only learn the identity of the person who started this mess, I'd be happy. I'd enjoy being able to confront the traitor."

"We'll think of something. You should focus your energy on the audit for now," Sam said, including himself in the process to assure Brandi that she was not alone.

Smiling, Brandi said, "Thanks for the support, Sam. Having you do the knight-in-shining-armor thing really helps."

"That's the least I could do for my fair lady in distress," Sam replied with a bow.

Rising, Brandi walked with him to the front of the shop. The customers greeted her warmly as she passed. In front of all of them, Sam placed a kiss on her cheek and left.

"That guy's in love with you," Susan proclaimed as Brandi joined her at the counter.

"I know," Brandi said with a shy smile.

"How do you feel about him?" Brad asked, observing the sparkle in Brandi's eyes.

"Confused. Only this morning I watched him leave with Ally," Brandi confessed.

"It's been one of those days," Susan commented.

"With luck, I won't have another one," Brandi concluded as she slipped into the crowd, leaving Susan and Brad to handle the register.

As she mingled with her customers, Brandi felt her spirits begin to rise. Over the Rainbow was thriving. Sales were brisk, the business checking account was full, and her bookkeeping was impeccable. She had nothing to fear except gossip and ill will, both of which she would overcome . . . especially with Sam at her side.

Chapter 11

An hour later, Mia rushed into the store, bringing a gush of cold air with her. She looked frazzled and very worried. Brandi was not only a client; she was her best friend. An attack on Brandi was an attack on her. And Mia was ready to do battle.

Speaking briefly to Susan and Brad, Mia marched to the back of the store. Customers parted to allow her to pass. Some frowned and wondered at Mia's brusque demeanor. Others, neighbors of Brandi's, had heard about the audit and understood completely. They nodded at each other, knowing that Brandi's buddy and support had arrived on the scene.

Tossing her coat into the chair, Mia stated without preamble, "We'll fix the SOB who did this. I'm sorry I couldn't get here sooner, but I was in Baltimore at a client's affair. Sam told me everything."

"Calm down." Brandi chuckled, feeling much better with the knowledge of Sam's support and affection and now Mia's. "You'll give yourself a heart attack. Besides, my CPA is pulling the information together right now. He says that this is a frivolous investigation based on absolutely nothing. Between the SBA files and my ledgers, we have all the proof we'll need to put this IRS business to bed. My attorney's drafting a letter as we speak. We'll use it as needed."

"That's good news!" Mia said, pacing the room, "but it doesn't push this issue from the minds of suppliers, who, by the way, have already called me for confirmation."

"Who called?" Brandi asked. "Were they satisfied with your answer?"

"Both of your book wholesalers phoned," Mia explained. "They believed me, I think. At any rate, they know that they can't do anything preemptive about it. The letter from your attorney's a good idea. Tell him to send it immediately."

Brandi smiled. "It was Sam's idea."

"Sam? How's everything on that front? I'm really sorry. I didn't know that Ally would throw herself at him like that," Mia said.

"Everything's fine, and you couldn't have known. She's your client, not your child," Brandi said. "Besides, Sam was free to push her away and didn't. He liked the attention."

"Men!" Mia stated with exasperation. "'You can't live with 'em, and you can't live without 'em.'"

"Sam's a good guy. He just didn't see this one coming. I'm not defending him, but I think Ally blindsided him," Brandi explained.

Settling into the chair, Mia exclaimed, "We'll have to take care of the SOB who tipped off the IRS and Miss Ally, too. Neither of them can get away with doing stuff like this to other people, especially not to nice people like you."

Brandi replied stoically, "Now that I've calmed down, I can see that there are worse things than disloyalty. I know my business is solvent and my books are squeaky clean. If you create a little ad campaign that shows Over the Rainbow is sound, we'll have covered all bases. You don't have to mention the IRS . . . just a nice little ad as usual."

"I'll design something tonight and bring it to you tomorrow morning. We can have it in the paper on Tuesday," Mia agreed, picking tiny dust particles from her skirt.

Speaking with her old confidence, Brandi stated, "Great, but let's hit the print and radio on Wednesday morning to coincide with the audit. I want everyone to know that Over the Rainbow is sound. This is one independent that won't fold under pressure."

Smiling at Brandi's energy, Mia asked, "And the Sam and Ally business? How will you handle that?"

"Cautiously for the moment. I don't plan to confront her. Sam says that he has told her of his feelings for me. I'll wait and see her reaction."

"Okay. I can't say that I agree with you, but I see your logic. I'd tear her hair out if I were in your position." Mia flexed her fingers as if feeling Ally's locks between them.

"No, I think low-key is better for the moment," Brandi insisted. "I don't want to give her any additional ammunition. She loves spreading news. If I made a move against her, she'd blow it up and pass it around."

"You might be right," Mia agreed reluctantly, "but I think I'll send her a little notice that our business relationship ends as of the first of the year."

"No, don't do that. I don't want her to think that your reaction to her is in direct relationship to the

Sam thing. Let it lie. There's no need for you to drop a client on my account."

"Okay, if you insist, but you're a better woman than I am. Depending on the way this shakes out, I still might drop her. I don't need a client like that. She'll stab me in the back one day, too."

"Well, so far, she's only acting catty," Brandi said. "Sam is grown, single, and fair game. Spreading gossip is ugly but not a criminal offence. However, I didn't expect it of her. She has always stayed to herself, not even attending neighborhood meetings. I didn't think that she even realized we existed. I don't know what brought her out this time."

"Brandi, look around you. Not everyone's nice, you know. Ally wants your shop space. Hers is much smaller. She's been interested in expanding for a long time. Don't forget, she has often encouraged the chains to buy out the block but without success. Customer loyalty is really strong in this neighborhood. If she gets you out of the picture and puts you into bankruptcy, she can take over your shop and expand . . . maybe even into Sam's, too. She might get him so confused that he'd move. She'd have both your shop and his then. She'd have that wall down so fast that the neighbors wouldn't even hear the bricks fall."

"Maybe you're right," Brandi conceded. "What's her goal . . . a shop like those on Connecticut Avenue? That takes a lot of money."

Looking at the ceiling, Mia replied, "I'm not supposed to tell you this, and you didn't hear it from me. Ally's loaded. The store's just something to do. She divorced a rock singer and made a mint. Then, she divorced a basketball player, one of your customers, as a matter of fact, and made another fortune."

Flabbergasted, Brandi sputtered, "Then, why does she want my little store and Sam, too? He's not wealthy."

Sighing, Mia explained, "Again, you did *not* hear this from me, but the rumor mill says that she personally designs those extreme outfits that she sells and ships them everywhere. I understand they're very popular in Los Angeles and Manhattan. The word is that the revitalization of downtown Silver Spring is about to spread south. This area is the next to pop. That's why companies like Nailor are interested in the neighborhood. Ally sees herself getting in on the ground floor and needs a bigger shop to do it. You know, she'll sell her creations to the rich and famous. She envisions herself operating one of those trendy Rodeo Drive or Fifth Avenue shops. Anyway, Sam's business is thriving, making money like mad. If she hooked up with him, she could control the coffee business, put him out to pasture, and move on to yet another bank account. You'd have heard all of this if you didn't work all the time. Everyone around here talks about her outrageous plans and lifestyle."

"Does Sam know this? She's something else."

"I don't know. He's as hopeless as you are. You both work too much. Life goes on around you, and you don't even see it."

"You'll have to tell him," Brandi said forcefully.

"Me? You're the one he loves. You tell him. I shouldn't have told you except that you're my best friend and Ally's been a real witch," Mia replied, examining her nails.

"I can't tell him. I'd look jealous or something," Brandi insisted.

"Maybe."

"No maybe about it. You know how men are. Sam's ego would blossom into something unrecognizable."

"Fine. I'll tell him to watch his back. He doesn't have to know about Ally's marital habits and expansion plans."

"Great. Anything else I should know?" Brandi asked.

"Not a thing. I'm out of here. We both have work to do. I'll see you tomorrow, relatively early," Mia said with a smile as she hugged Brandi.

"See ya, and thanks," Brandi called as her buddy left the office.

Despite the new sense of calm that flowed over her, Brandi knew that she had her work cut out for her. The fallout about the audit could still prove devastating to her business. Until the dust settled, she would not be able to breathe easily.

The ringing of the phone interrupted her thoughts. Brandi did not have to wait long to learn the caller's identity. The sound of the familiar voice sent chills down her spine.

"Oh, hello, Mr. Waters," Brandi said with as much cordiality as she could muster. "No, it's nothing serious . . . just a routine audit. Yes, I know that other independents have suffered from this kind of thing and folded, but Over the Rainbow isn't that kind of shop. That won't happen in my case. My books are in order. Thanks for your offer, but I really am not interested in selling to a big chain like yours. Much too impersonal. You're right, I might not get an offer this generous if the IRS finds a problem. However, you fail to understand my position here. My books are impeccable. That's right. Jealousy, the desire to occupy my space, greed . . . you name it. You'll be the first to know if I'm ever interested in selling. Thanks again. Bye."

Brandi hung up the phone and closed her eyes. The nightmare continued but on a different level. As she had anticipated, Mr. Waters, the marketing rep for the chain bookstore, Pages Galore, had called with an offer that was lower than his former ones but still generous. Even after ending the call, she could still feel him breathing down her neck. The only way to rid herself of the likes of him was to survive the Wednesday audit and let the world know that Over the Rainbow was sound. In the meantime, she would remain calm, take inquiring calls, and answer the myriad of questions. Whoever instigated the audit had certainly started a messy snowball rolling down the hill, and Ally had done her best to help it gather momentum by spreading the word.

The knowledge that someone disliked her enough to betray her was painful. She hoped sincerely that a chain store was behind the deed rather than someone she knew. Until she could learn more, Brandi would just have to wait, but at least she was not alone. With Sam at her side, Brandi knew that she would survive anything.

Chapter 12

Brandi had just locked her desk in preparation for leaving her office as the fax phone started to ring. The solitude was getting to her, and she needed to be with people to take her mind off her troubles. Wandering through the shop was just what she needed. However, the spitting of the ink on the paper forced her to stay.

The sight of the book distributor's letterhead was not a surprise. The person who betrayed her had worked very efficiently. Even her major creditor had heard and was taking a preemptive strike against her. After all these years with a perfect payment history, the distributor was withholding further orders until she could produce a statement from the IRS that her books were in order and the shop was not in danger of closing.

Brandi immediately scribbled an FYI across the paper and faxed it to her attorney. She had a feeling that she would need his help in this matter. She wished that he could help her discover the identity of her detractor.

"I'm going for coffee. Interested?" Brandi asked Susan and Brad.

"Definitely . . . with two sugars," Brad replied.

"A latte slim for me, thanks," Susan said with a gentle smile.

Tossing her office keys to Susan, Brandi pulled her jacket from the coat tree behind the counter. She could tell from her assistant's kind expression that she did not need to explain her actions. Although the shop was full of customers, Brandi had to leave them to handle the sales themselves.

"Come and get me if you need me," Brandi stated without giving either Susan or Brad the opportunity to tease her. Their sly smiles said that they understood that their boss had more than coffee in mind.

Turning, she walked to the door and into the nippy afternoon air that smelled strangely of an unseasonably early snow. Brandi had loved snowy days as a child and still enjoyed the idea of them, although she hardly ever had time to sit and watch the flakes dance past her window. Now snow meant slippery sidewalks, backbreaking shoveling, and reduced revenue. However, the decrease in traffic into the shop allowed her to catch up on her reading and produce the recommended reading list that her customers enjoyed.

The crowd in Sam's shop was as thick as ever. Smiling, Brandi spotted a number of people reading magazines and books that they had recently purchased at her shop. She liked the symbiotic relationship that had developed between Over the Rainbow and Where Worlds Meet. She liked the idea of having a neighbor whose store complemented hers especially since the proprietor was the man she loved.

Brandi joined the take-out queue as she scanned the menu posted over the counter. Although she always ordered hot chocolate, she read the list of specialty beverages while standing in line each time she entered the shop. One day, she would try something different but not now. At the moment, she needed the comfort of the familiar beverage.

The line slowly snaked its way to the counter. Sam, as usual, was busy filling cups. He appeared to know the visitors to his shop by their orders as much as by sight. He greeted each one with a smile and acknowledged each name as he filled orders.

After paying, Brandi moved along the counter to Sam's station. Watching him work, she observed the height of his cheekbones, the salt-and-pepper color of his hair, the slope of his nose, and his sturdy, muscular frame. He had once told her that he worked out every night regardless of the time that he returned home. It showed; Sam looked great. Although she had looked at Sam from every angle many times, she had only just begun to see him.

However, his efficiency and handsome appearance were not what drew Brandi to the shop that afternoon. She needed to speak with Sam, to hear him reassure her again that everything would be all right. She also wanted him to help her uncover the identity of the person who betrayed her, if at all possible. She needed to know the enemy among them.

Smiling at Brandi, Sam poured himself a cup of coffee and slipped the cup into the empty slot in the holder that he handed to her. Motioning toward his office, he pulled off his apron and instructed his assistant to take over the task of filling the orders. Walking around the counter, Sam joined Brandi at the office door. Unlocking it, he illuminated a room that was, if possible, more cluttered than hers. Without speaking, he cleaned a pile of papers from a chair for Brandi, then he sank into his rickety desk chair. His eyes took in every line of her tired face.

Sinking into the worn leather seat beside the badly scuffed desk, Brandi sipped the rich sweetness of the hot chocolate. She did not feel the need to speak although she had much to say. For the moment, she was content to sit and let Sam's calm attitude wash over her. The nearness of him made her feel safe.

To Sam, Brandi looked uncharacteristically fragile, and he felt an unfamiliar need to protect her. He knew that she never would have come to him on a busy workday if she did not badly need his support. He liked knowing that their relationship was on solid footing despite Ally's attempts to sidetrack him. Brandi's presence in his messy office empowered him to take on the world as her defender.

"I need help, Sam," Brandi stated simply.

"Name it," Sam replied without hesitation.

"I'm not falling apart; I'm still holding together by a very thin thread. Nothing has happened so far that I can't handle with the support of good friends and trained professionals. However, as you predicted, my main supplier is withholding further orders until this mess ends, and I received another offer for the store. You were right; it was many thousands lower than the original ones. After the IRS audit on Wednesday, the supplier will be content with proof of my solvency so that problem will be solved. I'm not concerned about the guy who made the ludicrous offer, since I've never entertained the notion of selling the store. However, for my peace of mind, I need to know who did this to me," Brandi explained, as she continued to hold her cup securely in her hands.

"Do you have a list of likely suspects?" Sam asked, as he reached for a pad of paper that lay across a stack of unopened mail.

"Only one," Brandi replied. "I don't want to put the blame on her until I'm sure. She had the motive and certainly relished spreading the news to everyone. I need to know with certainty before I confront her. Someone else might be to blame. She might only be a gossip with an evil streak."

"Or she might be the traitor among us."

"That's exactly what I need to know before I place the blame at her feet and demand a public apology."

"Okay. What do you want me to do?" Sam studied Brandi's dejected expression.

"Well, Ally seems to have taken a personal interest in you. Perhaps you could use it to your advantage, or rather mine. Maybe she'd tell you if she thinks you're on her side."

Sam shook his head. "I don't know about that, Brandi. I was pretty firm with her today. I made it perfectly clear that she suckered me once but won't do it again. She knows my feelings for you. I don't think she'd play along."

"Ally would if she felt she'd gain something from it. According to Mia, Ally has big plans," Brandi said.

"Mia stopped by to see me today, too. She told me some wild stuff, so I guess it's possible that Ally could be so intent on expanding her business that she'd try to ruin you and use me. Maybe I can convince her to confide in me," Sam said.

"Maybe you could make her think that she'd have

access to your shop if she were more straightforward with you," Brandi suggested.

"I'll try it. It can't hurt to ask her about her behavior toward me. She has really been coming on strong. I'd certainly like to learn her ulterior motives. A woman like Ally doesn't do anything without carefully choreographing her actions first," Sam agreed.

"Thanks, Sam. Don't commit yourself to anything dishonest or reprehensible on my account. Press her a little to see if she'll talk, that's all," Brandi said with a sad smile.

"I'll do what I can. Maybe I'll ask her to dinner tomorrow night. She might be more talkative away from the neighborhood. I'll let you know," Sam replied.

"Thanks. You're a pal." Brandi rose to leave.

Sam placed his hands on her shoulders to delay her departure. "Is that all I am to you? I don't blame you for being angry with me, but I'd hoped for a better place than that in your heart."

"You know you mean much more than that, Sam. It's just that my life is a mess right now, and I can't think straight. And remember, you compromised our budding relationship by giving mixed signals," Brandi said.

"I know. My behavior was . . . awful. I don't blame you for being hesitant. I'll make it up to you, Brandi. I want to be a fixture in your life. After all these years of working next door to you, I want to be more than a neighbor. I love you and have for a long time. I just didn't know how to change our status from professional to romantic."

Smiling, Brandi allowed Sam to pull her against

his chest. His strong arms made her feel secure and helped to push aside the feelings of desertion and betrayal. She could have remained in his arms the rest of the day if the shop had not demanded her attention. Maybe, after the mess ended, she would be able to surrender to the power of love completely.

The harsh realities of life looked less threatening with Sam's arms around her. Even his messy office did not look quite as shabby. His worn furniture took on an appearance of use rather than neglect. The stuffy aroma of clutter and old leather suddenly smelled inviting. Snuggling against him, Brandi marveled at the transformation that love could make in a pathetic little office.

Lifting her chin, Sam placed a gentle kiss on Brandi's lips. It was one of those lover's kisses about which she had read so often in romance novels. It warmed her entire body and made her tingle. It did not demand a response, but coaxed it from her. It did not press but lingered firmly. Brandi did not want Sam to stop kissing her, but she knew the sensation had to end. She wanted to stay in his arms forever.

A gentle knock at the door interrupted the magic of the moment. Still holding her hand, Sam opened the door. Susan, looking apologetic, waved and stepped inside.

"Sorry, Brandi," Susan said, "but we're swamped."

"I'll be right there," Brandi said with a smile as Susan hurried away.

Brandi turned her attention to Sam once more. "Gotta go. Work calls."

"Okay. Let's have a late dinner together after work."

Brandi declined with difficulty. "I don't think that's a good idea right now. Ally might hear about it and become suspicious of your motives."

"She's never here that late." He lightly stroked Brandi's cheek.

Firmly, Brandi replied, "She never comes to work early either, but she was here this morning. No, it's best if we don't see each other yet. Let's get to the bottom of this first. We'll have plenty of time later. Besides, despite that persuasive kiss, I still need to lay to rest the memory of Ally in your arms. That was a shock."

"Okay. We'll do it your way," Sam agreed reluctantly. "I want you unconditionally without any strings or hesitations. It's taken enough time to knock down that wall of Jericho between us, so I think I can wait a little longer."

Kissing him quickly, Brandi said, "Thanks, Sam. I'll see you later."

Brandi picked up the cups and rushed from the shop. As usual, she had dashed out without her gloves. The hot coffee felt good in her hands.

The shop was packed. To Brandi, it looked as if every customer she had ever served had decided to visit the store that afternoon. If the IRS agent could see the crowd, he would understand that all was well at Over the Rainbow.

Looking at the crowded shop, Brandi felt incredibly blessed. Suddenly, the IRS audit, the letter from her supplier, and the betrayal of one person did not matter anymore. She had a successful business, her health, her friends, and her man. Life was good despite the setback.

Chapter 13

The time passed without too much fanfare. Her attorney issued a strong letter to her creditors while her accountant prepared responses to all of the audit questions. Although she saw little of Sam, Brandi knew that he was working on her behalf.

"What do you think?" Mia asked as she produced the copy for a radio ad that mirrored the one in the paper. The double-team approach would put a stop to any further discussion of the audit.

"It's great! From the looks of this, there's no doubt that the shop is thriving. Send it on with my blessings. Thanks," Brandi replied, hugging her friend.

"It's as good as gone. I'll send one to the newspaper and a copy to your attorney as an FYI in case he needs more ammo to stop your creditors from balking.

Brandi sighed with relief. "It looks like everything's ready for the Wednesday meeting."

"How's Sam? Any news on that front?" Mia asked, lingering in the office.

"I haven't seen much of him. I've been too busy with the shop and the audit to ask if he's managed to pull any information from Ally. He hasn't come to visit, so I assume that he has nothing to share. I miss him, but it's best this way. I need to discover the traitor's identity before I can put this mess to rest."

"Don't go it alone. Call anytime," Mia said, packing her briefcase.

"I'm not alone. Susan and Brad have been super, and I know you and Doug are really working hard for me. Besides, Kevin visits often. Sometimes, I feel as if I'm imposing on him. He hasn't said anything, but I think he likes me . . . romantically. I don't want to lead him on. He knows that something had started between Sam and me before Ally burst in. I don't know if he thinks it's still viable, because he hasn't asked. He seems content to sit and talk, and I enjoy his company. I'm being careful with him just the same. He's a nice guy and a good friend."

"Well, keep me informed," Mia said, as she slipped from the office.

On the hour of the audit, Brandi's CPA arrived with boxes of supportive papers. Due to the volume of paper that Brandi would have needed to transport, the agent had agreed to meet in her office. Although she was on familiar ground, Brandi still felt incredibly nervous about the ordeal.

When he arrived, the IRS agent was impressed by the depth of the documentation that Brandi and her CPA could display in response to each charge against her. The audit consumed more than the two hours and left Brandi exhausted from the ordeal. Brandi, her CPA, her attorney, and the IRS agent holed up in her office, drank countless cups of coffee, and turned over reams of paper in search of any irregularity. From the impeccable SBA records to more recent tax filings to the current logs for Over the Rainbow, everything was in perfect order. Finding no trouble, the IRS agent used Brandi's computer to E-mail his report to the home office. He provided all the participants with a copy of the memo that cleared her name.

Draining the last drop from his cup, the agent pulled on his coat and said to Brandi, "I wish we could have met under more pleasant circumstances. You're a strong woman for having gone through this with such dignity. I applaud you. Never have I seen books kept in such perfect condition."

Rising, Brandi offered her hand and replied, "This ordeal would have been worse if it hadn't been for your gentleness. Thank you."

"Off the record, Ms. Owens, this kind of thing happens all the time. Try not to take it personally. It's hardly ever done by someone you know. It's over. I'd put it behind me if I were you. Enjoy your day," the IRS agent said.

The little man nodded to the others and left. As soon as the door closed behind him, Brandi fell apart. She slumped in her chair, covered her face with her hands, and wept. She had endured the tension for days, survived the prying into her personal and professional life, and maintained a stoic expression in the face of tremendous embarrassment. Now that the ordeal had ended, she could not hold back the tears any longer.

Her CPA and her attorney tried to console her but gave up when the gentle admonitions and flattery could not stem the tide of tears that cascaded down her face. They decided that Brandi needed a good cry to wash away the taint of the investigation and the pain of the betrayal, and she would have it.

The men stood helplessly watching her shoulders shudder with the expenditure of emotion.

In time the sobs grew less and finally stopped. Wiping the tears that had stopped coursing down her cheeks, Brandi thanked both of them for their help. As soon as they had left, Mia burst into the room without knocking. She had been waiting impatiently in the narrow passage between the main shop floor and the office.

"How'd it go?" Mia demanded, staring at the top of Brandi's head as her friend wept into a fresh handkerchief.

"Fine. It's over. I'm in the clear again," Brandi said, sniffing and without looking up.

"Then, why are you crying? You should be happy," Mia stated.

"I am!" Brandi sobbed loudly. "I'm just so tired that I can't help myself."

"Don't cry, little girl. It's over. Put it behind you," Mia advised softly as she pulled Brandi's head against the front of her suit, cradled her friend's shoulders, and rocked her gently.

"I don't know what's wrong with me," Brandi cried, dropping fresh tears on Mia's jacket. "I can't stop. I haven't slept much since this mess started, and I'm hungry. I must look awful."

Chuckling lightly, Mia stated, "You do need to pull yourself together, girl. I've definitely seen you looking better than you do at this moment. I'll take you to lunch. A drink or two might make you feel less pain. But at the rate you're crying you'll dilute the drinks."

"Very funny, but I'm too tired to eat. Let's get together later," Brandi muttered into the wet hand-kerchief.

Patting her shoulder, Mia said, "Since you're deter-mined to cry a river, I'll give you some information while you're doing it. Your book supplier called to say that he read the agent's findings and has reinstated your purchasing ability. Everything's turned out fine."

Lifting her head briefly, Brandi said, "Then the ads fit perfectly. The one in the paper looks like the typical business as usual. The one for the radio re-peats the message. It's great. Maybe we didn't need to run them."

Chucking softly, Mia replied, "No, you had to run the ad. The whole neighborhood was buzzing about the audit. Everyone had to see that it's no big deal and business as usual."

Sighing deeply, Brandi said, "I'm just so glad that my accounts were clean, and that it's over."

"It's over except for learning the creep's identity," Mia reminded her.

"At this moment, I don't even care about that. That person has to live with it forever. I'm free of it." Brandi frowned at her reflection in the mirror.

"You think the tears washed away all traces of the pain, but they really didn't," Mia counseled wisely. "You'll feel differently when they dry. You need to know the name of the person who put you through this torture. I hope Sam will be able to find out something helpful."

Touching up her tearstained makeup, Brandi said, "I hope I haven't misjudged Ally. Sam's task is to find out if she was involved. I hope with all my heart that someone from a large bookstore did this to remove competition. I hope that Ally only spread the mess that someone else created."

"I hope he learns something fast," Mia said. "Ally's not the nicest person in the world. I wouldn't put this whole thing past her. She's at the top of my likely suspects list. I'm glad that Kevin's relationship with her didn't last. He got out before she could do too much damage, although he seemed to have been crazy about her. For a while there, I actually thought that she cared for him, too. Silly me. I don't trust her."

"Don't forget that she's innocent until proven guilty. I hope she didn't do it," Brandi replied, adding a touch of lip gloss. "How dreadful do I look?"

"Not too bad considering you tried to end the drought by yourself," Mia teased.

"You're a big boost to my ego," Brandi countered, giving her friend another hug.

Together, the women left the office for the shop's main sales area. Susan and Brad threw their arms around her and hugged her hard. Most of the customers looked at them and smiled quizzically, thinking that it must be someone's birthday. The neighbors who knew of the audit sighed with relief that the ordeal had ended.

Smiling happily, Brandi spoke to both of them from her heart. "Thank you for your support. I don't know what I would have done without you."

Looking toward the door, Brandi spotted Sam and Kevin standing together. Both were tall, handsome men on whose shoulders she had leaned. Although Sam was the older of the two, he looked equally young and virile. However, the sight of only one of them could make her heart pound. Sam.

Brandi accepted the fact that those Friday and Saturday nights of standing in line for a cup of hot chocolate had not been only because of her desire for a fabulous beverage. She had wanted to see Sam, to catch a moment's conversation with him, and to have him to herself even as he continued to clean up for the night. She had denied her attraction for too long. Now she accepted the truth without question. She was in love with Sam.

If only Brandi could remove the sight of Sam with Ally the day her world hit a snag, she would be extremely happy. Unfortunately, she could still see Ally draped over Sam's arm. She could still hear Ally's voice speaking his name in a tone of ownership. Brandi did not know which she needed to know more . . . that Sam's interest in Ally had ended before it began or that Ally was not behind the audit. Now that the audit was over, she could concentrate on her personal life.

As Brandi looked past the two men and through the big front window, she saw Ally approaching the shop. Without hesitation, she burst into the store with an unknown gentleman at her side. She totally ignored Sam and Kevin as she rushed toward the counter where Brandi stood with Susan and Brad. Pushing her way to the counter, Ally grimaced in her best smile.

"I see that you've managed to convince the IRS that your records are in good order. Congratulations! I guess a big smile from an attractive woman still carries weight," Ally proclaimed in a sickly sweet tone.

In a voice laden with fatigue, Brandi replied, "I don't like the innuendo in that remark although I'm too tired today to discuss it with you. What brings you here? You don't usually leave your shop."

Smiling almost gleefully, Ally stated, "I wanted to introduce you to Larry Smith. He's the site manager for the new Hait Construction job. They purchased the parking lot behind us. It seems that you'll have something more ominous than an IRS audit to overcome soon. They're building space in the mall for a Pages Galore bookstore."

Extending her hand, Brandi said, "Welcome, Mr. Smith. There's always room for competition. I just hope the building won't be too out of character with our little neighborhood. As a resident as well as a shop owner, I'd hate to have a modern eyesore in this quaint little community."

"Don't worry about that, Miss Owens," Mr. Smith replied with a hearty shake. "We've designed a complex that's very much in keeping with this area. In fact, we've even taken parking into account and developed a plan that will accommodate customers' cars in an underground lot out of sight of the local homes. We won't inconvenience the neighbors one bit."

"Great. When will the stores open?" Brandi asked, shoving her hands into the pockets of her slacks.

Mr. Smith smiled. "We'll break ground the first of the year. If the weather holds, the first store should open in June."

"That's good news," Brandi said and added jokingly, "What kind of shops will move in? Will there be any competition of Ally?"

Joining the conversation with a smugness that made Brandi want to smack her, Ally said, "I'll be one of the first boutiques to open. I'm leaving this little row of shops for a larger, newer environment. Since it looks like you'll be here for a while at least, I have to move on."

"I hope you know what you're doing, Ally. It's difficult drawing customers to a new location," Brandi advised.

"Don't worry about me," Ally replied smugly. "My customers will follow me. I need a place that's a fitting showcase for my designs. This antiquated little strip simply isn't keeping up with my needs. By the way, Sam's moving, too. Both of us need more space. His coffee shop will fit in just right."

"Not so fast, Ally. I haven't signed a contract yet," Sam clarified, joining the conversation at the counter. "A lot of things have changed lately. I'm in the process of reevaluating my plans."

"Yes, Sam, dear. I know you say that, but you'll sign. The advantages are huge and far outweigh the inconvenience of having to pack up everything and move," Ally stated with a grin and then added for Brandi's benefit, "Besides, he'll be lonely without me. When two people are in love, they should spend as much time together as possible. We'll be neighbors without anyone between us."

"What?" Susan and Brad sputtered in unison. They could not believe that a relationship had sprung up between them considering Ally's behavior. They thought that Sam cared for Brandi since she had not told them of their little ploy.

Brandi looked from Sam to Ally. Remembering the conversation she had with him the day of the betrayal, she did not know if Sam was simply trying to penetrate Ally's defenses in order to determine her involvement in the IRS audit or if he really cared for Ally. Nothing in his expression or reaction to Ally's comment disclosed his feelings. For the moment, Brandi decided that she would play along and act pleased for the new couple.

"That's a good idea. Lovers should stay together," Brandi stated with a composed smile.

Kevin, who did not know about the arrangement between Sam and Brandi, did not agree. Speaking bluntly, he said, "That's the dumbest thing I've ever heard! Can't you see that Ally's using you to get at Brandi?"

"I don't remember asking your opinion, Kevin. In fact, I wouldn't waste my time with deception. Brandi and I are definitely not cut from the same cloth," Ally replied with a snap of her fingers.

"You're right about that. She's head and shoulders above you," Kevin said angrily.

"That's enough, Kevin," Sam warned. "It's not your place to criticize what Ally and I do. You're not privy to my thoughts or hers. Keep out of it, please."

"You're making a mistake thinking that you can forge a lasting relationship with Ally. She'll use you and throw you out when she finds someone else she'd rather have. She'll throw you over for another man in a heartbeat," Kevin continued without pausing.

"Okay, guys, let it go," Brandi interjected. "It's Sam's business who he dates. Good luck to you both. I hope your shops in the new mall will be a big success. I'll miss you, Sam, and wish I'd thought of combining our shops. Would have been logical, too. Just look at Cuppa Cuppa Coffee and Pages Galore. They often occupy the same space. I'm actually sur-

prised that they won't this time. I guess your reputation precedes you."

"That's nice of you, Brandi," Ally said, and then
added to Sam, "Let go. We have so much to discuss."

Pulling away, Sam replied, "I'll see you later. I
have a business to run."

"Fine," Ally responded with a huff. "I'll meet with
Mr. Smith alone and fill you in on the details."

Mr. Smith, who had been watching the exchange
with interest, allowed Ally to link arms with him and
propel him from the shop. Sam and Kevin followed
with each going in a different direction. Susan and
Brad could only exchange expressions of bewilder-
ment at the latest events.

Calmly, Brandi turned her attention to the cluster
of customers who had witnessed the minidrama that
Ally's announcement had created. No one could tell
her feelings from her expression. Brandi decided that
until she had the opportunity to speak with Sam
alone, she would act as if his liaison with Ally meant
nothing to her. No one except her staff and Mia knew
of the feelings that she and Sam shared. For a while,
Brandi would keep it that way. She saw no reason for
a public display of her feelings for him now.

For the first time since opening the store, Brandi
made wrong change and appeared distracted in her
work. Those who knew of the audit thought that the
stress of the day had played too heavily on her mind
and caused the mistakes. They overlooked her lack
of conversation as yet another result of the emotional and mental fatigue. They understood and
excused her.

However, Susan and Brad knew differently. They
had seen her with Sam the day the mess began and

knew that a relationship was developing between them. They did not know, however, that Brandi had solicited his help in finding out if Ally was the informant. From their perspective, they thought Brandi should be upset by Ally's announcement about the shop and Sam. They were surprised that she had not reacted like a woman scorned, but rather like someone suffering from mental fatigue.

Brandi spent the rest of the day in a fog. She desperately wanted to speak to Sam, but business was so brisk that she could not leave. She was so exhausted from stress and lack of sleep that the sandwich Susan bought tasted like sawdust instead of her favorite hot pastrami on whole wheat with mustard. She longed for a nap on the little cot in her office. But Brandi knew that she would not wake up until the next morning if she closed her eyes even for a moment. She should have been ecstatic about the IRS judgment, but Ally's announcements had dulled her enthusiasm. Once again, her life was on a tether, and someone else held the other end of the string. Until she could speak with Sam, the old nagging doubt about his interest in Ally would torture her.

Although she had a full calendar and many other clients, Mia breezed through the shop at closing time with a look of triumph on her face and Brandi's beloved carrot cake in her hands. She had been thinking about Ally all afternoon and thought that Brandi should take action immediately.

Brandi simply looked at her friend and said, "I'm too tired. I'll deal with it tomorrow."

"Tomorrow!" ally exclaimed, slamming her hand onto the counter with such force that the cake box popped open. "That woman tried to ruin you and still might depending on the sales volume of that new mall she has encouraged to open in your back-yard. She's parading your man around as if he belonged to her. I don't understand your hesitation."

"I have a lot of reasons, I guess," Brandi replied as she recounted the day's receipts. "First, I'm so tired that I can't think. This is the fourth time that I've counted these checks. Second, if Sam is involved with Ally, it's his business and not mine. It's better that I should find out now rather than after I've ordered the monogrammed towels. Third, we don't know if Ally really did anything other than gossip. Fourth . . . Oh, darn! I don't remember my next point. I'm too tired to think anymore."

"You amaze me!" Mia stated. "Aren't you at all worried about the new building? You should see the sign in the parking lot announcing its imminent arrival. It's huge."

Brandi looked up wearily. "It won't open until the summer. A lot can happen in that time. I can't do anything about it. Why should I worry? If I were to lie down in the path of the trucks, they'd drive over me, or at least around me, but they wouldn't turn away. My protests won't stop anything. Mr. Smith, the man responsible for the project, says that the architecture coordinates well with the neighborhood. If he's right, and I'm sure he is, I can't even start a protest on aesthetics."

"Have you seen the model?" Mia demanded.

"No, but I'm sure the community association president has. She doesn't let a clothespin get past her," Brandi responded with a yawn.

"Then I'll go talk with her," Mia proclaimed.

"Maybe this Mr. Smith snuck one past her. This might be the way to put a stop to the new building. One of us has to do something to stop this."

"Suit yourself," Brandi said. "The association president lives two doors to the right of me."

"Don't forget your cake," Mia reminded her as she slipped into her coat and marched from the shop.

During Mia's chattering, Susan and Brad had finished double-checking the day's receipts. Stuffing them into the bank deposit bag, they collected their things and prepared to leave. Each one took a big slice of the cake to eat later.

"Are you coming?" Susan asked from the door.

"Right behind you," Brandi replied as she locked the office door, flipped off the lights, picked up the cake box, and exited the building.

As they walked down the sidewalk, Brad inquired, "Aren't you buying your cup of hot chocolate tonight?"

"No, I'm going home. A slice of this cake is all I'll need tonight," Brandi replied without looking in the direction of Sam's shop.

Susan and Brad looked at each other with raised eyebrows. They did not know the reason behind the change in Brandi's pattern, and they would not ask. She had endured enough for one day without their prying into her business. Besides, Brandi always made her thoughts known in her own time. They could wait.

Waving good night, Brandi left them at the subway stop and then continued her walk home. The crisp air on her face helped to wake her up a little. The smell of the carrot cake actually made her feel hungry for the first time since the ordeal began. A cup of cocoa would go nicely with the cake, but she did not have the energy to turn around.

As she rounded the corner, Brandi could see Mia's car parked under the streetlight in front of the association president's house. She almost felt sorry for the woman who would have to listen to her friend's tirade at this hour of the night. Fortunately, Mia had not tried to drag Brandi with her.

The comforting aroma of spices greeted Brandi as she opened her front door, and the plaintive meowing of her cat soon followed. Quickly switching off the porch light, she walked to the kitchen. All she wanted was a slice of carrot cake and quiet. She would deal with Mia, Sam, and Ally in the morning.

Chapter 14

Brandi felt so much better after a good night's sleep. She had not slept so soundly since the IRS audit entered her life. For the first time in her working career, she did not wake up early to exercise. Not even her cat's insistent cries could wake her. As a matter of fact, if the alarm clock had not buzzed incessantly, she would have slept through the opening of the store.

Instead of going directly to the shop, Brandi circled the block to take a look at the sign in the old parking lot. She wanted to see the artist's rendition of the new commercial building for herself. Mia had been quite concerned about its impact on the old shopping strip and the stores. She had even been irritated that Brandi had not shared her reaction. In truth, Brandi had been too busy running her shop and dealing with the IRS to think about the competition that would come from the new shops. Maybe it was time that she did, but not that morning.

The old, abandoned parking lot looked much as it always did with the exception of the large sign planted at the sidewalk and the new chain-link fence that surrounded it. The lot had been abandoned for years with even skateboarders going elsewhere due to the ruts and holes in the surface. Litter had once peppered the lot, but the community association had banded together to form a weekly cleanup brigade that collected all the trash. At the moment, the faded blacktop waited for the bulldozers that would start the construction effort.

Turning toward her row of shops with their quaint facades, Brandi smiled affectionately. When spring came, she would organize a painting committee to restore the color to the wood trim and the shingles. The gingerbread trim and lead glass windows would sparkle once again. New benches in the little strip of park would be nice, too. If the old wanted to mesh with the new, it would need a fresh coat of paint.

Change did not come easy to the neighborhood. Three years earlier, her neighbors had been upset over the construction of two new houses. To their stubborn surprise, the architect had designed structures that looked as if they had always stood on their lots. In time, the residents of the little community had forgotten that they were new. The new and the old had blended seamlessly. As a matter of fact, the community association's president lived in one of the new houses. The neighborhood had been up in arms over nothing.

Walking to her shop, Brandi looked at the cheerful seasonally decorated windows of her neighbors. Everyone had used a theme that matched the merchandise they sold in the shop and coordinated with the old-world charm of the strip and neighborhood. Brandi loved the season even more this year than in the past now that the audit was behind her.

"Everything looks like Christmas. The shop decorations look great. Kevin's French horn is fabulous," Brandi declared as she slipped from her coat.

"All except Ally's, you mean," Susan snarled the name as if it tasted foul in her mouth.

"Ally's store needs to get in the holiday mood," Brad added. "She hasn't done anything yet and probably won't decorate this year now that she has moving on her mind. The mannequins in her shop window are still wearing the same outfits that they've worn since September."

"I guess it's just harder for some people to feel the joy," Brandi said.

"You're cheerful this morning. Have you seen Sam?" Susan asked.

"No, and I don't dare go to his shop. I'd really like a cup of cocoa, but I'm resisting the temptation," Brandi said.

"Don't you want to see him?" Susan studied Brandi's face for any change in expression.

Shrugging, Brandi replied, "Sure, but I don't know about his involvement with Ally. Until I do, I'll keep my distance. I can't completely let down my guard until I know for sure. That little warning voice speaking in my ear keeps reminding me to take it slow and wait it out. Until I've sorted out the Ally situation, I'd rather be safe than sorry."

Perching on her customary stool behind the counter with a trash can within easy reach, Brandi scanned and trashed advertisements, sales pamphlets, and miscellaneous junk. She slowed momentarily when she uncovered a beige envelope without a stamp. Finding her name on the front, she opened it and read the beautiful card that bore Sam's characteristically messy signature.

"What's that?" Susan demanded, leaning in for a closer look.

"It's a card from Sam. He left it here the day of the party at Mia's. It's beautiful," Brandi replied.

"He loves you. This proves it!" Susan gushed.

Looking confused, Brandi said, "Maybe he did then, but I don't know if he does now. Then, he looked forward to advancing our friendship. Now, Ally's hanging on his arm. I'm not sure he still feels the same way."

"Then ask him!"

"I will when the timing's right."

Sitting with her face in her hands, Brandi thought about Sam. He was complicated and transparent at the same time. A popular country song that she had heard at the grocery store said that men were works-in-progress. If that was true, Brandi wondered about the kind of man Sam would become if he ever reached completion.

Tossing the last of the junk mail into the trash can, Brandi wandered toward the back of the shop and her office, inspecting tables of books as she walked. Surveying the silent shop, she relished the last moments of solitude before the customers began to arrive. Adjusting the heat a notch, she stopped to fluff the throw pillows on the old sofa in the reading area.

As she unlocked the office door, the similarity between her life and Sam's struck forcefully. Brandi was always alone, too, except for her customers, Susan and Brad, and Mia. She really did not seek out other people although she was constantly surrounded by them. She was content with a few good friends.

Sinking into the old chair at her desk, Brandi muttered softly, "I am Sam."

At that moment, the telephone rang, jarring Brandi from her thoughts. Answering quickly, she was not surprised to find Mia on the other end. Her friend often rose early although she rarely got going until after downing a few cups of coffee.

Without preamble, Mia stated, "I thought you'd like to know that the community association approved the plans for the new building unanimously. There's no way to keep it from happening."

"I'm not surprised," Brandi confided. "The artist rendering is very attractive and compatible with the neighborhood."

"But it's so large and impersonal despite the attempt to make it look old and familiar," Mia complained.

Brandi commented, "Well, that's true, but the shopkeepers will make it feel more intimate by the way they display their merchandise. I think it'll make a lovely addition."

"I hope the new bookstore won't erode your profit margin too much. There's always that possibility," Mia continued with her doom-and-gloom speculations.

"It won't," Brandi countered. "Besides, competition is good for all of us. I won't be able to match prices with the larger shops, but I can offer services that they don't. I'm not worried."

"Far be it from me to worry when you don't," Mia whined.

Not wanting to beleaguer the point, Brandi changed the subject saying, "Do I remind you of anyone in particular?"

Without hesitation, Mia replied, "Yeah, Sam. Why?"

"Is the similarity that obvious?" Brandi demanded.

"It certainly is," Mia affirmed with a cluck of her tongue. "That's why I wanted you two to get together. You're so much alike that it's scary. Neither of you hangs out with any regularity. You're both content being alone. You don't really seem any more interested in getting married than he is, and he swore that he'd never do it again. The difficult task is in finding the differences between you. Are you just now realizing it?"

"I'm a slow study," Brandi said thoughtfully.

"Only on this one subject," Mia said. "You're on top of everything else. Even Doug, who never comments about anything and would certainly never play matchmaker, thinks that you and Sam belong together."

"That remains to be seen. Remember Ally?"

"She's a minor setback for a woman of your resourcefulness."

"A lot of this falls in Sam's lap, too, you know. He has to show that his interest in Ally is only data collecting at this point. That might not be the case."

"What does data collecting mean?" Mia sounded skeptical.

"Since Ally was all over Sam, I asked him to find out whatever he could about her involvement in the IRS audit. I suspect that she's the one who called in the tip."

"So do I. You think Sam will be able to get close enough to her to find out?"

"I sure do. If Ally got any closer to him, she'd become an appendage. She'll tell him what I need to know as a way of cementing their relationship."

"I hope he'll be more successful than I have. I haven't been able to uncover anything. The IRS doesn't kiss and tell," Mia said.

"But Ally does. Remember the gossip about her and Kevin when he first opened his shop? Everyone had her practically engaged to him before he could unpack the first trombone." Brandi chuckled.

"I sure do. She practically threw herself at him. The poor guy had to lock his door to keep her out. She visited him so frequently that he didn't get any work done. He phoned me to change the opening date of his store three times. The folks at the paper must have thought that I'd lost my mind."

"I wonder why their relationship didn't last. They dated for a while," Brandi mused.

"He wasn't flashy enough for her, I guess. Besides, he's really sweet on you, you know," Mia said.

"I know and I'm doing my best to put an end to it. He's a good friend, but that's all. I still wonder if he has feelings for her. I'm not the showy type either. I might be his rebound choice. You never know. He seems devoted to me, but his heart might really belong to Ally despite her odd behavior. Besides, if Kevin's too tame for Ally, why is she interested in Sam?" Brandi asked. "He's an old shoe kind of guy."

"I told you that it started out as purely business," Mia responded. "Ally saw a way to get what she wanted and she went for it. The audit gave her the means to move into your space. Now that it's over, she's using Sam as a means to an end. She thinks that he has a little money stashed away. However, according to your community association president, who by the way loves to gossip even more than I do, things with Ally aren't exactly what they seem."

"That's certainly a cryptic comment. What does that mean?"

"I don't know yet, although I'm looking into it. That's all your neighbor would disclose."

"Let me know whatever you uncover. It's time. I'd better unlock the front door before the customers wonder what happened to me."

Brandi did not have much opportunity to ponder the possible meaning of the community association president's remarks about Ally. Customers flowed through the door in a steady stream. She noted that many carried cups of Where Worlds Meet coffee, causing her to think that removing the wall between the two shops might not be a bad idea. If Sam did not move to the new shop, the combined store would help them weather the competition. One day, if the opportunity arose, she would suggest it.

Chapter 15

Although Sam was conspicuously absent in the shop from the time of the IRS audit until the first months of the new year, Kevin had become a fixture. He had started spending so much time in her shop that Brandi wondered if he was putting his financial security at risk. He had often spoken of the carelessness of his employees and, until recently, had rushed back to the store after even the shortest absence. Now Kevin often lingered over a cup of coffee and was underfoot so much that Brandi had to resist the urge to tell him to go away.

Brandi liked Kevin. He was one of those salt-of-the-earth guys who would do anything for people. He helped her box up the Christmas decorations and gleefully served chunks of the gingerbread house cake and cups of steaming coffee and cocoa. He hung countless yards of red and white paper streamers to decorate the shop for Valentine's Day, although he only placed a few little hearts in his shop window.

As soon as Kevin received the invitation to Mia's red and white party—she refused to call it a Valentine's Day party since everyone held those—he rushed to Brandi's shop and asked her to be his date although no one really needed one. Most of Mia's parties worked equally well for singles as for couples. Brandi was flattered but determined not to take advantage of his kindness, especially if his heart belonged to someone else, as did hers. Kevin appeared to be moving their relationship toward a new level while she was standing pat in the old one. As long as Brandi was unsure of Sam's behavior, she could only think of him.

Sam had learned nothing new about Ally's involvement in the IRS audit. In fact, his silence said that he either had uncovered nothing newsworthy or was beginning to enjoy Ally's company. Whenever Brandi ventured next door to ask him about Ally or his plans to move to the new building, she found Ally occupying a table near the counter. Seeing her, Brandi would quickly place her order and leave. For a woman who hardly spent any time in her own shop, she was a constant fixture in Where Worlds Meet. With Brandi not being able to do more than simply exchange glances with Sam, her visits had slowly dwindled. She preferred to send one of her staff on the coffee runs and stayed on her side of the wall.

Unlike Sam, Kevin had no difficulty showing his feelings. He brought her flowers and candies. He wrote her notes on music paper and composed songs that spoke of his affection. Susan and Brad often teased him about wearing his heart on his sleeve, and he never objected. In fact, Kevin smiled so broadly at the comments that Brandi felt embarrassed, knowing that his feelings were unrequited. She liked Kevin and enjoyed his company, but she could not summon anything deeper.

Sitting in her office one night after closing, Brandi stopped counting the receipts to look in

Kevin's direction. Standing beside the counter, he had been studying her so intently that she had miscounted twice. He always closed his shop earlier than she did and spent the rest of his evening waiting to walk her home. He had become a regular occupant of the sofa in the reading section. That night, however, he had lingered near the cash register . . . and Brandi.

"Kevin, you're a wonderful guy. You deserve someone who isn't preoccupied," Brandi said as she lightly patted his hand.

"I'm not complaining. I love being here with you. Now, finish your banking so we can go home. I want to talk with you about an idea I had, but this isn't the place for it," Kevin said, smiling broadly.

"I've finished," Brandi said, tucking the receipt bag into the safe and giving the tumbler a spin. "You could always keep your shop open longer, you know, rather than waiting for me every night."

"I tried that, but my customers don't seem to want to shop after hours. Hardly anyone came. I just wasted the electricity. Besides, I've been able to catch up on all my long-overdue reading. You're a good influence on me." Kevin helped Brandi into her coat.

"I just feel terrible keeping you waiting like this. You could have been at home relaxing by now." Brandi slipped on her gloves.

Kevin's hands lingered on her shoulders for an almost imperceptible moment longer. Slowly, he replied, "But I wouldn't have been happy there."

Looking deeply into his eyes, Brandi saw all the unspoken words of love. Sadly, she did not feel the same and could only look away. She was deeply fond of Kevin, but until Sam finished his sleuthing and returned to her side, Brandi could not give herself to another man. She was content with the business and the nightly walks home with Kevin.

Touching his cheek lightly, Brandi said, "Kevin, you know that I care for you, but I'm just too involved with the business to see past it right now. That IRS audit really turned me around. I don't think I've really recovered from the shock of possibly losing the shop."

Smiling, Kevin lightly kissed her gloved palm and replied, "I know, and I'm not asking for more. Your independence and your dedication to your work drew me to you when we first met years ago. My feelings for you are genuine and based on deep respect. I'm content with what we have at the moment."

"You've been a wonderful companion and a great help to me, but, Kevin, it's embarrassing sometimes. People are whispering that I'm stringing you along," Brandi protested lightly. She really did not want to hurt his feelings.

"We know the truth." Kevin turned off the shop lights. "I know that you still have someone else on you mind."

Involuntarily looking toward the lights streaming from Sam's shop window, Brandi commented, "I guess we're both hopeless romantics."

Matching his stride to hers, Kevin responded, "I prefer to think that we still believe in the power of love, and we're searching for the right person."

"And neither of us has been very successful. Love's so confusing," Brandi said softly as the cold night air nipped at her cheeks.

"But we could wake up tomorrow morning and

find that everything has worked out according to the greater plan of the universe." Kevin chuckled.

"You and that universal plan stuff," Brandi teased, increasing the pace against the cold. "That's what you said when they broke ground on the new building earlier than planned."

"I still think that fate decided to give us a warmer than usual winter so that the building construction could start early. We're ready for the challenge of the new shops. Our clients are firmly devoted to us. I'm not worried." Kevin took the key from Brandi's hand and unlocked her front door.

Tossing their coats onto the sofa, Brandi replied, "I hope we'll have time to put aside enough for the inevitable rainy day. I was hoping that my competition wouldn't appear until the slower months of summer. If the shops open in the spring, the impact on my bottom line might be a little more than I had anticipated."

"Don't worry. Whatever money you might lose during the spring you'll be able to recover in reduced salaries starting in May after Susan and Brad graduate," Kevin stated as he followed her into the kitchen to feed the cat.

"Don't remind me. I'll miss them terribly. They've been more like friends or siblings than employees. I couldn't have hired better assistants. We're so close. I don't think I'll immediately hire replacements. My mom says that she'd like to work with me for a while. She thinks that I'll take more time off if I know that I can depend on someone to care for the shop as much as I do."

"You can always hire new people after you see the summer sales volume. Your mom might have tired of the long hours by then. Hopefully, they'll be better than my assistants." Kevin scooped a handful of dry cat food into the bowl.

"I hope you know that you're confusing my cat. You feed him so often that he thinks you're his owner."

Kevin winked. "Maybe he's in touch with fate in a way that we're not."

Brandi chuckled. "That's possible, but I doubt it. His connection to fate depends on the frequency and quantity of his feedings. He's getting so fat that he can hardly walk."

For a few minutes, Brandi and Kevin shared the laughter of two old friends as they watched the pudgy cat waddle toward the bowl. She and Kevin were indeed wonderfully compatible, if only Brandi were free of the enchantment of Sam. However, at the moment, no one could hold a candle to Sam.

Kevin did not mind her devotion to both the shop and Sam. He had made time in his life to develop a relationship and did not object to spending it with her even if the waiting proved futile. He was aware that Brandi cared much more for Sam than she admitted. He saw the sadness in her eyes whenever someone mentioned Sam's relationship with Ally. The friendship that she gave him was enough to make Kevin happy even if it never amounted to more.

"Do you have any plans for Sunday?" Kevin asked as he lingered at the front door.

"Work. Why?"

"There's an exhibit at the National Gallery that I want to see and thought it might interest you. If you don't have any plans, we could go together." Kevin studied Brandi's face closely. This was the first time that he had asked her on a date, although he carefully worded his offer as a casual outing.

"I suppose I could ask Susan and Brad to cover for me. Okay. Let's go, but this isn't a date. We're just two friends sharing an enjoyable activity," Brandi agreed with a level of enthusiasm that surprised her.

"Of course it's not a date. Friends don't date. We'll ride the Metro. I'll meet you here and we'll walk to the stop together. See you tomorrow," Kevin said with a big happy grin as he opened the door.

Brandi closed and locked the door behind him with a sigh. She had not gone on a date since Mia's last botched attempt at matchmaking. She had not done anything social since the fall festival and the party fiasco at Mia's. She had begged off holiday parties, blaming work or the weather, because she did not want to encounter Sam and Ally.

"As long as we both know the rules and understand that it won't be a date, we're okay. Right, Midnight?" Brandi asked her cat as she bent to scratch him behind the ears.

The cat, her dependable companion, only purred louder. He understood everything, unlike men who failed to grasp the finer nuances of relationships and overlooked anything not directly related to sports, food, and sex. Brandi could count on Midnight to offer affection without expecting more than a bowl of food in return. He offered his love unconditionally, a quality often missing in human male-female relationships.

Switching off the light, Brandi made a mental note to ask Susan and Brad to run the store for her on Sunday. She knew they would not mind since both were working that day anyway. Besides, the store provided the excuse they still needed as a cover for the relationship that they pretended did not exist. Despite exchanging Christmas gifts, they had not taken their affection to the next level. Perhaps being alone in the shop decorated in honor of the month of love would inspire them.

By the time Sunday arrived, Brandi regretted her decision. Now that she had the day off, she could have used the time to sleep, clean her long-neglected house, become reacquainted with her cat, or read a book. Instead, she slipped into a pair of jeans, a thick sweater, and tennis shoes for a day at the art gallery.

Kevin rang her doorbell promptly at ten o'clock, helped Brandi into her coat, and led her to the Metro. He was so excited about their first nondate that he babbled constantly about nothing in particular for the entire ride from the Takoma Park Metro station across the street from their shops to the Smithsonian stop on the Mall. In all the years she had known him, Kevin had never said very much, but now he talked nonstop as if he needed to pull her into every aspect of his life. Finally, as they pressed through the cold wind on the Mall, Brandi could stand the steady drone of words no longer.

"Kevin, the wind is whistling past my ears so loudly that I can barely hear you unless I turn my head. Looking in your direction causes my collar to fall and the wind to hit my neck. Please stop talking for a while," Brandi begged through chattering teeth.

"You're right. I have been talking too much. I guess I'm nervous about our first date," Kevin agreed as they waited for the light to change and the traffic to stop.

"If you just remember that this is not a date, you won't feel the need to talk. Let's go . . . silently," Brandi instructed as she raced across the street and toward the I.M. Pei wing of the National Gallery of Art.

"Yes, ma'm," Kevin replied with a chuckle.

The interior of the marble structure, itself a work of art, was blissfully warm. Brandi removed a few of her layers and studied the mobiles that hung from the tall ceilings while Kevin waited in line for tickets to the popular exhibit. Finally joining her, he smiled but remained silent.

Standing in the serpentine line, Brandi remembered that she had not attended an exhibition at the gallery in four years. At that time, she and Mia had made the trip downtown to see the Monet exhibit, and she had loved every minute of the experience. Skimming the brochure of the current display, she hoped that the Rodin works had been as skillfully presented.

Inching forward, Brandi scanned the faces of the people in the line. Many were quite elderly, some were young couples with little children in their arms, but most appeared to be young professionals and art students. Regardless of their age, an almost reverent hush hung over them as they waited their turn to view the statues of the master.

"May I speak now?" Kevin asked with a youthful smile.

Brandi laughed. "Sure, but don't babble at me."

"I don't know why I was so nervous. I'm fine now. It must have been the cold. You're right, this is a nondate. I have no reason for nerves."

"Good. I'm glad to hear it. Have you ever seen Rodin's work?"

"Never, but I've always dreamed of traveling to Paris to view it."

Smiling, Brandi said, "My parents took me to see an exhibition in the gallery's main wing when I was a little girl. I remember thinking that his work was so huge. I wondered how anyone could spend so much time on any one project. I had a hard enough time practicing the piano let alone trying to produce something artistic from a slab of marble or bronze. I remember being very impressed. I wonder if the sculptures will look as big now."

Kevin chuckled. "Probably not. I remember returning to the shrine of the Immaculate Conception to view a mosaic that had knocked me off my feet when I was a kid. In my mind, it had filled the entire wall. I stopped in to see it while in grad school at Catholic University. I was so disappointed. It had shrunk to a manageable forty-eight-by-forty-eight inches."

"I guess memory distorts most things for good or bad," Brandi added softly.

Observing her closely, Kevin stated, "I guess there're some memories that we shouldn't dredge up."

With a little grin, Brandi replied, "That's for sure."

They had almost reached the front of the line when Brandi uttered a little startled sound. Coming toward them and approaching quickly were Sam and Ally, with her arm securely hooked through his. Brandi recovered quickly and willed her heart to stop pounding against her ribs.

Brandi had not seen Sam up close in ages. On seeing him now, memories that Brandi had sublimated rushed to her mind. She could feel his lips on hers and the strength of his arms around her. Her throat felt dry with the effort of not running to him. If Brandi had not been so shocked by the sight of fatigue that had replaced his familiar smile lines, she would have put aside her resolve and greeted him with a kiss despite Ally's presence or Kevin's watchful gaze.

Sam's tired face broke into a smile that quickly faded when he spotted Kevin at Brandi's side. He had heard the rumors that they were dating although he had not believed them. Now he thought he understood the reason that Brandi had been a stranger in his shop and in his life over the last few months.

Seeing them together, Sam decided that while he had been allowing Ally to drag him around in order to gain her confidence and learn her involvement in the IRS business, Brandi had fallen for another man. He felt the pit of his stomach tighten into a hard little ball and his fist clench in anger. He felt betrayed and determined to learn the truth.

In her usual overbearing way, Ally spoke first, saying, "I'm surprised to see you two here. You must be good for her, Kevin, because Brandi never leaves her shop for anything. Don't they look adorable together, Sam? They make a stunning couple. In fact, they're almost as well matched as we are."

"I'm trying to break her of that pattern. She needs an outlet for her creative energies after the difficult time she had in the fall," Kevin replied as he draped his arm protectively around Brandi's shoulders.

Brandi could see Sam flinch at the ownership stance. Stepping aside slightly, she said, "I haven't seen Rodin since I was a kid. Is the exhibit good?"

"It's wonderful. Sam even enjoyed it, and you know how he is about leaving his store. But he has changed so much. Sam accompanies me everywhere. He's afraid that another man will steal me from him," Ally bubbled, giving Sam a sugary sweet smile.

"You haven't come into my shop in a while, Brandi," Sam stated, ignoring Ally's closeness. "I have some information on that item I was trying to track down for you."

Kissing him lightly on the cheek, Ally said, "Oh, Sam, you know Brandi's too busy to socialize. That's why it's so surprising to see her out now. I hope she can afford to be away from the store today. I trust that she's left it in good hands. Besides, although she's been cleared of fraud in that IRS audit, she really needs to work hard and save as much as she can before the new shops open. That new bookstore will really give her a run for her money."

Brandi commented smoothly with a tone of superiority in her voice as she, too, momentarily ignored Ally, "Thanks, Sam. I'll come by tomorrow. Ally, if you mean the Pages Galore store, you don't need to worry about me. Larry Smith, the manager, stopped by to see me yesterday. We've known each other since the days of his owning an independent bookstore in Baltimore. I'm looking forward to working with him after all these years. Our customer base is sufficiently different that the proximity of our shops might help rather than harm one another."

"Well, that remains to be seen," Ally huffed at being one-upped by Brandi.

Sam smiled as Brandi's rapid and professional response silenced Ally's attempts at spreading mischief. He had learned nothing about her involvement in the IRS audit and had started to think that he never would. Ally was a sharp-tongued, brutal woman who did not hesitate to deliver low blows. As her escort to numerous social functions lately, Sam had seen her reduce several high-powered professionals to jelly. However, Ally had met her match in Brandi and disliked her for it.

As Brandi and Ally stood together, Sam marveled at the differences between the two professional women. Brandi's face carried none of Ally's sharpness. Her mouth was full and soft, not tight and mean. Her eyes sparkled warmly, unlike Ally's, which dissected everyone she met. Brandi spoke with expressive open movements of her hands; Ally held her arms rigidly at her sides, often with clenched fists. They were both successful, but one invited people to want to be in her presence while the other repelled everyone.

"It's our turn," Kevin announced as the hostess removed the velvet cord.

"Bye, Sam, Ally. See you later," Brandi called, reluctant to leave Sam's presence.

"Don't forget to pick up the information I have for you," Sam reminded her.

"I'll be there early tomorrow morning," Brandi replied as Kevin gently propelled her toward the exhibit's entrance.

Brandi entered the Rodin exhibit filled with conflicting emotions. Sam had looked so tired and unhappy that she felt a combination of pity for him and elation at his distress. She could read on his face the love that he still felt for her. All that she needed now was to hear him speak the words. She could hardly wait until their meeting the next day.

Smiling sadly, Kevin said, "For a moment, I thought the new spring in your step might be because of me. I guess I was wrong. You're still in love with Sam, aren't you? You don't have to answer that. It was written on your face and his."

"I'm sorry, Kevin, but I tried to warn you," Brandi replied, touching his hand lightly.

Sighing, Kevin remarked, "It's not your fault. You told me from the beginning that you didn't want a romantic involvement. I knew of your affection for Sam, but I guess I thought that I could win your heart. But I know now that I can't. I saw your face light up at the sight of Sam. There's nothing I can do to replace him. I'm a fatalist. You're meant for him, not for me. I'm just happy that we've had this time together. We'll always be friends."

"Thank you, Kevin, for being so understanding. Now, how about grabbing one of those great sidewalk vendor hot dogs? My treat."

On the ride home, Brandi and Kevin chatted happily about the exhibit the way old friends do when they have shared a wonderful experience. He unlocked her door and handed her the key. For the first time in weeks, he did not enter to feed the cat. Brandi could tell that he knew that their time together had ended.

"Thanks for going with me. It was nice having someone with whom to share the exhibit," Kevin said with only a touch of sadness in his voice. He had indeed enjoyed a wonderful afternoon despite the appearance of Sam and reality.

"I wouldn't have missed it. You're great company and a font of knowledge," Brandi stated lightheartedly.

"If you think this was good, wait until Manet comes to town. I'll really knock you off your feet then. Good night, Brandi," Kevin said as he lightly kissed her cheek.

"See you tomorrow," Brandi called from the doorway.

Kevin waved from the sidewalk without stopping. They both knew that the lovely little interlude would soon become a fond and cherished memory. Fortunately, their friendship would survive in the space where a romance would not grow.

Brandi leaned against the closed door. After a day in the huge museum with its vaulted ceilings and cool impersonal marble, her house looked even more cozy and inviting. She would feed the cat, grab a quick dinner, surf the Web, and go to bed early. The next day promised to be a busy one.

Chapter 16

Sam's shop had not changed in the days since Brandi's last visit. The lines of customers still reached to the door. The inviting fragrance of coffees continued to entice the taste buds. And Sam still managed to look harried despite being in complete control of the shop's operations.

Waiting her turn, Brandi watched Sam labor behind the counter. No one would have suspected that only a few minutes earlier he had been nervously checking the crowd in anticipation of her arrival. Now, with bent head, he looked engrossed in filling the stack of orders. The slips of red paper fluttered onto the counter, demanding his attention.

Placing her order, Brandi stepped closer to Sam's station. As if sensing her presence, he looked up briefly and smiled. They had been separated for much too long. The sight of her made his heart ache.

Brandi's heart fluttered like one of the order slips as their eyes met. She wanted to stop his flying hands and pull him close. Even though he had been working on her behalf, she had missed him terribly. Nothing would keep them apart any longer. If Sam agreed, they would put the investigation to rest.

A SPECIAL "THANK YOU" FROM ARABESQUE JUST FOR YOU!

Send this card back and you'll receive 4 FREE Arabesque Novels—a $25.96 value—absolutely FREE!

The introductory 4 Arabesque Romance books are yours FREE (plus $1.99 shipping & handling). If you wish to continue to receive 4 books every month, do nothing. Each month, we will send you 4 New Arabesque Romance Novels for your free examination. If you wish to keep them, pay just $18* (plus, $1.99 shipping & handling). If you decide not to continue, you owe nothing!

- Send no money now.
- Never an obligation.
- Books delivered to your door!

We hope that after receiving your FREE books you'll want to remain an Arabesque subscriber, but the choice is yours! So why not take advantage of this Arabesque offer, with no risk of any kind. You'll be glad you did!

In fact, we're so sure you will love your Arabesque novels, that we will send you an Arabesque Tote Bag FREE with your first paid shipment.

* Prices subject to change

THE "THANK YOU" GIFT INCLUDES:

- 4 books absolutely FREE (plus $1.99 for shipping and handling).
- A FREE newsletter, *Arabesque Romance News*, filled with author interviews, book previews, special offers, and more!
- No risks or obligations. You're free to cancel whenever you wish with no questions asked.

INTRODUCTORY OFFER CERTIFICATE

Yes! Please send me 4 FREE Arabesque novels (plus $1.99 for shipping & handling). I understand I am under no obligation to purchase any books, as explained on the back of this card. Send my free tote bag after my first regular paid shipment.

NAME _____

ADDRESS _____ APT. _____

CITY _____ STATE _____ ZIP _____

TELEPHONE ( ) _____

E-MAIL _____

SIGNATURE _____

Offer limited to one per household and not valid to current subscribers. All orders subject to approval. Terms, offer, & price subject to change. Tote bags available while supplies last.

Thank You!

AN084A

ARABESQUE

Accepting the four introductory books for FREE (plus $1.99 to offset the cost of shipping & handling) places you under no obligation to buy anything. You may keep the books and return the shipping statement marked "cancelled". If you do not cancel, about a month later we will send 4 additional Arabesque novels, and you will be billed the preferred subscriber's price of just $4.50 per title. That's $18.00* for all 4 books for a savings of almost 40% off the cover price (Plus $1.99 for shipping and handling). You may cancel at any time, but if you choose to continue, every month we'll send you 4 more books, which you may either purchase at the preferred discount price. . . or return to us and cancel your subscription.

THE ARABESQUE ROMANCE BOOK CLUB
P.O. BOX 5214
CLIFTON NJ 07015-5214

PLACE
STAMP
HERE

Handing Brandi her steaming cup of cocoa, Sam tossed his apron to one of his assistants and motioned with his head toward the back of the shop and his office. Again, Brandi's heart flipped. In a matter of minutes she would be alone with Sam again.

Taking her old familiar seat in his office, Brandi sipped her hot cocoa and waited. Turning toward her, Sam took the cup from her trembling fingers and pulled her into his arms. Instantly the trepidation faded as his lips sought hers. Brandi melted against him, putting all thought of the shop, Ally, and the IRS from her mind.

"Oh, Sam," Brandi breathed softly, "I was so afraid that things had changed between us."

Gazing into her eyes, Sam replied, "So was I, especially after seeing you with Kevin. That's why I decided to kiss you and tell you that I love more than anything. Business can wait."

Fighting back the tears, Brandi responded softly, "And I love you. I've really missed you. I've been so tempted to come in just to see you."

Sam chuckled. "You don't know the number of times that I've poured a cup of cocoa and started toward the door."

Brandi beamed. "You should have brought it over."

"I almost did on Friday. I got as far as your door and stopped."

"What stopped you?"

"The shop was packed, and Kevin was there. It just didn't seem to be the right time. I drank the cocoa myself. It was good, if I do say so myself." Sam pulled her closer and kissed her again.

"I love the way you taste of peppermint and coffee." Brandi sighed, laying her head on Sam's shoulder.

"It's the blend you like so much. I've been drinking it constantly while we've been apart. I'll bring some over tonight," Sam replied, gently massaging her shoulders.

"Tonight?"

"Tonight. It's about time we had a real date rather than only meeting in my office or yours. We have a lot to discuss, and I don't mean only Ally. I'll bring the coffee and biscotti," Sam explained.

"Do you think it's safe? What if Ally finds out? It'll blow our cover," Brandi said.

Speaking firmly, Sam stated, "As far as I'm concerned, this investigative stuff is for the birds. It's kept me away from you for too long. I've been stuck listening to Ally talk about herself while Kevin has been romancing my girl. You'll agree that we're ready for the next step as soon as you hear what I've uncovered."

Brandi was much too content to argue. She merely nodded and asked, "What time should I expect you?"

Sam said with a happy smile, "I'll walk you home after closing. Come over after you lock up. I don't want to take the chance that Kevin will ease his way into my space again."

"Don't worry about that. We're just friends," Brandi confided, looking into his eyes.

"Are you sure? You two were really enjoying each other's company at the museum," Sam said with a skeptical expression on his handsome face.

"Friends can enjoy each other without anything

else existing between them. He's given up hope of our relationship turning into something more. He knows that I'm in love with another man," Brandi replied with a big, happy smile.

"Anyone I know?" Sam teased.

"Umm. I'd say you have intimate knowledge of him. I'll see you tonight." Brandi picked up her cup and slipped from the office.

Sam smiled at her retreating back. He had never met a woman like Brandi. She was professional and womanly. She was serious and witty. She could cut him down with a frown and build him up with a smile. He was in love and incredibly happy. Now that they could spend time together, they would be able to build the relationship that he longed to share with her.

Once on the sidewalk, Brandi practically skipped back to the store. She enjoyed a happiness that she had not felt in weeks. She could handle anything as long as she had Sam by her side. If nothing else had come of their time apart, Brandi had learned that she had to have Sam in her life. Spending those few minutes with him had lifted her spirits higher than eating a box of chocolates.

"What's with you?" Susan demanded as soon as Brandi entered.

"I'm in love!" Brandi gushed.

"Oh, that. It's grossly overrated," Brad said with a sniff and a sideways glance at Susan.

"Ignore him. He's in one of his moods," Susan said. "Anyone we know?"

"I can't fight it any longer," Brandi gushed, hanging up her jacket. "It's Sam. I've decided that I'll never let anything come between us again. Not another woman, not another audit. Nothing will ever separate us again."

"It's about time," Susan exclaimed. "I suppose he finished his little project to your satisfaction?"

"I'll find out this evening when he walks me home, but I don't care anymore," Brandi explained. "This situation has continued too long. The audit unnerved me, and Ally's flirtation with Sam finished me off. It's time I shook myself out of this preoccupation with these insignificant matters and concentrated on the things that are important in life . . . like love."

"I vote for that!" Susan agreed.

"Until this evening, I have work to do. Give a holler if you need me. I have book orders to process," Brandi explained, waving her hand gaily.

"I can tell you won't get anything done," Susan teased.

Brandi smiled. "You're probably right, but I'll try."

Brandi giggled happily as she straightened a few books and vanished into the office. Tossing the empty cup into the nearest trash can, she settled into worn desk chair and tried to concentrate on the contents of the stacks of boxes that needed entry into the inventory database before making their way to the shelves. Forcing herself to concentrate, she managed to push Sam from her mind long enough to empty one box before someone knocked on the office door.

"Yes?" Brandi called absently.

"A package just arrived for you," Susan answered.

"Rats! Bring it in. That's all I need, another box of books," Brandi groaned.

Laying the long slender box on Brandi's desk, Susan said, "I don't think this one contains books."

Laughing happily, Brandi lifted the lid to expose a dozen red roses. The heady aroma immediately filled the cluttered office. Reading the card, she exclaimed, "I'm in love with a wonderful guy."

"I'd say that Sam has it bad." Susan chuckled as she backed from the office.

"So do I," Brandi whispered as she poured water from her mug into the white vase that accompanied the roses.

As Susan left, Brandi reluctantly returned her attention to the boxes of books and supplies for the shop. In all the years of running the bookstore, Brandi had never allowed anything to interfere with her ability to do her job. Even with the audit breathing down her neck and Ally's deceitful actions on her mind, she had always put the business ahead of her personal life. Now, for the first time, her mind strayed from work to Sam and the evening that lay ahead. She felt like a high school girl waiting for class to end so that she could see her boyfriend again.

Brandi had no way of knowing that Sam's efforts were equally as fruitless. He made incorrect change, spilled coffee grounds, and improperly mixed ingredients. Every time a customer entered the shop, he looked up to see if it was Brandi. Sometimes he forgot his place in the recipe and had to start over. He was a mess and could barely prevent himself from dragging Brandi from her shop and away with him for the afternoon. The evening would never come soon enough.

By the time Brandi closed her shop, she was a

bundle of nerves. The thought of an evening alone with Sam made her jumpy and fluttery inside. For the first time in her life, Brandi experienced the all-consuming power of love. No other relationship had ever had the same impact.

"I don't know how I made it through the day," Brandi confided to Susan as the last customer left the shop.

"It's a good thing that Mrs. Wilson is a regular. You practically pushed her out the door." Susan laughed as she threw the lock and turned the sign to read closed.

"Was I really that rude?" Brandi asked with a chuckle. "I'll have to apologize the next time she comes in."

"I guess even businesswomen forget their manners when they have a hot date planned for the evening," Susan teased.

"That's no excuse," Brandi stated. "I'm not a kid anymore and this is my livelihood. I should be in better control of myself than to run off regular customers, especially with competition moving into the neighborhood, but I simply couldn't help it."

"Speaking of competition, what have you heard about the new shops?" Brad asked as he joined the conversation.

"Not much. Construction is really ahead of schedule with some of the shops set to open at the end of next month and more to follow. By the summer, it'll be running at full tilt," Brandi replied, rechecking the day's receipts.

"The construction manager told me this morning at Sam's that the mall's owner has arranged for a big grand-opening celebration. He said the guy ordered a blimp to fly over the block. It'll have gigantic lettering, announcing the opening of the mall," Susan added.

"Really? That's a bit much for this quiet neighborhood. I wonder if he checked that out with the neighborhood association," Brandi said with a sniff. "Well, whatever he does will draw customers to us, too. Maybe we should hold another sidewalk festival and sale for the same weekend."

"That's a great idea. Customers will be able to visit both sides of the street. I'll get right on it tomorrow," Brad said.

"Call Mia for help," Brandi instructed as he assisted her into her coat. "She has all the information from the first one."

As the last one through the door and into the cold night air, Brandi flipped on the night-lights and locked the door behind them. She loved this time of night when the workday had ended and the street was quiet. The row of shops looked tranquil and inviting at that hour.

"I'll see you guys tomorrow," Brandi announced as they approached Sam's shop.

"Have a good evening," Susan called as she linked her arm through Brad's. Even in the darkness, Brandi could see his face break into a huge grin at her touch.

Inside Where Worlds Meet, the last customer was waiting for Sam to fill his order. Sam's eyes hungrily followed Brandi as he placed the final bran muffin of the day into the box and ushered the customer from the shop. Locking the door, he smiled and pulled her into his arms.

"It won't take me long tonight. I did a partial

closeout an hour ago," Sam said as he inhaled deeply of Brandi's sweetness.

Brandi sighed. "As long as I have a cup of cocoa, I can wait forever."

"One cup coming up. I'll join you at that table," Sam said as he hurried to gather the hot cup and the stack of receipts.

Sam placed the box of biscotti and the handful of receipts on the table. True to his word, he worked quickly despite the distraction of having Brandi so near. His hand rested periodically on hers as if to reassure himself that she had not vanished into the night.

The counting done and the shop locked, Brandi and Sam plunged into the cold night air for the walk to her house. Their breath made puffs of steam as they chatted about their day and their customers. By the time they reached the house, they had exhausted the small talk, and the cold had chilled their faces.

"Toss your coat on the sofa, and let's make another cup of hot chocolate. I'm frozen," Brandi instructed, leading the way to the kitchen.

"Where's that cat of yours?" Sam asked, surveying the living room.

"Just wait until I open the refrigerator door. He'll appear," Brandi called from the kitchen.

As Brandi heated the milk for the hot chocolate, Midnight appeared from his favorite perch at the upstairs window seat. He purred loudly and rubbed against her ankles. However, when the cat approached Sam, he stopped and sniffed the air. With a cautious meow, he waited for Sam to scratch his ears. Recognizing a friendly touch, Midnight dropped to the floor and waited for more attention. The man was not Kevin, but he gave good scratches just the same.

"You're in," Brandi said as she mixed the hot cocoa from the ingredients that Sam had brought from the shop. "If he hadn't accepted you, I'd have to put you out on this cold night."

"Thanks, Midnight," Sam said, pouring a saucer of milk for the cat.

"Now you've done it. We won't be able to get rid of him." Brandi laughed, handing a mug of steaming cocoa to Sam.

"I know an even better way to warm us up," Sam said, placing both cups on the counter.

Pulling a happily smiling Brandi into his arms, Sam gently enfolded her against his chest. His lips lightly tickled the hairs on her neck as his hands rubbed her back and shoulders. Tilting her face to his, he kissed first her cheeks, then her nose, and finally her lips. His mouth possessed hers with a force that left both of them weak and warm. The months of waiting and denying their love faded into a distant memory as they tasted each other's sweetness. The loneliness and the worry melted away.

Sam sighed into Brandi's neck. "You smell so good. Why did we wait so long?"

"I guess we were both afraid," Brandi admitted, looking deep into his eyes.

"Well, I'm not afraid anymore. Tonight is the beginning of a long life together," Sam promised.

"But what about Ally? She's still hanging over us," Brandi said as she led Sam toward the stairs.

"No, she isn't because I have a plan. I've thought of a way to solve all of our problems," Sam replied as he followed Brandi to the master bedroom at the top of the stairs.

"That's a major task. What's the plan?"

"Later. I'll tell you all the details later. Ally is definitely not on my mind at the moment." Sam pulled Brandi into his arms again.

Their lips and hands languidly caressed the familiar cheeks and backs. Allowing familiarity gained from long years of friendship to guide their new passion, Brandi and Sam explored the sensitive spots, lingering long enough to tease and titillate. As their clothing fell into a mingled pile on the floor, they slipped between the cool sheets. They quickly discovered that they could anticipate each other's reaction to a gentle touch and learned the way to thrill and excite to almost unbearable limits. When they could stand the exquisite pleasure no longer, Brandi and Sam's love liberated them to reach a degree of intimacy and passion that neither had ever experienced.

Lying exhausted in the circle of their bodies, they let the silence of the night and the strength of their love lull them to sleep. Neither heard the cat enter the room and assume his usual sleeping position at the foot of the bed. Even the last chiming of the grandfather clock at midnight could not disturb them.

Chapter 17

The next morning, Sam awoke to an empty bed. Stretching, he inhaled deeply of the mingled fragrance of Brandi's perfume and the combination of bacon, toast, eggs, and coffee. The sounds of domesticity and the singing of birds caused him to throw off the covers although it was only seven o'-clock.

Taking a quick shower, Sam rushed downstairs to join Brandi in the kitchen. She had set the table for breakfast, using a cheerful chintz pattern and coordinated place mats. The roses he had sent her, but had not noticed the previous night, filled a white vase. A pot of hot cocoa added its aroma to that of the breakfast treats.

"Good morning," Sam said as he filled the juice glasses.

"I thought you'd never wake up. Sleep well?" Brandi grinned, giving Midnight a sliver of bacon.

"Like a log. What time is it?" Sam asked, nuzzling Brandi's neck.

"Late enough. We have to open our shops, don't forget. This isn't a holiday," Brandi reminded him, placing delighted kisses on the corners of his lips.

With a sigh, they separated and she set the plates of scrambled eggs on the table.

Sam slathered jelly on his toast. "It should be. This is the first day of the rest of our lives together. We should celebrate by calling in sick."

"Not on a Saturday. You know the staff can't handle the crowd without us."

"That's too bad. I could sure enjoy a repeat of last night's celebratory activities," Sam teased.

Grinning and blushing, Brandi replied, "I think we could arrange that for tonight."

"I'm a lucky man. I'm in love with a wonderful woman who loves me back. She's a good cook and a fantastic lover. What more could a man want!"

Laughing, Brandi said, "And I'm a lucky woman. My man not only loves me, he likes my cat. I'm in heaven."

They ate in contented silence for a while with only the sound of the purring cat between them. The comforting ambiance of domesticity embraced them and turned the hurried breakfast into one that they would remember for the rest of their lives. For the moment, the world and work were far away.

Sipping his cocoa, Sam said, "I don't want to break the spell of the moment, but we need to talk and the clock's ticking."

"Is this about Ally?" Brandi sipped the last of her cocoa.

"Sure is. I overhead a conversation that helped me to figure out her involvement in the IRS audit and a way to straighten out this mess. I had planned to tell you last night, but the evening's activities pushed that idea from my mind." Sam grinned.

"I'm listening." Brandi laced her fingers with his.

Placing his mug on the table, Sam said, "Ally only capitalized on the audit, but she didn't snitch on you. The IRS agent asked her for directions to your shop. Ally decided to put the audit to use by passing the information on, hoping to drive you out of business so that she could occupy your store. However, she didn't want to dirty her hands by actually informing on you herself. She was afraid that the agent might reveal her name and the word would get around that she was the one who tipped off the IRS. She saw an opportunity and took advantage of it."

"Really? Ally didn't phone the IRS? She had everyone thinking that she was the tipster while all the time she was innocent," Brandi replied incredulously.

"That's right. She didn't do it. I don't know who did, but it wasn't Ally. I don't know if even she knows who did."

"I've judged her unfairly. So have Susan, Brad, and Kevin . . . and you too. She seemed like the likely suspect," Brandi said, resting heavily in Sam's strong arms.

Kissing her fully on the lips, Sam replied, "Her behavior and joy at your distress certainly led us to believe in her guilt. When you escaped unscathed, she decided to latch on to me. If she couldn't take advantage of the audit putting you out of business, she decided to reel me in, combine the shops, buy me out or divorce me if we got that far, and then dump the coffee business. She just wanted a huge shop for those strange outfits of hers."

"How does the new shopping mall fit into the

equation?" Brandi asked as she stacked the dish-washer.

"That caught her off guard. As soon as she heard about it, she decided to modify her plan a bit. Instead of simply enlarging the shop she talked nonstop about each of us opening a place in the new mall and leaving the old strip. She became obsessed with the idea."

"Why would she need you to do that?"

Explaining quickly, Sam replied, "She doesn't, but she's determined to keep us apart. She's envious of your relationship with me and the neighborhood. That plus the desire for a larger space was her motivation from the beginning. Ally's even said that a combined shop really wouldn't work because of the possibility of ruining her creations. The new digs would give her as much space as she wanted plus a plush location to satisfy her champagne tastes."

"So she didn't tip off the IRS, she only tried to steal you away from me," Brandi mused.

"Isn't that enough?" Sam demanded.

"Of course, but it's not a hanging offense. Women do that all the time. Besides, our relationship hadn't exactly blossomed then. In many ways, Ally did us a favor. She united us against a common foe . . . her. We might not be standing here now if we had allowed time to take its course. We've had six years and nothing happened," Brandi remarked.

"Well, plenty will happen from now on," Sam replied, kissing her soundly.

"So, now what?" Brandi asked.

Leaning against the counter, Sam stated, "I'm not seeing her again. We know all we need to know about her involvement in the IRS mess and her plans. You've survived the audit and come out on top. Ally's efforts have backfired. Your business is stronger than ever. We're together. Ally's counting on the new bookstore eating into your profits, but that's just a little added something in her mind."

"That could happen, but I'm not worried." Brandi snuggled against him. "The manager's an old friend, and he doesn't think that we'll interfere that much with each other. As a matter of fact, we might actually help each other. The proximity of the mall might lure people to our shops that don't visit the neighborhood now. Our personal touches might be enough to keep them with us. But I'm still confused. If Ally didn't finger me to the IRS, who did?"

Stroking her arm gently, Sam replied, "I don't know. We'll have to keep on the lookout. The only thing we know with certainty is that the audit was not a random act. The agent told you that someone had phoned in a tip. We might never know who did it."

"Or the person might strike again," Brandi said.

Pulling Brandi into his arms, Sam said, "That's possible. We'll have to be watchful. This thing with Ally produced two good results. We're together, which might not have happened if she hadn't connived to profit from the IRS audit. The other was her idea about combining our shops. It's a great marketing idea that'll keep both of us in business and give us more free time for a life together. The big chains do it all the time, team beverages with books, I mean. We're doing it now, but our customers have to walk outside to reach us. We should think about knocking down that wall as soon as possible."

Lightly kissing his lips, Brandi said, "I'll do more

than think about it, I'm ready to put it into action. Actually, the idea has crossed my mind many times. Every time it rains or the weather's bad, I feel sorry for our customers as they make that mad dash between shops. Removing the wall would solve that problem and help with staffing issues."

"Okay! We've solved that problem, now let's tackle the personal one," Sam suggested.

"What personal problem?"

"We'll be business partners but nothing else. It's time to combine our living arrangement, too. Let's get married." Sam looked deeply into Brandi's eyes.

"What?" Brandi sounded incredulous.

"Let's combine not only our shops but our lives. No one will be able to interfere then. We love each other. It seems like a logical solution to me."

Turning toward Sam, Brandi replied, "I love you, and you're right. However, I need a little more time. We've only just started dating."

"That's a technicality," Sam grumbled.

"Just the same, I want roses and long walks and deep conversations before I say 'I do,'" Brandi replied, as they locked the front door.

"Marriage won't change that," Sam protested.

"Yeah, right. That's not what I've heard," Brandi retorted, chuckling. "You know better than that."

"Let me rephrase. Marriage to the right person will enrich our lives, not diminish them. We'll live like the characters in the fairy tales . . . happily ever after," Sam held tightly to Brandi's hand.

Smiling happily into Sam's eyes, Brandi said, "I'm in no hurry to march down the aisle until I know all of the skeletons in your closets."

Linking arms, Brandi and Sam walked the short

distance to their shops in deep thought. Now that Ally was out of the picture, Sam had a new obstacle in the way of his happiness . . . Brandi. Somehow, he knew that he would enjoy overcoming her objections.

eistic, without friends upon it. Frequently, they felt excited at the idea of the . . . she had once obtained inside view of the operations of . . . Brandi felt confident now that she would enjoy the journey to . . . publication.

Chapter 18

Brandi could hardly wait to share the good news with Susan, Brad, and her mother. She knew that they would be as happy as she was about the turn of events. As they readied the store for the day's first customers, she told them about Ally, the IRS, and Sam.

"Gosh, Brandi, she's really an opportunist of the highest caliber," Susan commented.

"How long have you known about this?" Brad asked.

"Sam told me last night, but I've suspected it from the beginning. Actually, Mia had heard something similar," Brandi replied. "It's the only logical reason that made sense, plus, of course, wanting Sam for herself. Sam's been helping me uncover her motives."

"You mean that all this time you and Sam have been working together? We thought Ally'd broken you up," Brad said.

Smiling, Brandi responded with a wink, "Actually, things did get a little dicey for a while, but because of jealousies rather than Ally. Besides, you're not the only ones that can keep a secret."

Susan and Brad blushed and looked at each

other. "Touché!" Susan said as she linked her arm through Brad's.

"How long have you known about us?" Brad sputtered.

Brandi laughed. "I've probably known longer than you have. You two fought it forever. I've never seen two people resist falling in love as much as you did."

"We had good role models," Brad said.

"Why didn't you tell us earlier? When did you start dating him again? When's the wedding?" Susan demanded.

Brandi held up her hands. "Not so fast! I can't even think!"

"Okay. Start wherever you'd like, just fill in the blank spots," Brad said.

Perching on the closest stool, Brandi replied, "We met only a few times so that Ally wouldn't see us. Sam felt awful about the audit and wanted to help even though that dance with Ally and her behavior toward him had put a hold on our relationship. I became jealous, which was not smart. Sam's a good man. I never should have doubted him. Anyway, he offered to gain Ally's confidence and find out if she had any connection with the audit. In the meantime, Kevin popped into the picture and made Sam think that we had a thing going. We're just friends, but Ally encouraged Sam to believe that I didn't want to see him anymore. He became confused."

"But when did he tell you that he loved you and about Ally? We were with you until closing last night," Susan stated with her hands on her hips.

Brandi replied with a shy smile, "He told me everything over breakfast this morning at my house.

He's a real good guy. Even believing that our relationship had ended, he still continued to work to help me."

"From the expression on his face and yours, I'd say that your relationship is back on track. Are you going to get married?" Susan demanded.

Blushing, Brandi said, "I'm happy to inform you that Sam and I are officially together. He's wonderful. I love him . . . he loves me . . . all's right with the world. We're taking it one step at a time. I'm not rushing into anything as serious as marriage."

Mrs. Owens sighed. "I'm so glad, it's about time you realized that Sam's a gem."

"He's perfect for you, and he loves you so much," Susan gushed tearfully.

Brandi laughed. "If you're going to come apart like this, what'll you do if we ever make the trip down the aisle."

"I can't help it if I'm the sentimental type," Susan said, sniffing.

"Don't ever go to a romantic movie with her. It's embarrassing," Brad said.

Casting him a dirty look, Susan dragged Brad from the shop. It was their turn to buy the morning coffee. Brandi was happy to see that their relationship appeared to be making progress, too. The Valentine's Day decorations added to the feeling of love in the air.

"Your father will be so pleased," Mrs. Owens commented, alone at the front of the shop with her daughter. "He had almost given up the idea of being able to escort you down the aisle."

"He shouldn't rent the tux yet," Brandi advised her mom. "Sam and I need to get to know each other on a personal level before the wedding bells start ringing."

"That won't take any time at all. You'll make a beautiful bride." Mrs. Owens sighed happily. "Have you phoned Mia? She'll just die!"

"No, but I will in a few minutes. Just think, I managed to fall in love with the man of my choice without Mia's help," Brandi said.

"She'll never believe that she didn't have something to do with it. After all, that horrible party that started the whole thing with Ally was at Mia's house," Mrs. Owens reminded Brandi.

Brandi chuckled. "True. Well, maybe Mia and Doug do deserve a little credit."

Before Brandi could attack the day's work, Susan and Brad returned with the drinks. Their cheeks were flushed from more than the walk from Sam's shop. They giggled like children sharing a secret. To Brandi's surprise, Sam accompanied them.

Before removing her coat, Susan blurted, "Ally's tapped out!"

Glancing quickly at Sam, Brandi demanded, "Where'd you hear that?"

"At Sam's. She fired her assistants this morning. They couldn't wait to spread the news," Susan replied with a shrug.

"She never mentioned any problems to me," Sam said.

With a cocky assurance, Susan said, "According to her assistants, the landlord has given her one month to become current on her rent or she's out. Her assistants said that after Ally fired them, she locked the door and went home."

Leaning confidentially toward Brandi and Sam,

Brad added, "We heard that she's three months in arrears on her rent. She has until the first of March to pay up."

"That's terrible!" Brandi cried. "If this is true, she must be devastated. That explains why she'd be so set on capturing you, Sam. She needed your money to front her business in the new mall, or at least to cover the expenses in this one."

"So it was my savings she was after. And I thought it was my sexy smile," Sam replied lightly.

"We'll all have to help her," Brandi suggested. "I'll canvass the neighbors to see if anyone's interested in joining me in the effort. Maybe we can think of some way to approach her with assistance while still giving her a way to save face."

Susan stared at Brandi with an open mouth. Pulling herself together, she demanded, "You'd do this for a woman who spread rumors and tried to steal your man?"

Placing her cup on the counter, Brandi said, "I know what you're thinking, but look at it this way. Ally didn't start the IRS audit; someone else did that. All she did was spread the word and try to muscle in on Sam. I wouldn't have used her tactics, but she was desperate. She saw a way of saving her business and expanding it and used it. Besides, Sam and I are together now, and that's all that matters. If Ally hadn't tried to push us apart, we might not have found each other. In a strange way, she did us a favor. At this point, I'm more concerned about having an empty store on the block as the new mall opens. The timing's dreadful. We have to look as if we're thriving, not falling apart. I'm not really that generous. I'm doing it as much for us as for Ally."

"Let's hope the others will feel the same way," Sam said, heading toward the door.

"They will as soon as they learn the truth about the audit. We'll have to help Ally if we want to look prosperous," Brandi explained. "That reminds me. We need to paint the shop fronts as soon as the weather warms up a bit more. We can't look run-down with the new shops opening across the street."

"By the way, we're looking into the logistics of combining our shops," Sam interjected.

"That's great!" Susan and Brad exclaimed simultaneously.

Shrugging, Brandi replied, "We share the same customers anyway. We've both been thinking about making the suggestion but never got around to it. It really doesn't make sense that customers have to go outside in the rain and snow for their coffee when they could simply move between the shops."

Peeking under her bangs, Susan asked, "Brandi wouldn't tell me, but does this mean that you and Brandi will combine forces personally, too?"

"Nosy!" Brad scolded.

"Okay, so what else is new?" Susan replied and repeated her question.

Smiling indulgently, Sam replied, "I've proposed, but the lady hasn't responded. The store idea isn't firm either. We have to consult with the landlord first about structural concerns. I don't think we'll encounter any opposition or problems."

"What'll you call it if it happens?" Brad asked.

"I don't think we'll have to change the name, just push the letter together." Brandi slipped her arm through Sam's.

"I'm lost," Susan declared.

"Just think about it . . . Over the Rainbow Where Worlds Meet has a nice ring to it. Neither of us will lose our identity, and our customers won't become confused," Brandi said as she walked with Sam to the door.

"I like it," Susan proclaimed.

"Me too," Mrs. Owens chimed in.

"I don't want to be the only holdout. I guess I like it, too," Brad admitted.

"Then it's settled," Sam stated, kissing Brandi and closing the door.

Smiling happily, Brandi vanished into the office to phone Mia. She could only imagine her buddy's reaction to the news. For so long, Mia had tried unsuccessfully to arrange Brandi's life, and now suddenly all of the pieces were falling into place.

"Which news do you want first . . . the good or the best?" Brandi asked as soon as she heard Mia's voice.

Mia laughed. "The best, of course."

"Are you sitting down?"

"I am now. What is it?"

"Sam and I have reconciled. We're an item," Brandi stated smugly.

"What! It's about time!" Mia screeched. "When did this happen?"

"Last night. He came over. We talked. He explained about Ally, who, by the way, didn't contact the IRS. We made up, and life is wonderful," Brandi gushed.

"I knew that one day my work would bear fruit," Mia stated, taking credit for the romance as expected.

"You were right."

"I'll get dressed and come over. I need to hear more about Ally."

"There's another problem with her and the block, but I'll fill you in when I see you. See you later."

Brandi tried to turn her mind to work, but soon found the task futile. Writing Sam's name in the thin layer of dust on her desk, she thought about her neighbor and lover. Sam had arrived to save her like a hero from a novel. He was her knight in slightly tarnished armor. He made her feel secure and protected. Although she was perfectly capable of providing for herself and had for years, Sam made her feel complete in a way that, as yet, she could not explain. It felt good, and she liked the feeling.

Chapter 19

With the exception of Kevin, none of the other proprietors felt inclined toward helping Ally. She had repeatedly snubbed them and insulted them to the point that they could not muster the compassion or time to help her. She had carried herself above them. Not even the need to keep the block intact could convince them otherwise.

Hanging up the phone, Brandi sat deep in thought for a few minutes. She had to think of a way to help Ally while uniting the shop owners. Perhaps increasing everyone's exposure and revenue would be the way to go. With shops in the new mall just weeks away from opening, she had to do something fast.

The ringing phone put a halt to her ruminations. Listening closely, Brandi nodded as Sam repeated all that he had learned from his conversation with Ally. Perhaps the conversation would lead to a solution.

Speaking quickly, Sam relayed his conversation with Ally, saying, "Ally admits to being tapped out. She also says that she's not interested in reopening her shop on this block regardless of our support. She's looking to explore other options. I don't know if a new shop is still in the works, but the old one is finished."

"Did you tell her about us?" Brandi asked, twirling a pencil through her fingers.

"Sure did," Sam replied enthusiastically. "She was really surprised. I didn't tell her about our plans for combining the shops, but I mentioned that we've talked through our differences and are doing fine now."

"I bet she was shocked." Brandi chuckled dryly.

"Yeah, she said it won't work out. I didn't quite understand what she meant, but Ally said that once another woman enters the scene, the damage is too great to overcome."

Brandi stated, "I've heard that one, too, but I don't buy it. Besides, we've more or less been together all along. We hit a bump in the road momentarily, but we've overcome it."

"I think it's a good sign that our love affair sprang from our professional relationship. We work together well, and we certainly fit just right," Sam said with a deepening of his voice at the memory of their lovemaking.

"We have a lot in common. The exciting thing is that we've just tapped the surface," Brandi said, ignoring the veiled reference to the previous night's pleasurable activities.

Laughing, Sam said, "That was a clever little bit of sidestepping. Let's give our assistants the thrill of running the shops alone tomorrow and do something fun together. Now that Ally's out of our life, we deserve a break."

"Okay. What'll we do?"

"Following an enjoyable repeat of last night, we'll

see what arises in the morning and play it by ear," Sam said suggestively.

Brandi giggled. "Why, Sam! I didn't know you had such a well-developed sense of the double entendre."

"There's a lot you don't know about me, Miss Brandi," Sam joked. "Like you said, we've only scratched the surface. I'm eager to learn all of your hot spots and to teach you a few of mine. Let's stay at my place tonight and head for Williamsburg tomorrow. We'll make a day of it."

"That sounds great!" Brandi agreed happily. "I haven't been there in ages. I'll need to go home for a few things. Pick me up there."

"No way! I'm not letting you out of my sight. We'll drive to your house. I'll feed the cat while you pack a bag. You're mine until Monday morning. I'm not going to miss a single minute."

Brandi sighed. "I never realized that you were so possessive."

"That's what love can do to a man."

"Love? Who said anything about love? I thought we were talking about a sexual romp as part of an enjoyable weekend," Brandi teased.

Speaking seriously, Sam said, "Sex is only part of it, an enjoyable part, but not the whole. Loving you makes everything better . . . sweeter. The coffee and cocoa, the meals, and the physical closeness are all better because I love you."

"Oh, Sam! I love you too. This weekend will be wonderful. I just know all of our days will be perfect."

"I'll certainly do everything I can to make them memorable, despite the cold weather."

"Oh, but what about Ally? So, her clerks were only partially correct. Ally doesn't really want the store anyway. I'd hate to see her shop close. I don't want customers to think that we're running scared of the chain stores."

"You've got a point. I guess we can find someone else to move into the space or encourage one of her neighbors to expand into it," Sam mused.

Brandi suggested, "It might be hard to get someone to rent here when the new mall will soon open across the street. Maybe Kevin would be interested in expanding into the vacated space now when he learns that she's not coming back."

"You could talk with him about the idea since he was at least willing to help her," Sam offered. "It's not as nice a fit as our shops, but it might work."

"I'll call him now, and I'll see you after closing tonight," Brandi agreed quickly.

Sam laughed. "I can't wait. By the way, I seem to remember that Kevin's sweet on you. Let's not forget that we're an item now."

"Kevin only thought he was. He's one of those men who loves being in love. He's a great guy who deserves someone who'll return his affection. I wasn't the right woman for the job. I couldn't keep my mind on him and off you. Besides, he once had a weakness for Ally. Maybe he still does. That would explain his interest in helping her."

"As long as he remembers that you're my woman, everything will be okay," Sam said firmly.

"I'll see you tonight. Don't worry. We're cool," Brandi said as she ended the conversation and finished the last of the work on her desk.

A few minutes later, Brandi waved to Susan and

Brad as she rushed from the shop and hurried in the cold to Kevin's store. On the first and third weekends of the month, he sponsored a jam session that attracted amateur and professional musicians. Kevin and his shop had been featured often in the paper and local magazines. It was one of the places to visit on the weekends.

"Hey, Brandi. What's up? Still thinking of ways to help Ally?" Kevin asked over the background cacophony of instruments.

"I sure am," Brandi explained as she eased closer to the counter. "However, I'm thinking more about the impact of having an empty store on the block at the time that the new mall opens. It doesn't give a good impression of our little neighborhood that shops are closing before the competition even arrives."

"Yeah, I thought of that, too, as soon as you mentioned Ally's problems. That's why I'm willing to help her. I'd really be helping myself," Kevin said.

"I'd hate to see that shop next to you sit empty," Brandi mused with a slight hint in her voice. "It might be hard to rent once the new mall opens."

Kevin chuckled. "I know what you're getting at, and I've been thinking the same thing."

"Really?"

Nodding, Kevin replied, "Yeah. My shop's full to overflowing with inventory and customers, as you can see. I can hardly move in here most days. I need more space, but I don't want to move to the mall and lose the charm of this place. The new mall will be too vinyl and concrete for my taste even with the efforts to copy the old look. I like the old hardwood floors and the paneled walls we have here. I haven't run the figures, but if I can manage the increased rent, I might be interested in knocking down that wall between the shops and expanding."

"That's great news! It'll solve the vacancy problem quickly," Brandi said as she watched his assistants skillfully handle the huge volume of customers.

"I'll let you know after I speak with my accountant. When do you think she'll move out?" Kevin asked.

"Sam says that she's already notified the management office that she'll officially move the last of her stuff from the shop by the end of the month. However, I just peeked in on my way here, and it looks completely empty to me. I didn't see a mannequin anywhere unless they're in the back room," Brandi replied as she absentmindedly played the thumb piano.

"You're not interested in expanding your shop? You're as cramped for space as I am."

Feeling a little uncomfortable disclosing her plans to a man who only recently showed a personal interest in her, Brandi said, "Sam and I are discussing the possibility of combining our shops since we share most of the same customers. Books and brew seem a logical pair. It's always worked so well that I created a reading section for people who want to read their purchase in the shop while sipping coffee rather than going home or returning to Sam's. The older single people really like it."

"You're right, it's a good match in many ways," Kevin said with a smile that relieved the tension.

"I have to get back to the shop. It's good to know that we can solve this problem so quickly. Let me know what you decide," Brandi said as she stepped over a box of sheet music and headed toward the door.

"I will. It won't be a hard decision. I really need the space. I'm really glad that I might be able to preserve the integrity of the block." Kevin waved, turning his attention to the next customer in line.

Rather than returning to her shop, Brandi walked past the door and entered Sam's. From a peek in the window, she knew that Over the Rainbow was in Susan's and Brad's capable hands. They would look for her if an emergency arose.

As always, the aroma of coffee and cocoa made Brandi's mouth water. Rather than wait in line, Brandi signaled to Sam to join her in his office. Smiling, he grabbed two cups and followed.

"What did he say?" Sam asked, lightly brushing her fingers as he handed Brandi her order.

Tingling from his touch, Brandi answered, "He's interested in the expansion idea and will check its feasibility. He agreed that a vacancy on the block would give the wrong impression."

"Great. It looks as if the problem's solved," Sam said, taking Brandi in his arms.

"The financial one seems to be. He needs the space worse than I do. Since Ally's determined to leave, maybe a going-away party would be the best idea. Despite her best efforts to alienate all of us, she was still a member of our block for a long time. It would show that we hold no hard feelings toward her despite her part in the unpleasantness," Brandi said, snuggling against his chest.

"Let's put our heads together tonight," Sam suggested as he kissed her lips tenderly.

"I'll see you later. I think I'm blushing. Look what

you've done to me, Sam. You've turned me into the kind of woman who blushes when she sees the man she loves," Brandi said with a smile as she eased from his arms.

"It's very becoming. Tonight, you'll have to show me where it starts," Sam teased as Brandi's cheeks flamed.

"What's happened to Ally? There's a very cryptic note on the door about closing permanently," Mrs. Wilson asked as she paid for her purchase of children's books for her grandchild.

Susan replied quickly as she bagged the books, "I understand that she decided to spend her time elsewhere."

"That's a shame. I'm too old to wear those extreme outfits that she carried, but I liked to look at them. The colors were quite vivid. Who'll move into the empty store?" Mrs. Wilson asked.

"We don't know yet, but I'm sure it won't stand vacant for long," Brad replied, handing her the change.

"That's good news. It wouldn't look good to have an empty store when that mall opens. It would give this block a run-down appearance." Mrs. Wilson nodded emphatically.

"Don't worry. That won't happen." Brandi added a couple of lollipops to the bag.

"Thanks, dear," Mrs. Wilson said as she buttoned her coat. "You always add such a nice personal touch to everything. Don't you worry about that bookstore in the mall. None of your customers would think of buying anything in there."

"Thank you. I hope you're right," Brandi replied with a big smile.

"You let me know if they do, and I'll take care of them," Mrs. Wilson said firmly, waving the cane she carried over her arm.

Brandi watched as the dowager of the neighborhood braced herself against the cold air and stepped from the shop. She was a woman of authority and dedication who worked constantly for the revitalization of the block. When the city government refused the community association's request for improved lighting, Mrs. Wilson made a few calls. The city installed the lights within two weeks. Perhaps her influence would touch the purse strings of the residents and ensure continued success of the shops on the block as well.

With thoughts of her financial future and the evening with Sam on her mind, Brandi decided to leave the counter to Susan and Brad. Easing toward the office, she stopped to speak with customers along the way. Reaching her office, Brandi found a callback slip lying on her chair. Kevin had called back while she was at Sam's. Returning his call, she sat with crossed fingers as she listened.

"It's a go," Kevin said. "My accountant confirmed that my cash flow will allow expansion into Ally's shop. I'll call her as a courtesy, and then the realtor to make the arrangements."

"That's great," Brandi said. "Are you sure you don't feel pressured to make the move?"

"Not at all. I've wanted to do this for some time. As a matter of fact, I briefly entertained the idea of moving to the new mall for the additional space but decided against it. Now, with Ally's shop available, I can double my space and save money over the rental in the new building. I'm ready. Combining shops is a great idea for you, too. You'd gain a little more room by knocking down the wall, eliminating the reading spaces, and making better use of unused corners."

"We're thinking about it but haven't come to a decision yet. The business end of it makes sense. It's the emotional side that we're still sorting out."

Chuckling, Kevin said, "As much as I've avoided the issue, everyone knows that you two have a thing for each other. I've seen the way you look at each other myself. Joining forces professionally would only add to the romance."

"I'm sure there are statistics somewhere that would contradict that opinion." Brandi chuckled. "Being together twenty-four-seven, might be too much. We'll see."

"As you reminded me, a good business opportunity does not come along every day. Carpe diem! I'll talk to you later," Kevin concluded in a voice that showed no heartache at not being able to win Brandi's heart.

Brandi knew that Kevin was right about the professional angle, but she was not so confident about the romantic element. Her relationship with Sam was too new and untested. Still, they had known each other for years and shared customers. Perhaps the romantic element would not adversely affect the business venture. Returning to her work, Brandi made a mental note to bring up the idea with Sam again that evening. This was certainly the best time to make a change, with the new mall on the verge of opening. However, book orders forced her to push further thoughts from her mind.

Sam, too, had been visualizing the new combined space. He could envision the movement between the book and the coffee sides of the new shop. Being practical, he knew that they would have to reposition the register to prevent people from leaving without paying for reading material. However, that was a small price to pay for increased revenue, customer convenience, and a direct view of Brandi.

Later that night as Brandi lay satisfied in Sam's arms, they discussed the feasibility of combining their stores. She carefully considered the wording of her questions and comments so that she would not sound as if she lacked trust in him. Considering the total abandonment of her reserves that she had only minutes ago exhibited, Brandi hoped that Sam understood clearly that she loved him with her entire being.

Running her fingers across his chest, Brandi said, "I know it makes sense professionally and would certainly give better service to our customers, but do you think the change would put too much stress on us?"

Gently massaging her shoulder, Sam replied, "I think we can handle it. We're grown up. I enjoy being with you more than I can ever say. It'll be great being able to look across the room to see you any time I want. Besides, we've both heard the customers grumbling about having to go outside in the rain. For their convenience alone, it's worth the change."

"You don't worry about the twenty-four-seven to-getherness having a negative effect on our relationship?" Brandi asked as she leaned on her elbow to study his face.

"No, if anything, it'll bring us closer together," Sam replied, kissing the tip of her nose.

"I've heard of couples that broke up because of job tension. They just couldn't stand being together all the time.

"I'm sure that has happened, but it doesn't have to happen to us. Look at Mia and Doug. They spend a lot of time together, and their marriage is great."

"True, but they've been lovers since college. Neither of them can bear to be away from the other for too long."

"I hate being away from you, too. This way, you'll be in my sight every minute. I'll know when another man tries to put the moves on the woman I love," Sam said, pulling her back onto his shoulder.

Playing with the hair that ran downward from his belly button, Brandi continued, "I'd like more time with you, too, but I'm concerned about the pressure. What if absence, in this case the wall, really does make the heart grow fonder? What if too much togetherness breeds contempt?"

Speaking confidently, Sam replied, "It won't. I really don't see that all that much will change. We'll knock out the wall and remove the sitting areas in both shops. You don't need those sofas if customers have access to the tables. That's the only real change."

"We have to keep one sofa," Brandi objected as she warmed to the idea of change. "I have two elderly lovebirds who regularly sit and chat in my shop. I can't disturb their meeting place."

"They haven't gotten married yet?" Sam exclaimed. "He's slower than I am."

Chuckling, Brandi said, "I think the spring will bring about a change in their living arrangements. The courtship has really heated up lately."

"Good, then after they get married we can ditch the sofa."

For a while, Brandi and Sam lay silently in each other's arms. They listened to the breathing of the furnace and watched the flickering of the candles that filled the bedroom with a romantic yellow glow. The idea of merging the shops seemed to have gelled until Brandi thought of one more obstacle.

"We won't have to fire anyone, will we?" Brandi asked, breaking the spell.

"What?" Sam asked sleepily. "No, I don't think so. If we need to reduce our staff, we'll wait until Susan and Brad leave for grad school and not replace them."

"Good. I wouldn't want to do that. We both have good people working for us who shouldn't have to suffer because we make a change in our operation."

"Can we go to sleep now? We have to get up early for our trip to Williamsburg." Sam yawned.

"Would you mind terribly if we didn't go? I don't feel like being around a lot of people. I'm in crowds every day. I'd rather stay here alone with you. I'll make onion soup and French bread. We can watch TV or read. I just feel like vegging out."

"Fine with me, but I thought you wanted to tour the town and shop." Sam adjusted the covers around her shoulders.

"Not anymore." Brandi yawned. "I'm too content where I am."

Instead of an answer, Brandi heard deep breathing and the beginning of a snore. Snuggling against Sam's warmth, she decided that her fears about their future were unjustified. They were completely comfortable together. The usual shyness of the first date had not happened. The awkwardness of nudity had not been an issue. The nervousness of sharing the shower had not arisen. They were a perfect match that should have happened years ago.

As the cat settled into his usual spot at the foot of the bed, Brandi sighed and closed her eyes. The IRS audit was behind her. The incident with Ally had ended. The idea to merge their shops had become a reality. Their life together was off to a good start. Brandi felt more content than she had in weeks.

Chapter 20

The weeks passed quickly as the wall between the shops fell to make way for the expansion that would make both stores more customer-friendly. With each passing day, Brandi and Sam discovered more little things to love about each other and found their bond solidifying. Sam seldom returned to his condo at night, preferring the warmth of Brandi's bed to his solitary one. Living together had become their norm although neither had discussed the arrangement that seemed so natural. They ate a hurried breakfast together every morning before making the dash to the stores. They left the shops in the hands of their assistants at dinnertime and escaped for a quiet meal at home. In between, they visited as often as possible under the pretext of inspecting the ever-widening space where the wall once stood.

In order to make the noisy transition as pleasant as possible, the construction crew erected blue plastic sheets in both shops with the intent of blocking the view and stopping the flow of dust. The sheeting reduced customer space in both shops, but it helped to keep the dust from infiltrating the coffee machines and covering the books. The crew did most of the work during the day when customer traffic was at its lightest. By the time the city's inspectors arrived for their final visit at the beginning of the month, the floor had been repaired, the ceiling painted, and the seating rearranged. It was impossible to tell that Over the Rainbow Where Worlds Meet had not occupied that space forever.

"Don't they look cute?" Mrs. Wilson whispered, pointing at Sam and Brandi with her cane.

"Darling. It's about time, too. They've been alone too long. They're perfect for each other. I told you that when they first opened their shops," Mrs. Harrison said in an equally conspiratorial tone.

"You told me? I'm the one who noticed them first. The day Sam moved in here I told you that he was the man for Brandi. Your memory's slipping."

"My memory's fine. You're the one with advancing senility. Don't you remember that I invited Brandi and Sam to my house the week after he opened the shop? I was trying to get them together then."

"Yes, but I invited them to dinner the night he arrived. I remember I fixed a wonderful pot roast, macaroni and cheese, and kale."

"How can you remember what you cooked six years ago when you don't remember to pick up your dry cleaning unless you pin a note to your coat?"

"At least I didn't leave the house without my teeth," Mrs. Wilson snapped at her best friend.

"That only happened once," Mrs. Harris conceded with a sulk.

"I rest my case," Mrs. Wilson proclaimed triumphantly.

Mia, of course, planned a grand celebration to advertise the union of the shops and perhaps the couple. She and Doug helped Brandi and Sam decorate with red and white streamers that played up the Valentine's Day theme as well as the romance that filled the air. Mia ordered sandwiches, cookies, and a lovely cake in which the names of both shops came together within a red heart.

Standing next to Susan on the first weekend after the expansion, Brandi whispered, "You'd think this was my wedding day. I haven't seen Mia this excited since our college graduation. She wasn't this giddy when she married Doug."

Chuckling, Susan replied, "She's all energy. You'd think this was her shop."

"That's the way she's always been," Brandi explained. "She becomes so involved with her friends that all of our triumphs and failures become hers."

Leaning toward them, Brad added, "From the looks of this crowd, I'd say that this is definitely a success. Your mom and dad seem to be enjoying themselves, too."

"I didn't know it, but the expansion has been a dream of theirs, too. It seems as if everyone wanted the relationship with Sam to happen, although Mia's the only one who really pushed it," Brandi said.

Brad laughed. "Susan and I tried, but we didn't have much luck. You were as difficult to move as the wall."

"This is the best party." Mrs. Owens carried another tray of sandwiches to the tables on Sam's side of the shop.

"I'd enjoy it more if your mother would let me sit for a while," Mr. Owens griped, following her with a heavy punch bowl.

"You'll have plenty of time to relax when we get

home," Mrs. Owens retorted, urging her husband through the crowd.

At that moment, Mia joined them on her way to the office for more cookies. Rushing past, she exclaimed, "Isn't this the best turnout ever? Even with threatening skies and cold weather, you're drawing them in by the hundreds."

Brandi laughed at her friend's enthusiasm. "I think you're exaggerating a bit, but it's definitely crowded in here."

"I'd better check on the caterers. I hope we'll have enough food!" Mia said as she dashed away.

Brandi sighed. "Poor Sam. He's so busy he doesn't even have time to enjoy the moment."

"What about poor us?" Brad quipped. "This is the first time that I've been able to sit down since coming to work this morning."

"You spoke too soon," Susan said as the line of customers picked up again.

They worked in silence until the crowd thinned in late afternoon. Leaving the counter to Susan and Brad, Brandi eased across the room to the coffee shop side. Sam had just filled the last of many orders and was sipping a glass of cold water.

"Care to join me?" Sam asked, offering a second glass.

"I can only sit for a few minutes. I've never been so busy or so tired," Brandi replied as she gratefully sipped the water.

Smiling, Sam teased, "I'll make you forget all about the fatigue once I get you home."

"Really? What are you offering?" Brandi winked.

"Maybe a full-body massage or a foot rub followed by the best loving you've ever had." Sam grinned.

"You're on, but I bet you'll fall asleep before I do."

Laughing, Sam said, "You're probably right. I'm beat. But this is our big day, and we're going to celebrate."

"This is the first of many big days," Brandi said, correcting him gently.

Before Sam could respond, a bell tinkled in the distance, signalling that Susan needed help at the register. Turning to Sam, Brandi said as she hurried away, "It works. That was a great idea. It's much more discreet than shouting."

"Yeah, but it serves the same purpose. It takes you away from me." Sam lightly kissed her cheek.

"See you later." Brandi sighed and slipped away.

Sam watched as Brandi hurried toward her half of the shop. Although he knew that she was needed, he hated for her to leave him. Just being with Brandi made his heart flutter and his face feel warm. Her love gave him a true purpose in life. Without her, Sam felt lost.

The impatient sound in his assistant's voice pulled Sam from his reverie. Smiling, he could not remember a time when he had felt so content. He hoped the joy would last forever.

Brandi, too, felt more at ease than she had in ages. When she felt stressed, she could look across the room and see the man whose presence made her forget her cares. Looking around the expanded shop, she saw a dream come true and knew that only by loving Sam could the transformation have been possible.

Despite the winter weather, customers packed the shop until closing. She was too busy checking out customers, cataloging books, and refilling empty shelves to worry about the competing bookstore that would soon open. If business remained this brisk, she would have to clean out the messy office to create larger warehouse space.

As the grandfather clock signaled closing, Mia and Doug flopped cross-legged on the floor in front of the counter. They waited in an exhausted heap as Brandi locked the door behind the last customer. They were too tired to leave.

Mia nodded. "I don't think I've ever seen so many people in one shop in my life."

"I didn't know people could eat so many sandwiches," Mrs. Owens exclaimed, joining them.

"What about punch? They consumed buckets of it." Mr. Owens rubbed his sore shoulders.

"I'd say that your publicity paid handsome dividends," Doug said with pride at his wife's success.

Sam joined them on the bookstore side of the store. "We couldn't have done it without you."

"I never imagined that combining shops and impending mall competition would result in sales volumes like these," Brandi said, taking a break from recounting the day's receipts.

Susan added, "Everyone came . . . all of the regular customers, the kids, the other shop owners, and people I've never seen before. It was an amazing day. And to think we worried that the new mall would put us out of business."

Ever cautious, Sam replied, "It still can. The more shops that open, the more curious people will become about the mall. We'll have to see what the next weeks bring. I don't expect this level of success every weekend."

"I hate to mention the name, but I didn't see Ally," Brad added.

Mia moaned as she forced herself to stand on aching legs. "I didn't either. Maybe she doesn't consider herself part of the neighborhood anymore. I've tried to contact her, but she never returns my calls."

"Let's not ruin the day by looking for trouble," Brandi suggested.

"Agreed," Sam said. "Let's go to Brandi's for a little champagne to toast our successful partnership."

Moving as quickly as the fatigue would allow, the eight of them closed the shop and bundled up against the cold night. Looking back on the row of shops from the vantage point of across the street, Brandi smiled and hugged Sam. The sign that ran the width of both shops announced their professional partnership. The strength of Sam's arms holding her close proclaimed the personal one.

Once inside the warm house, Brandi and Sam served glasses of champagne to their friends. Even as fatigue lined their faces, nothing could dull the moment. Taking turns, they each offered a toast to the successful opening of Over the Rainbow Where Worlds Meet.

Sam started the round of toasts by saying, "Here's to continued success."

"To fabulous business consultants without whom we couldn't have pulled this off," Brandi added.

"To long-overdue good ideas," Susan said.

Brad intoned, "To a profitable union."

"To love and romance."

"Mia!" Brandi said.

"Well, it seemed appropriate," Mia protested.

"To endless years of happiness together," Mrs. Owens added.

"To good books and great coffee," Mr. Owens said.

"To good friends and happy times," Doug concluded.

They drank heartily and then said good night. As Brandi and Sam waved good-bye, Sam said, "This is the beginning of another chapter for us, you know. I think we should make our living arrangement as official as our working partnership."

"What are you saying? Do we need to visit our attorney again?" Brandi asked as they climbed the stairs.

Sam smiled. "No, I was thinking more in the line of a minister saying a few words over our folded hands."

"On the surface that sounds like a good idea. However, what is the real incentive for doing it? I understood the business sense of combining our shops, but what's in it for me if we unite our lives?" Brandi asked with a teasing tone in her voice.

Pulling her toward him, Sam replied, "I can't speak for you, but for me, it's not having to sleep alone again and holding the woman I love in my arms every night. It's waking up to see you lying next to me. It's sitting across the breakfast table from you. It's having kids, watching them grow up, and growing old together."

Nestling against his chest, Brandi replied, "Those sound like good reasons to me."

Looking at her closely, Sam demanded, "Then you'll marry me?"

"I suppose it depends on the way you state the

terms of the agreement." Brandi sank into the chair by the closet.

Taking the hint, Sam knelt at her feet, took her hands in his, and asked solemnly, "I bring a heart that overflows with love. I promise to take care of you and to love you with my life for as long as we live. I ask only that you will do me the honor of becoming my wife."

"Dear Sam, I give you myself, my love, and all that I am from now until forever." Brandi spoke softly as tears of happiness coursed down her cheeks.

Leading her upstairs, Sam flipped off the lights. His heart pounded as he led Brandi toward the bed. His fingers shook with emotion as he unbuttoned her sweater and eased it over her shoulders. He looked at her body as if seeing it for the first time and studied every ridge and curve. His hands slowly caressed her skin and fingered her hair. His lips traced gentle kisses along her neck and shoulders, down to her breasts, and along the flat surface of her stomach.

Tossing her slacks onto the pile of clothing on the floor, Sam gently kissed the face of the woman he loved while his hands traced the sweetness of her body. Although they had made love many times since they started living together, Sam wanted this time to be different. They had turned a new page in their relationship, and he wanted to remember this night for the rest of his life.

Brandi closed her eyes and felt the warmth of Sam's hands on her skin. She shuddered in the warm bedroom. Her lips parted slightly to welcome his. Her hands caressed his skin and held him close. Dropping onto the bed, Brandi pulled him to her as he tossed the hastily discarded condom wrapper onto the floor.

When neither of them could stand the exquisite sensations any longer, Sam made slow, tantalizing love to Brandi until she cried out in rapture. Their legs and arms interwove in the ancient dance. Time passed and fatigue vanished.

Lying satisfied in each other's arms, they breathed deeply of the sweetness of their intertwined bodies. Their arms and legs remained locked long after their breathing slowed to soft flutters. Neither could think of any reason to move.

Chapter 21

The next morning, Brandi and Sam awoke to sounds of sirens in the usually quiet neighborhood. Grabbing her robe, Brandi rushed onto the front porch as Sam joined her. Peering through the space between the houses, they saw that the fire engines were speeding away from the residential section and toward the shops. They looked at each other as a shopkeeper's worst nightmare swept through their minds. Quickly throwing on their clothing, they rushed from the house and raced the few blocks to the strip.

Even before they reached the commercial section, they could feel the heat of the flames and hear the crackling of the wood. The police had cordoned off the block and would not allow anyone to enter the area. Standing on the corner across from the burning strip mall, Brandi covered her face and wept for the lovely row of shops that had been completely engulfed in flames. Sam held her tightly against his chest as he watched the firefighters bravely fight the losing battle. The shops were old, and the blaze was too hot. All was lost.

Neighbors joined them on the corner and wept in disbelief. The shops had been a permanent fixture in the Takoma Park neighborhood since the first resident had moved into her house. Mrs. Wilson had raised her children within walking distance of the stores that no longer occupied the block. In their place lay ashes and smoldering timbers.

"It's gone!" Mrs. Wilson lamented. "After all these years, it's gone. Your new store. What will we do? You've just opened your combined business, and now it's gone."

"We'll rebuild," Sam stated resolutely.

"How, Sam? We don't own the strip," Brandi reminded him gently. "The owner's old and has been thinking of selling for a long time. He might not be willing to rebuild."

"We'll think of something," Sam replied firmly.

They watched in silence as the firefighters inspected the remains of the block, rolled up their hoses, and rumbled away in their trucks. The sun struggled to shine through the smoke that filled the sky. Now that the fire was out, Brandi felt cold. She could not bear the thought of crossing the street. Turning her back on the devastation, she slowly walked home. She would phone Susan, Brad, and Sam's employees and tell them not to come to work. The shop was closed.

Sam stayed behind a little longer. With the firefighters gone, the police encircled the block with crime scene tape. It would remain until the fire department finished the investigation that it had already started.

"Was it the wiring?" Sam asked the inspector.

"We're not sure yet, but it doesn't look like it," the inspector replied.

"Then what caused it?" Sam demanded.

"I won't know for sure until after the lab processes the evidence, but I'm not ruling out arson." The man filled his bag with charred fragments from what only hours ago had been Sam's shop.

"Arson? Who would have done a thing like that?" Sam asked himself more than the inspector.

Seeing the expression of disbelief on Sam's face, the inspector said, "That's only my guess. We'll know more after we complete the investigation. For now, phone your insurance company and give this number. I'm awfully sorry."

"Thanks." Sam accepted the inspector's card on which appeared the case number for the investigation.

Walking farther along his side of the tape, Sam tried to find anything that would remind them of their shop and plans. In the midst of the debris, he saw twisted metal coffee machines, conduit, and furniture legs but little else. Brandi's side was even more depressing; all of her precious books had burned beyond recognition. Water collected in large puddles on the spot that used to house the beautiful antique checkout counter. The heat had even melted their new sign. Over the Rainbow Where Worlds Meet was no more.

Slowly, Sam dragged himself away from the ruins. As he trudged tiredly toward Brandi's house, he thought about the inspector's words. An arson fire. If the inspector was right, someone had set fire to the row of shops.

Silence greeted him as Sam slowly opened the door. He did not want to see the pain on Brandi's face for the loss of her shop . . . their shop. They had put so much of themselves and their lives into it that he could not bear to see her sad eyes and watch the tears flow down her face again. It was gone. They would rebuild. Nothing would be the same.

"I'm in here," Brandi called from the kitchen.

"I wanted a closer look. I'm sorry I did it now," Sam said, accepting the cup of brew. Brandi was freshly showered and beautiful but very sad.

Brandi leaned against the counter. "I phoned the insurance company. They'll need the case ID number from the fire department."

"I'll call them back with it," Sam said softly.

"There's nothing left, is there?" Brandi struggled to hold back the tears.

"No, nothing. Not even our new sign survived." Sam studied her set face.

Brandi's shoulders slowly began to sag and her hands to tremble. Hot tears tumbled down her cheeks as her composure crumbled. Sam immediately took her into his arms. The last shreds of her bravery collapsed as she melted against him.

"All we worked for . . . everything's gone." Brandi sobbed.

"I know, but at least no one was hurt. We're still strong and healthy. We can rebuild," Sam said as he cradled her against his chest.

"I know, but that shop was my life for so long," Brandi whispered.

"You have this life now," Sam said gently.

Drawing comfort from his strength, Brandi said, "What would I do without you, Sam? You're so calm and brave. Your life's work is gone, too, but you're still holding it together."

"I have you. Nothing else is important anymore. We can always open another shop. As long as we're together, we can do anything." Sam kissed her lightly, tasting the salt from her tears.

Looking into his dear face, Brandi felt a wonderful sense of comfort filling her heart. Her shop was gone. That life had ended. However, her life with Sam had only just begun.

"What caused it?" Brandi asked, drying her tears.

Not wanting to tell her what he had learned, Sam hedged. "The inspector wasn't sure."

Blowing her nose noisily, Brandi studied his face. "You're holding back. What did the inspector say?"

"He's not sure," Sam lied unsuccessfully.

"But what does he think?" Brandi insisted, laying her hand firmly on Sam's arm.

Looking into her now calm face, Sam replied, "He thinks it was arson. He's been investigating a series of residential fires and thinks this one fits the pattern. It's possible that the arsonist is expanding his targets to include neighborhood businesses."

"Someone set fire to the block to burn us out? Who would have done something like that?" Brandi demanded rhetorically, her eyes big with disbelief.

"They'll find out soon enough. Maybe even make the connection to the residential fires."

"Now what do we do? What if the owner won't rebuild? I've already called my students to tell them that I've canceled the tutoring sessions until further notice, but there's no way that we can notify all of our customers about the fire. They'll be devastated if they arrive to find the place a smoldering pile of rubble," Brandi cried.

"Let's take one thing at a time. Sam pulled her into his arms again. "First, the insurance company will cover the replacement of our inventory minus the deductible. We have the backup disks here and can print off the information whenever the claims adjustor wants it."

"What a nightmare!" Brandi moaned, and slipped into the nearest kitchen chair.

"Next, we can always relocate to the new mall while they still have vacancies."

"I don't want to move. I like it here."

"But that's no longer an option," Sam said softly.

Tears began to flow down Brandi's cheeks again as the reality of Sam's words penetrated her resistance. Their shop, their lovely block no longer existed. Someone had destroyed a row of shops that had stood in the same spots since WW II. Now it was gone, and she could not fight against that stark reality.

"I guess someone should call Mr. Reynolds, the owner," Brandi suggested.

Gently rubbing her shoulders, Sam replied, "I ran into the community association president on the way home. She called him as soon as she saw the flames. He's old and living in Florida. He told her that he'll wait to hear from the fire department before making any decision."

"What do we do now?" Brandi cried.

"We call our staff and Mia and Doug and have them meet us here in a couple of hours with their cell phones. We'll phone as many customers as we can to tell them about the fire. We'll send a mailing to the ones we can't reach."

"It's a good thing that we did all the open-house preparation from here. At least we have the disks with their mailing addresses."

"Don't forget that Mia has copies, too."

"Okay, so our mailing lists are intact. But what do we do after that? I'm used to going to work every day. What'll we do with ourselves?"

Speaking with a confidence that came from keeping Brandi calm rather than from his own emotions, Sam said, "Just in case Mr. Reynolds doesn't want to rebuild, we'll look for new rental space. We might even see what owning rather than renting would cost us since we plan to run this business forever."

"And to think that only yesterday we thought that 'forever' might only last until the chain stores in the mall could put us out of business. Who knew that a fire would beat them to it?" Brandi asked dryly.

"For our mental health, let's go look for new rental space. It'll keep us occupied."

Sighing, Brandi agreed, saying, "Okay, but you need to take a shower first. You smell of smoke and your face is sooty."

Aware of his appearance for the first time since returning from the ruins of their block, Sam nodded and walked up the stairs. At the landing, he turned and said, "I think you should take a look at the remains of the shop. It'll give you closure. We'll go there first and then make the calls."

"It'll make me angry." Brandi pounded her fist on the table.

"That's good, too. I'll be back in a few minutes," Sam said as he reached the top step.

Brandi sat staring at the remains of her coffee. The sludge at the bottom of her cup was all that was left of a good brew, one of Sam's best that an arsonist had reduced to charred beans and dust. With a heavy sigh, she forced herself to rise, rinse her cup, eat some toast and yogurt, and drag her coat from the closet. Deciding that she wanted to leave something at the site for her customers and the curious, she quickly crafted a sign and found a plant support on which to attach it. After all these years and all the love, the shop deserved a proper farewell.

Sam did not ask about the sign, knowing that Brandi would share it with him in her own time. Helping her into her coat, he quickly locked the door and led her the short distance to the spot on which their shop once stood. They could feel the heat from the rubble as they approached.

Tears once again filled Brandi's eyes as she gazed upon the twisted remains and the ashes of her beloved store. Here she had proven that she could run a successful business, touched the hearts of many and been touched by them, and fallen in love. Now it was gone. Neighbors and customers embraced her tearfully as they paid their respects to the shop. Already bouquets of flowers tried to add a touch of color to the decay.

Bending slowly, Brandi pushed the stake into the soil. Stepping back, she read the hastily composed sentiment once more. It said just enough. *At the end of the storm, you'll find us Over the Rainbow Where Worlds Meet. We'll be back.*

As Brandi and Sam turned to leave, Kevin approached them. He too had found nothing but ashes to remind him of his successful music business. His face was ashen from soot and pain.

"What a mess!" Kevin said.

"We'll survive," Sam said.

"Yeah, but it won't be the same."

"Maybe it'll be better," Brandi offered. Her words sounded brave, but her voice was hollow.

Kevin said, "I heard that the fire marshal suspects arson."

Sam nodded. "I heard it, too."

"I wonder who would have done such a thing," Kevin said, watching the puffs of steam rising from the void.

Shaking her head, Brandi replied, "I don't want to think that anyone who ever visited our shops would have done this to us. The inspector thinks it might be connected with the other fires that have plagued Washington. We'll have to wait and see."

"You're right. We have enough on our plates already," Kevin agreed.

"After we phone a few customers, we're going out looking for a new rental space. Regardless of the owner's decision, we'll need to set up shop somewhere before we deplete our savings," Sam announced.

"Sounds like a good idea to me. Old man Reynolds might not want to rebuild. Even if he does, he might not be in any hurry. I don't know how long I can survive on the money I'll make from giving music lessons while I wait for him to do it," Kevin said as he embraced another tearful customer.

"Why don't you have your staff join us at my house shortly? Bring cell phones. We can divide up the lists and make the calls faster," Brandi suggested.

Looking from one to the other, Kevin smiled and said, "I'll see if they're willing. They were rather shook-up, too. They might want to start their job search immediately. At any rate, I'll meet you there."

As Kevin vanished into the crowd of customers gathered on the sidewalk behind the police tape, Sam pulled Brandi against his chest. The wind felt especially cold without the row of shops to block it. The air reeked of the acrid smell of smoke. To top it off, freezing rain had begun to fall.

"Let's go home," Brandi said. "I've seen enough."

Holding hands, Brandi and Sam picked their way home through the debris that had spilled onto the sidewalk. They would make calls, accept and offer words of comfort, and start their search for a new location. If they had to move, they would survive, but Brandi was worried about the neighborhood. Her neighbors depended on the shops as a place to meet and exchange information. Over the years, the block had become much more than a simple strip of shops. The people who shopped there were neighbors and friends. If the shops did not rise from the ashes, the neighborhood would feel the loss. Not even the mall and its chain stores would be able to fill the void.

"A penny for your thoughts," Sam offered.

Brandi sighed. "I was just thinking about the neighborhood without the shops. They were an integral part of the life of this community. I know something will grow up in its place, but it won't be the same. That quaint little strip of shops added so much charm to the neighborhood."

"Let's not think about that now. Let's focus on the positive."

"Which is?"

"No one was hurt. And we love each other. We'll get through this together." Sam opened the door.

Smiling, Brandi entered the warmth of her house, made all the more comforting by having Sam behind her. After the others arrived, they would tackle the tasks at hand. Until then, she would enjoy the silence and Sam.

Chapter 22

When Brandi awoke the next morning, she immediately thought that she had overslept and was late opening the shop. Slowly, the realization that she had nowhere to go filtered through the first fog of awakening. With a heavy heart, she turned toward Sam, who lay awake and silently staring at the ceiling but not speaking.

"It feels strange not having to go anywhere on a work day," Brandi said softly.

Pulling her against his shoulder, Sam agreed, "I know. I've been lying here planning a day that doesn't need to be planned. Other than checking out rental space, I don't have inventory to do or coffee machines to maintain. It's eerie."

Gently stroking his chest, Brandi said, "We work hard and grouse about not having enough time for ourselves or for a vacation, but now that we have all the time in the world, we don't know what to do with it."

"I can think of something," Sam said as he gently massaged her shoulders.

Brandi moaned her agreement as his fingers explored her sensitive points. She reveled in the delicious kisses that caused sparks of anticipation to course through her body. She pulled him closer and opened herself to him as her exploring fingers caused a groan of pleasure to escape from his parted lips. She clung to his muscular back and matched her rhythm to his, forgetting all thoughts of the store, the fire, and the future. For the moment, the only thing that mattered was their union and the exquisite sensations that made her arch her back to meet his demanding thrusts.

Sam lost himself in the joy of Brandi's abandonment. Never had he known a woman who gave of herself so freely, whose body fit his so perfectly, and whose energy was so completely matched to his. The expression of love and rapture on her face excited him to new heights. He longed to fill her with himself and never let her go. He loved her with a totality that was almost frightening. He knew that he would spend the rest of his days loving and protecting her.

Their moist bodies lay intertwined, barely covered by the sheets, as Brandi and Sam rested in each other's embrace. The ugliness of the world had vanished. The magnitude of their love had replaced the fear of the unknown. Together, they would persevere against any hardship and uncertainty.

Reaching into the drawer of his nightstand, Sam extracted a small velvet box. He had planned to give it to her at dinner, but the fire had taken preeminence. Lying with Brandi's head against his chest seemed the perfect moment to present it to her. He saw no reason to wait.

Feeling clumsy and awkward, Sam simply said, "This is for you. I hope you like it. I'd planned to drop it into a champagne glass or something equally as clichéd, but right now seems like a good time to give it to you."

"Oh, Sam!" Brandi said breathlessly as she peered at the impressive sparkling diamond that spoke of their promise to love each other eternally. "It's stunning, but can we afford this extravagance after the fire? It's lovely, but I really don't need anything so grand. A simple gold wedding band with a matching one for you would be enough."

"We can afford it," Sam assured her, slipping it onto her finger. "I want you to have something that will always remind you that I love you more than you could ever imagine."

"I don't need this ring, beautiful as it is, to remind me of that. All I have to do is look at your dear face," Brandi said as she drew his face to hers and kissed him gently.

"I hope you see it. I hope the world sees that you mean more to me than life itself," Sam whispered.

"Oh, Sam, our world is right here. As long as we know that we love each other, nothing else matters," Brandi replied, holding him close.

For a long while, they lay together, locked in each other's arms. Life was their bed, their bodies, and their love. The harsh world outside could not threaten them as long as they had each other.

Teasing, Sam whispered into her sweet-smelling neck, "By the way, I don't wear rings."

"What?" Brandi demanded, rising on her elbow to stare into his face.

"I don't like jewelry. It looks great on you, but it's not my style."

"What exactly are you telling me?" Brandi tugged on his chest hairs.

Holding her fingers, Sam replied, "I don't think I'll wear a wedding ring."

"A married man needs a wedding ring," Brandi stated firmly.

Sam smiled. "It won't make me more married. I love you and belong to you already. I don't need a piece of gold to remind me."

"My father wore one. My grandfather wore one. My husband should wear one."

"My father didn't. My grandfather died before I was born, so I don't know about him. My brothers don't wear one."

"Let's just say that you'll start a new tradition in the family. You'll wear one and so will your son," Brandi said with a tight smile.

Continuing the argument, Sam said, "I know plenty of guys who wear them and still cheat on their wives. They're not more married because of the ring."

Unrelenting, Brandi stated, "I know men like that, too, but you're not one of them. You'd never do anything like that."

"That's right. So I don't need the ring."

Feeling her frustration growing, Brandi tried another approach. "The ring's significance is in its symbolic nature. As a symbol of our love, it will show the world that we are happily united forever."

"I don't need that symbol any more than you need that engagement ring. We love each other; we don't need anything else," Sam replied, carefully gauging the extent to which he could continue to push the discussion.

The glittering diamond provided the next point of the argument. Seizing the advantage, Brandi stated,

"I want you to wear a wedding ring for the same reason that you want me to wear this engagement ring."

Sam chuckled. "Betrayed by my own generosity. If it means that much to you, I'll change my old habits and wear a wedding band."

"Thank you." Brandi peppered his face with happy kisses as her fingers explored his warmth.

"We'll never leave this bed if you continue to do that." Sam laughed huskily.

"That's okay with me," Brandi said as she rolled onto her back and took Sam with her.

The ringing of the phone an hour later disturbed the lovers' sleep. Untangling herself from Sam's arms and legs, Brandi answered. Listening carefully, she stored the fire marshal's words in a place in her memory from which they would never escape.

Turning to Sam, Brandi said, "The fire marshal's report says that the fire was the result of a deliberate act of arson. The investigators found the remains of a gasoline can in Kevin's shop. They think the blaze started there."

They stared at each other silently for a long moment. Neither could speak in the face of the horrible reality. Someone deliberately put an end to their dreams and livelihood.

Finally, Sam voiced their shared thought, saying, "The investigator said that there's been a string of residential fires lately. This one might be related. I hope the fire department is right about the connection to the other fires."

"So do I. As awful as this is, it would be worse if

someone we knew has done this to us," Brandi remarked sadly.

"Let's not think the worst. Until the fire department discovers more evidence, we'll just assume that the fire was a random act of violence."

"Good. Now let's get going. Random violence or otherwise, we need to find a shop," Brandi said as she threw off the covers.

"Hey!" Sam protested as the cool air hit his naked flesh. "Show a guy a little kindness!"

Laughing, Brandi tossed Sam his robe and darted into the bathroom for a quick shower. He followed immediately and turned the simple act of cleansing into a languid expression of love and sensuality. By the time they had finished showering, they had put the fire from their minds.

Brandi and Sam spent the remainder of the day touring malls and shopping centers. They quickly confirmed that the largest ones were too impersonal and the smallest were often run-down and in need of more than cosmetic repair. They wanted to remain as close to the neighborhood as possible but resisted the idea of considering the new mall due to the rumor of exorbitant rents. Finally, when they could find nothing closer than three miles away, they decided to consider their new neighbor. At least their relocation would not pose a hardship to their customers and Brandi's students if they found a suitable space in the new mall.

The mall's interior was surprisingly homey. Instead of tiled floors and ceilings, the builder had installed hardwood floors and left the ceiling beams exposed. He had accentuated the dark-stained wood with hanging lights and interesting banners that depicted scenes from famous sites in Washington. The mall was huge but not cavernous due to the casual flow of the halls and the almost random placement of the shops. Shoppers strolled leisurely from one section to another and entered a different wing at junctions rather than cold right angles. The mall felt more like an old town than a shopping center.

"I'm impressed," Sam said as they reached the end of their tour.

"I am, too," Brandi conceded reluctantly and continued, "I haven't seen any of our regular customers, have you?"

"No, but give 'em time. They'll come. The fire's still the main topic of conversation. In a few days, they'll need coffee and reading material. The CVS provides both."

"That's even more reason for us to act quickly. The longer we stay closed, the harder it'll be for us to win them back once they see that this place isn't occupied by monsters. I still don't want to open a shop here," Brandi said as she eased Sam toward the exit.

"Me either. Let's phone Mr. Reynolds as soon as we can. Maybe he's come to a decision," Sam suggested as they walked past the charred remains of their shop and headed home.

Sighing, Brandi said, "Even if we could scrape together the money to buy and rebuild, it would take forever. I don't think we can spare that much time. We'll have to rent."

"Let's not make a decision before we have all the facts. It didn't take long to build the new mall. The winter weather cooperated for them. It's almost spring. We might get a break, too." Sam tugged her away from the twisted remains.

Wiping a tear, Brandi said, "I still can't believe that my shop is gone."

"We'll survive and prosper, Brandi. Don't worry." Sam kissed her cold cheek lightly.

Pushing against the wind, they arrived home as the sun was setting. As Mia and Doug opened the door to welcome them inside, Brandi and Sam looked at each other in confusion. They did not remember inviting their best friends to dinner. Smiling, Mia and Doug looked like people with a barely concealed secret as they held cups of steaming coffee in their hands.

"We took the liberty of letting ourselves in," Mia explained as she hung up Brandi's coat.

Doug added, "And of inviting a few people to join us."

Suddenly, the living room filled with laughing people, carrying trays of food and drinks and stringing balloons and streamers on the banister and door frames. As they worked, they cast furtive glances at Brandi and Sam, while not stopping their activities. They opened folding tables and spread them with festive red tablecloths. They set the tables with white and red china and sparkling stemware. After arranging heaping serving bowls and trays of food on the tables, they encircled Brandi and Sam.

"Surprise!" they shouted in unison as their laughter rang though the house.

"I don't understand," Brandi said to Mia.

"These are just a few of your closest friends, neighbors, and customers who wanted to do something to let you two know that you're loved. They phoned me and here they are!" Mia exclaimed as she swept her arms around the room.

Brandi and Sam looked from each other to the room jammed with familiar and dear faces. Mrs. Wilson, sporting a shining new wedding band and holding her husband's hand tightly, smiled through her tears. Children of all ages stood beside their parents and waved happily. Couples who normally inhabited seats in the coffee shop stood near the steps. Older people for whom the shop was a second home smiled gently. People stood on the stairs, overflowed into the kitchen and dining room, and continued to pour through the front door, bearing still more platters of food.

Susan wiped the tears that streaked her makeup, and Brad struggled to retain his composure as they stepped forward carrying baskets and boxes filled to the brim with envelopes. Handing them to Brandi and Sam, they hugged their bosses and stepped back. Silence fell over the crowd as everyone waited for their friends to examine the contents.

"Open a few of the envelopes," Doug instructed as he relieved them of the load.

Obeying silently, Brandi and Sam opened first one and then another envelope that contained not only notes of genuine affection for the shop owners and sympathy for their losses, but checks as well. The amounts varied according to the givers' finances, but all of the envelopes held the outpouring of love from their neighbors.

Mrs. Wilson stepped forward and said, "We wanted to do something to help the two people who have given so much to this neighborhood. If it hadn't been for your devotion to the block, those shops would have crumbled to dust years ago. You brought them back to life and gave us a place to call home. This is just the beginning. Use it to start rebuilding our block. We love you."

Brandi's eyes again filled with tears as Sam threw his arm protectively around her shoulders. Just when they felt at their lowest, their customers and friends had rallied to help them find a way to start over. For a few minutes, they stood speechless.

"Your generosity is overwhelming," Sam stated with great difficulty.

"We don't know how to thank you enough," Brandi added, struggling to speak through her tears. "But we weren't the only ones who were burned out. Kevin lost his shop, too. And the dry cleaners and the bank."

"Don't worry about me," Kevin said as he pushed through the crowd. "They've already been very generous."

Brad shared the latest neighborhood news, saying, "The bank sent its architect to take a look at the place today. They'll return and will put up some of the financing. I spoke with Mr. Franklin, too. He says that he's ready to retire from the dry-cleaning business. He'd been thinking about it for a while but didn't want to do anything now with the mall opening. The fire has liberated him. As soon as his insurance company pays off, he's heading to Florida to be with his son and grandchildren."

"That's not the end of it. We've been busy while you guys were out goofing off," Mia said with a huge smile as she nudged Doug to take over the presentations.

Rubbing his ribs, Doug said, "We talked with Mr. Reynolds this afternoon. He's not interested in rebuilding and wants to sell the land. He's offered us a price that we couldn't refuse."

"You're the new landlord?" Brandi asked with disbelief.

Mia laughed. "Yeah. Isn't it something? Who'da thought that we'd join the establishment?"

"But we're not the only owners," Doug explained. "You, Sam, Kevin, and your parents also own shares, as well as the community association and the bank. The deal calls for all of us being equal partners."

"But the cost? Do we have the cash flow to cover it?" Sam asked.

"We'll have bigger shops that'll only cost us a few hundred more each month in mortgage than we pay now in rent," Kevin added.

Looking at each other in disbelief, Brandi and Sam could only smile with pleasure. In the wake of the destruction of their shops, their dream of ownership had come true. Not only would their shop rise from the ashes, it would be something that they would own and could pass down to their children.

As Brandi fought back tears of happiness, Sam shook hands with Doug and said, "This is wonderful news."

"All that's left now is the rebuilding. These contributions should help with that," Mia said.

"When do we start?" Brandi asked.

"The fire marshal gave the go-ahead today. We'll have plans by the end of next week," Brad said.

Brandi sighed. "I can't believe it."

Becoming impatient, the dowager Mrs. Wilson said, "Enough talk. Let's eat. I hate to see good food go to waste."

Immediately, the house filled with the hum of

happy people mingling and eating. A CD played softly in the background. TV trays appeared for anyone who did not feel comfortable with the juggling act of buffet-style dining. Brandi and Sam accepted plates of food from Susan and Brad. Claiming a seat on the stairs, they ate in silence and watched their friends. They had always loved the neighborhood, but never more than at that moment when everyone was assembled for a common cause. Their beloved shop was gone, but their future was incredibly sunny.

Later that night after the neighbors had restored the house to order and departed, Brandi and Sam slipped into bed. They were exhausted in a good way. Their hearts had never been so full of love.

Holding her close, Sam said, "Now that we're engaged and pinching pennies for the rebuilding, I think I'll sell this condo. We don't need two places. I'm just wasting money. We'll use the proceeds to pay off the mortgage on this house. It makes sense for us to settle here. It's home."

"That's a great idea. It'll be our house. I can't imagine living anywhere else anyway. This is a perfect neighborhood for raising kids," Brandi purred contentedly.

"How many do you want?" Sam asked, kissing her gently.

"At least a zillion. I love children," Brandi gushed.

Sam laughed. "That many? I hope I'm man enough for the task."

"I'd settle for two." Brandi snuggled against his shoulder.

Locking her fingers through his, she added, "We really are blessed with wonderful friends."

"Not many people would have an entire neighborhood stand up with them at a time like this. They could have abandoned us in favor of the new mall."

"I always knew this was a great place to live and work, but I never understood until today just how much we depend on each other. I don't think I've ever been so happy," Brandi whispered as tears filled her eyes again.

"I certainly hope the police find the arsonist. I'd hate to rebuild only to have it happen again."

"Don't think such things! Lightning and fire don't strike the same place twice. But I agree. I'll feel great relief when we know who did this."

"Why do you think we haven't heard from Ally?" Sam asked. "Everyone has reached out to us except for her."

"Maybe she moved away or divorced herself from us completely. I don't know. She wasn't exactly anyone's favorite person. Besides, she's unpredictable. Kevin's kept in touch with her. He probably knows where she is. They used to be an item. It was a while ago, but you never know," Brandi said sleepily.

"Do you think—?" Sam started.

"No."

"How do you know what I was going to say?"

Brandi sighed. "I don't want to think about her or anything else right now. I'm too tired and too happy."

"Agreed," Sam muttered, holding her close.

Sam allowed Brandi's gentle snoring and the sounds of the house at peace to quiet his thoughts. It was difficult to feel anything but happy with a wonderful woman like Brandi in his arms and a bright future in front of him. As the cat settled on the foot of the bed, Sam closed his eyes and slipped into a sound sleep.

Chapter 23

The days passed quickly as the new business partners worked in harmony to restore their beloved block. The architect suggested rebuilding in the same style as the original shops in order to reconstruct the charm and appeal of the old structure. No one objected to the retro look, not even the bank, which would hide new technology and security within the framework of crystal chandeliers, dark paneling, and wood floors. Brandi, Sam, and Kevin were thrilled that their old décor would return. Kevin even pulled a collection of vintage musical instruments from his attic to adorn his shop window.

Construction, of course, did not progress without hitches. The weather turned unexpectedly cold and snowy in March. Heavy rains in April slowed progress to a crawl. City inspectors took their sweet time approving completed work, and a strike at the furniture manufacturer promised a delay in the delivery of the custom counters. However, despite the setbacks, the warm weather of May had everyone talking about the grand opening of the restored shops.

Enjoying one of their few moments alone in their living room, Brandi and Sam discussed the string of grand-opening delays and the impact on their future. It seemed as if their entire life revolved around the return of Over the Rainbow Where Worlds Meet. Since the shop had been an integral part of their past, it was only fitting that it would take center stage in their future.

Brandi snuggled against Sam and said, "Do you think we'll do it this time?"

"What? Get married or open the shop?" Sam asked, teasing.

"Both."

Sam sighed. "We'll get married all right, but at the rate we're going we'll be ancient by the time we've said our I-dos if we wait to time the event to coincide with the reopening of our shop." Sam sighed.

"I can't think of anywhere I'd rather have the ceremony," Brandi said. "Besides, maybe we've finally reached the end of the delays. They can't continue forever."

"I wouldn't count on it. I talked with the construction foreman today. He says that they'll need at least one more week, maybe two. We've decided to add a two-week cushion, bringing us to June."

Brandi yawned. "Did you tell the others?"

"Sure did," Sam replied with a stretch. "Mia changed the copy for the newspaper ad again, and Doug rescheduled the caterer for the first Saturday in June."

"I guess the wedding arrangements are the only parts that aren't set." Brandi watched the flickering fire.

"We could take care of that this week if you'd only say the word. We could fly to Vegas for the weekend," Sam suggested, studying Brandi's face.

"As tempting as that sounds, I'm determined to have the ceremony in the shop. We met there, so we should get married there," Brandi stated firmly.

"We could get married right here on the steps or in front of the fireplace," Sam suggested.

"That's a good idea, but it's not my dream." Brandi sighed. "Since the moment I fell in love with you, I've known that we'd get married in our shop. At the time, I thought we'd have the ceremony in my store and then walk next door to yours for the reception. Now that we've combined the stores, the locale is even more ideal. I know I'm asking a lot of you to wait, but I've always dreamed of holding our wedding there. June isn't that far away."

"I don't mind waiting. In my mind, we're already married anyway. Nothing can make me love you more." Sam pulled Brandi closer and handed her a glass of wine.

"You're so wonderful, Sam, and so understanding," Brandi said happily.

Chuckling, Sam remarked, "But if you change your mind, we could get married right here in our house."

Looking into his very serious eyes, Brandi replied, "That's a tempting idea, but I'm going to stick to our plans for a while longer."

"Do you realize that this is the first evening we've had together since the rebuilding process began? What happened to the free time we thought we'd have?" Sam asked.

"It vanished. I think I'm more tired from the meetings and discussions than I ever was from putting in a day's work at the shop," Brandi remarked as she led the way to bed.

* * *

Next morning, Brandi and Sam awoke to the now
unfamiliar sound of birds chirping in the trees. Construction noises had sent away the few that had
returned since the completion of the mall. Now that
the men were doing the interior work, the feathered
neighbors had returned and reclaimed the area.

Smiling, Brandi and Sam quickly showered and
dressed. They needed to see for themselves that construction on the block of shops was nearing
completion. Neither could believe that they were only
weeks away from the most important day in their lives.

Rushing along the quiet streets, Brandi and Sam
met their neighbors, who also wanted to see the construction progress. They had supervised the laying
of every brick. It was time to celebrate.

As the spring sun filled the sky, pushing away the
last of April's clouds, Brandi, Sam, and their partners stood across the street from the row of shops.
They had stood there countless numbers of times in
the past and looked at the decorations in the old
shop windows. Now they gazed at the completed
structure that they owned and loved. The builders
had even hung the signs over the doorways. The
shops would soon be alive with people sharing moments and shopping.

The old shops had character; the new shops had
charm. Instead of exterior trim that would require
periodic painting, the builder had used siding that
mirrored painted wood. Instead of a composite roof
that would eventually leak and need replacing, a
new deep brown tin roof topped the structure.

The construction crew had replaced the sidewalks,
too. Gone was the drab gray cement, replaced by
deep red brick-like material guaranteed to last a life-

time. After much debate, the city had agreed to replace the old worn-out streetlights with new ones that looked antique but would provide bright security lighting. The block's transformation was stunning.

Crossing the street in a mass of humanity, Brandi, Sam, and the neighbors approached the block of shops solemnly. Even the children did not speak. Everyone was stunned by the change in the familiar block from comfortable to ashes to renewal. While the men crawled around the exterior, they had missed its beauty. Now, with them inside, the block shimmered and shone.

"Do we dare look inside?" Mrs. Wilson whispered at Brandi's elbow. Although she had been married for months, she had refused to change her name. She had insisted that a woman did not need to change all of her credentials and vital records just because she had remarried. She was and would always be Mrs. Wilson. Her new husband, Mr. Nelson, did not mind. He had waited so long to make her his bride that he hardly noticed the resistance to conformity. Besides, he liked a woman with spunk.

"I don't see why we shouldn't. We own it," Brandi replied with a big smile.

"My golly, you're right!" Mrs. Wilson exclaimed loudly. "Let's go!"

Brandishing her cane like a charging warrior, Mrs. Wilson led the crowd onto the sidewalk and to the shops' doors. They positioned themselves along the row so that they could peer into the huge display windows. Being careful not to leave prints on the glass, they moved from one shop to the other, gazing at the boxes of hardwood flooring to be laid, the cabinets to be hung, and the chandeliers to be assembled. Although much still remained to be done before they could occupy the shops, Brandi and Sam were thrilled with the progress.

"Finally, we can get married," Sam proclaimed.

"You two haven't gotten married yet? I heard that you'd eloped," Mrs. Wilson said, without taking her eyes from the unfinished interior of Over the Rainbow Where Worlds Meet.

"Brandi refused to marry me until we could have the ceremony in the shop," Sam replied as he helped Mrs. Wilson step to the next window.

"That's the most ridiculous thing I've ever heard. Young people should get married. Heck, even old ones shouldn't take forever to get on with it," Mrs. Wilson fussed, looking over her glasses at Brandi.

Giving Sam a look, Brandi explained, "I wanted to have the ceremony in the shop because that's where we met. It's so romantic that way!"

"Posh!" Mrs. Wilson exclaimed with an affectionate chuckle.

"You were invited to the wedding," Sam reminded her.

Mrs. Wilson sniffed. "I know that, but I had hoped that you children had changed your minds about the hoopla and just done it."

"Sam wanted to, but I dragged my feet," Brandi replied, defending her fiancé.

"He should have clubbed you with my cane and dragged you off," Mrs. Wilson said before moving to another window.

Sam laughed. "Believe me, I thought of it."

The group continued its survey of the building's progress. Sam served as their secretary and jotted down anything that might require the builder's attention. Although the outside appeared finished, they saw spots that needed a little caulking and drain spouts that needed lengthening to take rainwater farther from the structure. However, they were mostly pleased that the shops were almost ready for occupancy. The bank would return to the anchor site on the right corner. Sam and Brandi's shop would occupy the enlarged location to the left of it. Kevin's music shop would have a position left of theirs. The new dry cleaner, a tenant, would finish out the block.

"I'm hungry," Sam said, closing the notebook that contained everyone's comments.

"Let's go home. I've seen enough. If I stay here any longer, I'll join those guys and hang the lighting fixtures myself," Brandi said as she slipped her arm through Sam's.

Waving good-bye to their friends, they crossed the street and disappeared down the block. On the walk home, Sam said, "I haven't seen your wedding gown yet. Where is it?"

Snorting, Brandi said, "And you won't until our wedding day. Besides, it's still at the boutique."

"Don't you think you should bring it home? Unless, of course, you've only been stalling and don't plan to marry me," Sam said with a touch of impatience in his voice.

Kissing him lightly on the cheek, Brandi replied, "Mia, Susan, and I have already made the appointment for our final fittings."

"You haven't done that already?" Sam asked incredulously. "We were supposed to have been married by now."

Shrugging, Brandi said, "I didn't see the point in having a final fitting only to find out that the dress wouldn't fit by the time we finally got married. I was afraid I'd gain weight sitting around all day. I had no idea that I'd be on the go as much as I have with the building construction. We've had so many date changes. I'm glad I didn't select anything with a seasonal theme."

"When you bring the gown home, stash it where I won't see it. It's bad luck to see the dress before the wedding," Sam declared, unlocking the front door.

"Who says?"

"The bride magazines."

"How do you know that?"

"You're not the only one who reads those things. You leave them in the bathroom. I read 'em."

"Well, well, well. You are a surprising man," Brandi said with her hands on her hips.

"Good. I'm glad there are still a few things about me that you don't know." Sam pulled her close and kissed her soundly.

"I thought you were hungry," Brandi quipped with a purr.

"I am. Let's go upstairs." Sam took her by the hand and led the way.

Laughing, Brandi followed Sam to their bedroom. Locked in his arms, nothing else mattered, not the shops or the fitting or the grand opening. She was content to spend the rest of her life in his embrace. Sam forgot his physical hunger as Brandi's love filled him with delight. She was all he needed forever.

Chapter 24

With the shop construction nearing completion and occupancy only weeks away, Brandi could finally turn her attention to wedding preparations. Although she had survived the tedium of one fitting, she had always been too busy to return for the final one. She was the kind of person who was used to being constantly in motion and found standing still while someone pinned and marked her gown a painfully boring experience.

Even worse had been the preliminary makeup session on which Mia had insisted. Brandi enjoyed wearing a little bit of blush, lip gloss, and mascara; however, the excessive amount that the makeup artist insisted upon applying to her face was more than she could stand. She had creamed her face as soon as she returned home.

Unable to delay the final fitting any longer, Brandi met Mia and Susan in the bridal department of one of the area's most famous department stores. Carrying the dyed-to-match shoes in a bag, she looked like all the other harried brides who had lists of last-minute items to handle before the big day arrived. She could feel the other women's nervous energy mingling with her own as she stepped off the escalator.

Scanning the anxious faces, Brandi finally spotted her two friends, patiently flipping through bridal magazines. She wished that she could feel that relaxed with so much to do. Although the ever-capable Mia was in charge of the catering and the decorations, Brandi still worried needlessly about the possibility of running out of food or a disaster befalling the cake.

Doug had the responsibility of transporting the minister from his church six blocks from the store. However, she worried that he would forget to pick him up at the last minute. So much could go wrong at weddings and usually did. With so many variations of the plans in peoples' minds, a misstep was even more probable.

Brandi forced her face into a happy smile as she approached her friends. "I hope you haven't been waiting long. I had a few last-minute items to discuss with the builder. The men are working overtime this weekend and every weekend until they deliver the building to us," she said, kissing both of them on the cheek.

Susan, bubbling with positive energy, replied, "Isn't it wonderful! The wedding day's finally here! It seemed as if it would never come."

Mia interjected, "Yes, but it has, and this fitting is the last thing that we have to do. I've taken care of everything else."

"If they would just bring out the gowns, we could get on with it," Brandi commented impatiently.

"Look," Susan said, pointing. "Here they come!"

Rising, the three women followed the saleswomen

into separate dressing rooms off a common area that contained the fitting platform and the walls of mirrors. Taking a deep breath, Brandi tried to calm her nerves. For the first time since falling in love with Sam and deciding to marry him, she felt fluttery. She knew that she was making the right decision, but it was such a big and final step that her stomach lurched as she slipped from her slacks and sweater into the layers of shimmering satin. She actually felt a little light-headed as the saleswoman placed the veil upon her head.

Holding her head up and her shoulders back, Brandi stepped forward for Susan's and Mia's inspection. They wore stunning shades of mauve, but were nothing compared to the vision that Brandi created as she glided toward them. Her creamy satin gown brought out the highlights in her skin tone. Her nervousness added a beguiling blush to her cheeks.

"Oh my! You look more beautiful than I've ever seen you. You should be on the cover of a magazine. I'd forgotten that the gown was so gorgeous," Mia gushed as sentimental tears filled her eyes.

"You're absolutely radiant! Did you change your makeup or are you feverish?" Susan asked.

"I think I'm going to be sick," Brandi muttered and sank onto the platform on which she should have stepped.

Smiling, the sales manager said sympathetically, "That's a very normal reaction for a bride. You're making a big step. You're a successful business-woman, and now you're becoming a man's wife. Mixed emotions are perfectly healthy at this time."

"Just keep telling yourself that you love Sam," Mia suggested.

"I do love him. It's the public display that I dread. I wish we had simply slipped away and gotten married. We've had plenty of time, and we should have done it. Sam wanted to, but I insisted on this wedding business. Now look at me. I'm a mess!" Brandi moaned as she gratefully accepted the glass of iced tea from the sales manager.

"Your parents would have been so disappointed, not to mention the neighbors, the customers, and me," Susan said.

"I know, but I wouldn't be sitting here now feeling as if I'm about to heave," Brandi said.

Mia said softly, "I've never known you to be like this. You're always so confident."

"I'm not into show, you know that. I've always wanted a small wedding in the shop. This has grown into an extravaganza. It would have been better if we'd eloped as Mrs. Wilson suggested, or gotten married in our house. This wedding will be a circus."

"All weddings take on a life of their own," Susan said, trying to console her boss.

"You would have regretted not living your dream if you'd changed you plans. Just go with the flow and enjoy the moment of celebrity. It's not every day that a woman has the stage to herself. This is your day. Work it," Mia insisted, kissing her friend's damp forehead.

"You're right. I'm feeling much better. Let's get on with this fitting. I have a makeup consultation this afternoon in a half hour," Brandi said with a feeble smile.

"If it makes you feel any better, Miss Owens, you make a lovely bride," the seamstress stated as she made a few minor adjustments through the waist and bust.

"Just wait until Sam sees you. He'll just die!" Susan gushed, turning slowly for the seamstress, who marked the length of her hem.

"Let's hope not!" Brandi said. "I've waited a long time for this moment. I don't want anything to spoil it."

The happy laughter filled the fitting room as Brandi settled into the mode of the pampered bride. Despite her objection to the fuss, she liked the vision she saw in the mirror. Sam would definitely be pleased, too.

As soon as the fitting ended, Brandi changed into her slacks and sweater without hesitation. Although her gown was beautiful with its full skirt and beaded bodice, she felt more comfortable in tailored clothing than in the yards of fabric that made up her wedding dress. The veil was a concession to her mother, who had been horrified by the idea that Brandi had not planned to wear one. To her, all brides, regardless of the fashion magazines and latest trends, needed to wear a veil and a white gown. She grudgingly agreed that the cream color of Brandi's gown suited her complexion better than the stark-white gown would have, but that was her only concession.

Both of Brandi's parents had initially been shocked that she had decided to hold the ceremony in the shop rather than in a church. They had dreamed of seeing their little girl walk down the long burgundy aisle to the delight of the myriad guests. Despite the romantic element of marrying in the place in which they met, the Owens had only reluctantly accepted their grown daughter's decision.

As a matter of fact, Brandi's parents had thought that the fire and the construction delays might cause her to change her mind. However, once they realized that Brandi was set on the location, they had acquiesced. After all, it was her big day, her wedding, and the beginning of her life with Sam.

As soon as they shed the gowns, Brandi and her friends rushed downstairs to the makeup department. They followed one of the representatives to the room that the store furnished for private makeup consultations. Over the course of the years, brides, models, and celebrities had used the room for their special sessions.

Sinking into a fabulously comfortable chair within a room that sparkled of white marble and gleaming mirrors, Brandi waited as the makeup artist transformed her from a minimalist to a supermodel whose face was made up to perfection. Squinting into the mirror, Brandi looked for herself under the powder.

"Am I supposed to be able to do this myself?" Brandi asked skeptically.

"Don't worry. I've hired Serge to do it for you that morning. You won't have to lift a finger," Mia replied with a smile at the skilled artist who was outlining her eyes.

Brandi chuckled. "That's good. It would take me all day to do this. I'd probably look like a clown for the effort."

"Where's the camera? We need a shot of the beauty in that chair!" Susan said as she waited her turn for a transformation.

"Why am I doing this?" Brandi asked Mia, who sat beside her in rapturous enjoyment of the makeover.

"Are you still fussing about this?" Mia demanded without taking her eyes from the mirror in front of her.

"I'm a perfectly competent, resourceful business-woman. I don't understand why I'm putting myself through this makeover and pretence. I like the way I look. I don't need all of this powder to change my looks. Sam loves me the way I am. I love myself without all of this," Brandi complained.

"You don't have to do it if you don't want to. I thought you might find it relaxing and enjoy the change," Mia said.

Sighing, Brandi responded, "I don't mean only this. I'm talking about making these drastic changes in my life."

"You call getting married drastic?" Susan chimed in from her seat on the other side of Brandi.

"Yes, don't you?" Brandi exclaimed. "Just look at all the changes in my life. I'm going from being a happy and successful solo act to a duo. What if I'm making a mistake? What if Sam isn't the right man for me? What if he ruins my business? What if he sells my house from under me? What if all this makeup makes me turn into a large zit?"

"You're losing it, kid. You love Sam. You have a raging case of premarriage jitters." Susan chuckled, looking at Brandi's tortured reflection in the mirror.

"You're so young that you don't know how treach-erous men can be. You think marriage is a bed of roses. A man can turn on you in a minute," Brandi retorted.

"Get a grip, girl! Sam wouldn't do anything like

that, and you know it," Mia stated firmly. "I think the fact that he paid off the mortgage on your house is a true sign that he's in it for the long haul. He's stated from the start that he wants to be an equal partner."

"That's the way it looks now, but anything's possible after marriage. He's on his best behavior at the moment. He might change overnight," Brandi insisted stubbornly.

"And you really believe that?" Susan asked.

"No . . . I don't, but it could happen. I'm just nervous, I guess. My life was so wonderful as it was. I don't know what the future as a married woman will be."

"You'll be every bit as happy as I am," Mia said as she studied the new style of her hair.

"But Sam might not be as perfect as Doug," Brandi said.

"He's acted pretty good so far," Susan said. "He really came to your aid during the audit. He's been a rock since the fire."

Agreeing reluctantly, Brandi said, "You're right. He has been wonderful! I couldn't have asked for a better or truer friend. That's when I first realized that I had fallen in love with him. He showed a warmth and compassion that I'd never seen in him or any other man. I don't know how I would have made it through the rebuilding without him. He held me up when I thought that my world would collapse."

"You're just afraid of the unknown," Mia said. "You've been single and doing your own thing for so long that you're not sure you'll be able to make the change. You'll do just fine. You don't really doubt

Sam, you doubt *your* ability to work within a relationship."

"I'm afraid all right," Brandi stated emphatically. "I'm scared to death that I'll make a horrible wife. I'll turn into a shrew and nag him all the time. I'll spend more time thinking about myself than about him and us. I just know I'll make his life miserable. Sam deserves better than being married to me. I'll make a mess of raising our children. I guess that's why I delayed having the final fitting for the gown. I don't want to mess up a perfect relationship."

"You'll be a wonderful wife, and a great mom," Susan said. "Just look at the way you've mothered Brad and me."

"It's just that I've dated a few less than perfect men. Now that I have a great guy in my life, I'm afraid that he'll turn out to be one of them in disguise . . . a wolf in sheep's clothing. It'll be too late then. I'll be stuck. What if I can't find myself under the weight of marriage any better than I can see my face under this makeup?"

"Let's address each issue separately," Mia advised calmly. "Marriage is demanding, but it's not a prison sentence. Yes, I remember all too well some of the frogs you've kissed, but Sam isn't one of them. You've known him for six years and not once in that time has he shown strange or erratic behavior. He's a rock. Only a man who loves a woman completely would have put himself at risk for criticism by helping you in the Ally situation. He loves only you. I think he showed that admirably.

"Next, you've grown in the years you've known him and even more in the months that you've lived with him. You've become less fixated on work and more relaxed. Some of that type-A personality has softened. You're more fun. You smell the flowers now. Sam's the reason for that change. You might not realize it, but he's given you a grounding that you haven't had in your life. None of your other relationships have had that effect. As for the makeup, don't wear it if you don't like it. That's an easy one to settle."

"Madame, if I might make a comment . . ." the makeup artist interrupted.

Answering for Brandi, Mia said, "Please do. You've heard this same conversation hundreds of times. Tell her that everything will be just fine."

Smiling, the makeup artist replied, "I can't promise that your prince won't develop a few warts, but I'm fairly confident that your marriage will be a happy one. From what you've said, you've already weighed all the options, made a pros-and-cons list, and decided to marry this man. It sounds like he's been in your corner for a while. You're not a kid; you know what you're doing. It's just time that you stopped second-guessing yourself. Relax and enjoy your day."

"See!" Susan said.

"However, there is one thing about which I have the utmost confidence," the makeup artist added with a smile. "This makeup will not turn you into a zit. It's great stuff."

Laughing, Brandi said, "I guess that settles it. I don't have a thing to worry about."

At that moment, a waiter arrived with flutes of champagne and plates of luscious red strawberries. Finally allowing herself to relax, Brandi sipped and nibbled as Mia regaled them with anecdotes from her wedding to Doug. According to Mia, the minor glitches and near disasters that seemed huge at the moment had become laughable with the passage of time. Remembering the day, even Brandi had to laugh at the way time changed the horror of the broken heel on Mia's right shoe and her limping down the aisle into a funny story.

"Stop! My sides are killing me!" Brandi said as she clutched her sides and laughed even harder.

"See? I told you that distance makes everything look better." Mia dabbed at the tears that clung to her lashes.

"You're right. It's all the planning that's getting me down. I have a wedding to arrange while contributing to the rebuilding of my business. That's quite a load. We should have eloped. Sam suggested it, but I resisted. We should have done it. I should have taken my rock by the hand and skipped town," Brandi explained.

"Eloped! I should say not," Susan said. "You would have cheated all of us out of the party of the decade."

"I don't think it'll be that impressive," Brandi muttered as she sipped the champagne.

Reluctantly agreeing, Susan said, "Well, maybe not that big, but it'll certainly mean a lot to the neighborhood. It's all the neighbors have talked about for months. Everyone will be there."

"Thank you all for your support," Brandi said, looking at her friends. "I'm not worried about Sam or giving up myself. I know I've changed for the better since falling in love with him. I feel calm with him and I didn't without him. I don't know if the festivities will be the talk of the town, but I intend to enjoy every minute of my day."

"That's my girl!" Mia said.

* * *

Meeting Sam at home for a cozy dinner at their favorite restaurant, Brandi studied the man she loved across the glow of the candles. As she sipped of the wine that perfectly complemented the roasted Cornish hens, she could not understand the reason for her misgivings. Sam's strength had seen her through hard times. He had been her source of strength when her own had flagged.

Brandi loved Sam with her entire being and could plainly see that he felt the same way. Nothing, not the destruction of the shop, the fire, or the changes in her life, could make her abandon her feelings toward him. She knew that there would be ups and downs in the years to come, but, together, they would overcome them and grow stronger for them.

Chapter 25

Between making final wedding plans and putting the finishing touches on the shop's reopening, Brandi was so busy that she could hardly think. She saw Sam briefly as they touched base on progress during the day and at night as they fell exhausted into bed. She missed their conversations in one office or the other. They would have much to discuss once life calmed down again.

The entire neighborhood was excited about the reopening of Over the Rainbow Where Worlds Meet and the other shops in the block. For the first time, the residents of the little community felt a financial as well as personal ownership in the success of the stores and were prepared to assume the responsibility of ownership. Mia had placed a large ad in the paper to announce the opening gala and hoped, like everyone else, that the customers would come.

However, the night before the big grand reopening and the week before the wedding, a strange feeling of panic hit Brandi as she was getting dressed for bed. Rushing into the bathroom where Sam stood shaving, she looked in panic at the face she loved more than anything in the world. Seeing her distress, Sam quickly washed the foam from his face.

"What if no one comes?" Brandi cried. "What if we open the shop tomorrow morning and no one comes?"

Sam sighed with relief. "Oh, that. I thought you were having doubts about marrying me again."

"No, I'm over that. That's ancient history. I've decided that, if this union of ours is a mistake, I'll simply make the next fifty years of your life miserable. No, I'm worried about the store," Brandi replied with a slight smile.

Even freshly washed without a speck of makeup, Brandi was the most beautiful woman that Sam had ever seen. Looking into her eyes, he searched for words that would put her mind at ease. Finding none, he pulled her into his arms and tried to kiss away the worry.

"I'm serious, Sam," Brandi protested as she leaned against his chest.

"So am I."

"I'm worried," Brandi whispered.

"And I'm wondering if it's bad luck to make love to the owner of a bookstore the night before the grand reopening," Sam said as he picked her up and headed toward their bed.

"But, Sam!" Brandi protested weakly.

"Just relax. I'll make you forget all about the shop."

Brandi did not mention the shop again as Sam's finger quickly loosened the tiny pearl buttons down the front of her nightshirt. She did not complain when his lips burned hot against her stomach or nibbled her ears. She did not argue as his hands explored the familiar terrain of her body.

Under Sam's gentle loving, Brandi put aside all

thoughts except those of loving him. She pulled him against her hungrily, tossing his damp towel, which had barely covered his loins, onto the rug. Her hands explored his body with a sense of urgency and ownership. She loved every angle and curve. The warmth of his skin warmed her hands and soul.

Brandi no longer thought about the shop as Sam joined with her, and they matched their rhythm to the music of love. Making love to Sam was not only a physical pleasure but a spiritual and emotional one. He filled her body with his, her heart with his tenderness, and her soul with his compassion. Loving Sam made Brandi feel complete. She had not lost her individually in finding him; she had discovered a greater depth for love within herself.

Tingling with spent passion and cradled against his chest, Brandi ran her fingers over his moist skin. Sam's muscles rippled with strength even while at rest. The physical work of unloading boxes of supplies had hardened his body and trimmed the love handles from his waist, giving him the physique of a bodybuilder.

Yawning, Sam said, "I can read your fingertips."

"What?"

"You've written the name of our shop on my chest at least five times. It'll become a tattoo if you do it again," Sam said, bringing her hand to his lips.

"I didn't even know I was doing it." Brandi sighed and snuggled even closer.

"At least you haven't called me by that name," Sam said as he changed his voice into a falsetto and added, "'Faster, Over the Rainbow Where Worlds Meet! Yes! Rainbow! Yes! Harder, Meet!'"

"Very funny!" Brandi laughed as she playfully slapped his flat, hard belly.

Chuckling, Sam pulled her against him and said, "It'll be okay. Everyone will come back. Business will be booming once again. I predict that by the end of this week you'll be complaining about not having enough time at home anymore."

"I hope you're right, but I've already planned for that possibility."

"What do you mean?" Sam demanded, studying her face curiously.

"I don't intend to spend my evenings in the shop while my handsome husband sits alone at home. Susan and Brad will run the shop at night until they leave for grad school."

"Oh, really? Isn't that a little premature? What makes you think that I want to spend my evenings with you? I'm used to working late, too, you know. I like the peace and quiet of the evening hours," Sam joked.

Rather than answer, Brandi kissed Sam slowly, allowing her tongue to tease his while her hands caressed his groin. Involuntarily, Sam groaned as his body responded to her tantalizing fingers. His fingers gently explored her sweetness.

"You win," Sam muttered. "I'll stay home nights."

All conversation ended as their bodies connected once again. Before the sensation coursing through her body blocked out all thought, Brandi decided that spending the rest of her life with Sam would definitely have its benefits. The union would definitely prove to be one of the best decisions she had ever made.

Chapter 26

The next morning, they awoke to the chiming of the grandfather clock in the hall. Its dulcet tones teamed perfectly with those of the corner church bell. Rising, they rushed to shower and dress. Smiling broadly and chatting gaily, they made their rumpled bed, fed the cat, gobbled a bowl of oatmeal, and dashed out the door. It would not do for the shop proprietors to miss the dedication ceremony.

The neighbors had festooned the block housing the row of shops with banners, streamers, and balloons. Overhead, the weather cooperated by giving them the bluest sky anyone could ever remember seeing. A gentle breeze filled the air with a mixture of floral scents from neighboring gardens. Takoma Park was ready to welcome the return of the shops.

Everyone in the neighborhood had assembled for the dedication. Many of the women carried plates and bowls of goodies for munching as customers browsed the shops, even though they all knew that Mia had hired one of the area's best caterers. Everyone was thrilled that all of the hard work would finally bear fruit. The shops were ready to open and give the neighborhood a central gathering point once again.

Stepping onto a platform constructed in the middle of the square for the occasion, the community association president waited for Kevin's jazz band to finish the last tune. Smiling happily and waving to the assembled throng, she brandished an enormous pair of brass scissors with which she intended to cut the dedication ribbon. As everyone turned their attention to her, the association president rapped an equally large gavel on the podium and waited for silence.

"This is a wonderful day for all of us," the president began. "For the first time in the history of this community, we own not only our homes but our shops. As we take this step into history, let's take a moment to thank God for His many blessings. Join me in a moment of reflection before the joyous ribbon cutting."

Stepping from the platform with Kevin's assistance, the president walked to the ribbon that hung symbolically between the poles of the new sign that announced the existence of the shops to passersby. Gripping the scissors with both hands, she snipped until the bright yellow ribbon finally broke. The crowd cheered loudly as the ends flapped in the warm breeze.

The procession formed a line behind the community association president and regally made its way from one store to the other. The band played gaily in the background. At each door, the proprietor waved an oversized ceremonial key that magically unlocked the shop to its first visitor. The same happened until each shop had reopened.

Brandi and Sam had selected Mrs. Wilson to be the first customer in their newly restored shop. Proudly the older woman took her place beside them as the

band played "Somewhere Over the Rainbow" as
Brandi and Sam unlocked the door, turned on the
lights, and ushered her inside.

"My stars!" Mrs. Wilson exclaimed as the band
moved toward the bank. "It's more gorgeous than I
had dreamed it would be."

Hugging her thin shoulders, Sam said, "And
you're our first customer. Would you like cream and
sugar with your coffee this morning, Mrs. Wilson?"

Smiling broadly, Mrs. Wilson replied, "No, thank
you, Sam. I'd like a cup of your hot cocoa, if you'd
please. No one makes it like you do. I've been
dreaming about the first taste of your special brew
since the fire shut us down."

"Cocoa it is," Sam responded with a deep formal
bow.

"Here's your newspaper, Mrs. Wilson. I'll show
you to the reading section," Brandi said, linking her
arm through the older woman's.

Mrs. Wilson complimented every item as she wandered through the shop. The new decorations had
the look of age and gentle care but were anything but
familiar to the shop's oldest and most loyal customer.
Brandi knew that Mrs. Wilson would like the changes
as soon as she got used to them.

"Which would you prefer, the chair or the sofa?"
Brandi asked as she pointed to the matching blue
leather sofa and wing chairs in the cozy reading corner.

"It's so lovely," Mrs. Wilson said, sinking into one
of the wing chairs and resting her feet on the ottoman. "I'll never be able to rise. You'll have to call
my husband to walk me home tonight."

Brandi grinned. "You can have any level of service you'd like on our special day."

"Well then, I'd like to dance at your wedding." Mrs. Wilson winked mischievously.

"And you will. In one week, I'll marry that handsome guy over there." Brandi smiled and, to her surprise, blushed—she felt exactly like a bride.

"It's about time!" Mrs. Wilson stated firmly. "Between the audit and the fire, you've had no time to think of yourself. You need to settle down, and Sam's the perfect man for you. I'll dust off my dancing shoes as soon as I go home."

"What's this about dancing shoes?" Sam asked as he handed Mrs. Wilson a cup of steaming cocoa.

"We were talking about the wedding." Brandi smiled shyly.

Turning his attention to Mrs. Wilson, Sam said, "You'll have to save a dance for me. That is, if you can fight off the other men."

"You know that I only have eyes for you, my husband, and this cocoa, but not necessarily in that order." Mrs. Wilson laughed and turned her attention to enjoying every sip of the brew.

Sam laughed as he returned to his side of the shop. Customers, long deprived of his delicious creations, had created a line that reached out the door and down the sidewalk. Others, contentedly holding cups in their hands, filled each table, stood along the perimeter, and lingered in the newly created square. As Sam had predicted, people flocked to the shop in happy numbers.

Returning to the front of the bookstore, Brandi discovered that her side of the shop had filled to capacity also. Susan and Brad stood surrounded by patrons who purchased books, magazines, and newspapers as if starved for information. As Brandi passed through them, everyone greeted her warmly, patting her on the back, kissing her cheek, and giving their praise for the new décor.

"Brandi, could I have a minute?" Frank Henderson from Nailor asked as she passed.

Brandi smiled happily. "Of course, Frank. I haven't seen you since the festival. I guess you've been busy opening new malls."

"That's putting it mildly," Frank said as his smile flickered and faded.

"Should we go to my office?" Brandi asked.

"No, here's fine," Frank replied. "I need to tell something that I discovered the other day."

"What is it, Frank?" Brandi felt her curiosity increasing.

"It's about the audit," Frank began. "I've discovered who phoned in the tip."

"Who?" Brandi asked, her fingers tightly gripping his arm.

"My assistant." Frank looked miserable. "He was new and thought he'd make an impression on everyone by removing the competition. Well, he did, but not the kind he wanted. He phoned your book supplier, too. It took a while to get all the facts, but I fired him yesterday. I'm terribly sorry."

Momentarily, Brandi closed her eyes to stop the room from swaying. Life had a way of laying a heavy burden and, just as quickly, lifting it. For a moment, Brandi felt as if she would take flight.

"Brandi, are you okay?" Frank demanded, studying her closely.

Brushing tears from her lashes, Brandi replied,

"I'm better than you could ever imagine, Frank. Thanks for lifting a tremendous weight. You don't know what you've done for me. Stay awhile and party with us."

"I'll do that. Good luck, Brandi, but you won't need it. You have everything already," Frank stated and walked away.

Brandi squared her shoulders and breathed deeply. For the first time since the fall, she felt light and boundless. Nothing remained of the terrible months that threatened to crush her. She had Sam's love, a restored shop, and closure to the nightmares. Seeing Sam across the room, Brandi smiled and waved as she squeezed through the crowd. She could hardly wait to share Frank's news. It was a day of celebrations.

Later in the day, as expected, Mia breezed into the shop at the height of the morning's excitement. Her eyes sparkled with pleasure as she surveyed her best friend's new establishment. Finding Brandi in the reading section, she rushed to her side and gave her a big hug.

"It's glorious!" Mia gushed. "So old and yet so modern at the same time. I was afraid the new cash register would look out of place in this old décor, but the cabinet disguises it perfectly. It's wonderful to see the old shop back in business. This is really your day. I'm so happy for you. All the pieces have fallen into place so well . . . the audit, the reopening. I could just cry."

"It's a miracle. I'm so blessed," Brandi agreed.

Linking arms, the friends walked to the counter from which they could survey the entire shop. Overhead brass and glass lighting in the style of libraries from the early 1900s lighted both the new upstairs section and the downstairs. Tall ladders, reminiscent of the old days, provided access to the top shelves more efficiently and attractively than the folding metal one that Brandi usually lugged from the back room or the wobbly wooden one she had relied on for years. The rich paneling and floors reflected the light and added a period charm to the room. The only missing component was the lady librarian to shush the conversation.

"Now that the shops are back in business, let's put the finishing touches on those wedding plans," Mia suggested with a wink.

"I don't think there's much more to do. You've handled everything with your usual efficiency." Brandi chuckled. "If I remember correctly, you even dragged a reluctant bride for a final fitting."

"Humor me for a minute. I have a need to run down the list. I don't want to miss any of the details for my buddy's wedding," Mia insisted. "The caterer's ready for next Wednesday. So is the string quartet. Doug will pick up the minister and bring him here. I'll get the gowns today as soon as I leave here. Did I forget anything?"

"What about the flowers?" Brandi asked, smiling at her friend's thoroughness.

"I'll have them here and in the refrigerator early on Wednesday. Anything else?" Mia asked again.

"No, I don't think so. We have the rings and the license. We're ready. It's finally going to happen." Brandi laughed, remembering the recent panic that had gripped her and now seemed so unnecessary.

"Then it's done. I'll call you later tonight. Let me

know if you think of anything else," Mia replied as
she pressed through the crowd.

As much as Brandi loved her friend, she was always happy to see Mia leave. Mia was such high
energy that she made Brandi tired. She was also
compulsively neat and well organized, which Brandi
was not. They had different philosophies on life,
too. Brandi had finally realized that they would undoubtedly forget a few of the small details for the
wedding, and she was ready to overlook the omis-
sion. Mia wanted to anticipate every possible mishap
and plan around it. Those differences had probably
added to the success of their long friendship. Each
was willing to ignore the other's traits while being
supportive and encouraging.

The press of customers quickly put the upcoming
wedding far from Brandi's mind. She and her assistants were so busy that they could not leave the
register for lunch until very late in the afternoon.
When it was finally her turn, Brandi joined Sam in his
office for a quick meal. He was also too busy to stay
long in the peace and quiet of his new workspace.

"So much for a slower pace of life," Sam said as
handed her half of the huge pastrami and cheese
sandwich he had packed the previous night.

"Don't complain. They could have stayed away.
Then we'd have another song to sing. We've been
out of business for a long time," Brandi stated,
chuckling.

Sipping his aromatic special brew, Sam said, "I'm
not really complaining. Actually, I'm glad to be back
at work. I enjoyed our time together, but the lack of
cash flow was beginning to worry me. I'm on the

verge of becoming a married man. I have responsibilities."

"I don't drink with men in committed relationships," Brandi teased. "I guess I'd better leave before you fiancée arrives."

"I don't think anyone would begrudge me a few minutes with the most beautiful woman in the world." Sam gazed lovingly into Brandi's smiling eyes.

With no further need for conversation, they sipped their brews in silence. The smell of new leather and wood made the freshly restored uncluttered office inviting in its newness. They had ordered enough bookshelves and file cabinets to enable Sam to remain organized despite his tendency to hoard catalogs and product flyers.

"Have you seen Kevin? Any idea how his shop's doing?" Brandi asked, breaking the glorious silence.

"One of his assistants rushed in a few hours ago. He ordered six coffees and left quickly but said that the shop was packed and jammed. According to him, the register hasn't stopped ringing," Sam said.

Wiping her mouth and tossing the balled up napkin into the trash can, Brandi stated, "If business continues like this through the evening, I think this will be the highest sales-volume day I've ever had. People aren't just buying single copies, they're bringing armloads to the counter. Even the kids seem to have saved their money for today. Comic books are flying off the shelf."

"I'd say that the neighborhood is giving us a good welcome-back present," Sam added as they left the office and returned to the beehive of activity.

"Let's hope it continues," Brandi said.

Sam laughed. "That's for sure. I need money to pay for that honeymoon trip."

"Where are we going?" Brandi asked for the hundredth time.

"You'll find out when we arrive at the airport," Sam joked, pulling her close for a lingering kiss.

Clearing her throat, Susan said, "Brandi, Sam, sorry to interrupt, but the fire marshal's here to see you."

"Finally, some closure," Sam stated, taking Brandi by the hand and leading her toward the door.

"I'm sorry, folks. I didn't know that you were having a party. I guess I should have called ahead or mailed the information, but I was in the area and thought I'd deliver the report in person," the marshal said.

"It's our grand reopening. Come into the office. It'll be quiet there," Brandi said, leading the way to the back of her section of the shop.

Motioning to a chair, Brandi and Sam perched on the new leather sofa together. Holding hands, they waited as the marshal pulled his glasses from his shirt pocket and opened the battered briefcase. Their sense of anticipation increased as he opened the folder that contained the news for which they had been waiting.

Clearing his throat, the marshal scanned the report and announced, "We have apprehended the arsonist. Although yours was a commercial, not residential fire, the MO was the same. The perpetrator broke into the establishment, doused the interior with gasoline, and left the can on the scene. From other evidence left at the scene, we were able to link this fire to the residential fires in surrounding areas.

We have apprehended the man in whose garage we found a stash of similar gasoline cans. He has confessed to this arson and the others. I've filed a report with your insurance company. Here's a copy for your file."

The relief was palpable in the room as Sam said, "You don't know how happy we are to have this information. It's great to have closure as we move forward with the new shop. Thank you."

"Have you shared your findings with Kevin, the owner of Drums and Bugles?" Brandi asked, accepting the folder from the marshal.

"Yes, ma'am, I interrupted his celebration first," the marshal replied, smiling.

"Don't feel that you interfered in any way. Your news has given us even more reason to celebrate," Sam said, leading the marshal to the refreshments.

"Stay awhile and relax," Brandi suggested.

"No, thanks, I have much more to do before I can go home tonight. Thanks for the offer. Enjoy your new shop," the marshal said as he squeezed through the crowd and vanished into the courtyard.

"Wait'll we tell the others. This is a great day!" Sam beamed.

"You tell Susan and Brad, and I'll find Mia and Doug," Brandi suggested.

"Have you forgotten something?" Sam asked, holding her by the arm.

"No, I don't think so," Brandi replied, looking puzzled.

"You plan to walk away from your fiancé without giving him a good-bye kiss on this special day armed with this fabulous news?" Sam teased.

Chuckling, Brandi wrapped her arms around

him, kissed him soundly, and said, "We'd better get used to kissing a lot, because every day will be this special."

"I agree," Sam replied, pulling her close again.

After months of almost devastating events, life had finally returned to a firm path. The shop appeared to be on its way toward incredible success at selling both coffee and books. The audit was behind her and all but forgotten. The fire marshal had just delivered fabulous news. Everyone was well and happy. Neither of them could ask for more.

As the hours flew and the customers finally went home, Brandi left the cash register to Susan and Brad. She had not sat down since the late lunch with Sam and had not touched the pile of work that covered her desk. While her assistants handled the last of the customers and closed the register for the evening, she would spend her time updating computer files and ordering merchandise.

Just as Brandi had begun to relax, the door burst open and her mother and father entered. They had booked a trip to Las Vegas with a group of friends, not thinking that delays would affect the shop's reopening. Both of them appeared breathless as if they had been rushing to beat the clock.

"Sorry we're late," her mother stated as she sank into the empty chair beside the desk.

"The traffic back from the airport was terrible," her father added, casually leaning against the wall.

"Did you enjoy your trip?" Brandi asked as she studied their happy faces.

"We certainly did. I won quite a bit of money," her mother said.

"You and Sam will have to go with us the next

time. You've got to see your mother in action at the crap table. She's a piece of work," her father stated proudly.

Picking lint from her sweater, Mrs. Owens added, "We tried to get here sooner, but Route 50 was backed up. I'm sorry that we missed the crowds. Susan said that people were packed in here like sardines. I would have liked to have seen that."

"You didn't need to rush. You could have waited. The shop will be here for a long time, thank God." Brandi smiled at her proud mother.

"There's no way that I would have missed the grand reopening after all the trouble you've been through to make it perfection. Susan said the outpouring of support was overwhelming. Besides, I wanted to see if I had invested my money wisely," her mother said proudly.

Smiling softly, Brandi replied, "The neighborhood definitely poured its love on us today. Everyone came out. It's incredibly heartwarming."

"I can think of one person who I hope was a no-show," Mr. Owens said.

Turning toward him, Brandi asked, "You mean Ally, don't you? Well, she didn't and I'm glad. The people wouldn't have been nice to her at all. They're still mad at her for spreading the gossip about the audit."

"And you're not? I feel like pulling her hair out one strand at a time," her mother retorted.

Brandi shrugged ."I was over it even before I got the best news today. She showed a very nasty side of her personality by engaging in gossip, but she really had nothing to do with the audit. An employee of Nailor phoned the IRS."

"You mean that Ally's in the clear?" Mrs. Owens demanded incredulously.

"That's right. She shouldn't have become involved in the mess, but something good came of it. I got Sam. He might not have broken from his shell if he hadn't felt the need to help me in my time of need. Even though I wanted to, I doubt that I would have stepped from the store long enough to break my silence. I wouldn't be getting married next week either, and Dad wouldn't be giving me away."

"Well, I still hope she has the sense to stay away from the wedding. The gossip she spread hurt as much as or more than the audit itself. If she hadn't told everyone about it, the audit would have come and gone with no one being the wiser," her mother stated, clicking her nails together angrily.

"It's over now, Mom. Let it go. Besides, she might come with Kevin. They've been seeing a lot of each other since the fire, so I hear. She helped him redecorate and he's helping her work through her issues. I understand she's in therapy."

Chiming in, her father said, "Brandi's right, dear. It's time to move on."

"She'd better steer clear of me! It wasn't just the gossip. She tried to steal Sam from you," her mother added with a snarl.

Shaking her head, Brandi said, "She couldn't steal someone that I didn't have. As a matter of fact, the combination of the audit and Ally made me realize my feelings for Sam. In a way, Ally did me a favor."

"Still, she's one nasty chick," Mrs. Owens insisted.

"I almost forgot to tell you the rest of the news. The fire marshal stopped by a while ago with his report. They've caught the arsonist. He confessed to setting the fire here and the residential ones. It's over."

"What a relief!" Mrs. Owens exclaimed. "I don't think I could have stood it if it had been someone you knew."

"That's great news, baby. You've been through so much. It couldn't have come at a better time," Mr. Owens stated, kissing his daughter happily.

In an effort to divert her mother's attention from the topic of Ally, Brandi offered, "Let me show you around the shop. You haven't had the ten-cent tour yet. You've been gone for a week. The store's changed a lot in a week."

Smiling proudly, Brandi led her steaming mother through the shop. Her father followed at a safe distance. He knew not to cross his wife when she was angry. Both of them offered praise as Brandi explained their reasoning for removing a beam here and adding a staircase there. By the time Brandi's mother had finished the tour, she was in a much better mood. She was even willing to join Brandi and Sam at their house for a glass of wine to celebrate their partnership, after they closed the shop. Her father was clearly relieved and breathing more calmly. His wife of thirty-five years was a handful when angry.

Brandi quickly finished the night's business and sent Susan and Brad on their way. She felt good being back in the routine of the life she loved so dearly. Opening her own shop, dealing with her clients, and closing up were all components of her very enjoyable lifestyle. She was happy to have everything back the way it should be. With Sam across the room from her, life was perfect.

Sam, too, was in a wonderful mood. Sharing

Brandi's happiness had given him more reason to rejoice at their good fortune. He sang in his rich baritone as he cleaned the last of the coffee urns and finished checking the register. Locking the office door, he joined Brandi and her parents for the walk home.

The night was sweet and warm as the foursome walked homeward. Husband and wife and the engaged couple chatted happily until they reached the door and then continued their animated discussion inside over glasses of perfectly chilled white wine. Rather than make the drive home, Brandi's parents accepted the invitation to stay the night. They had seen enough of highways for one day.

"Are you sure we won't be a burden? Daddy can always drive us home," Mrs. Owens said as they sipped a glass of wine.

"You're no trouble at all. Just relax. Drive home tomorrow," Brandi replied as she patted the demanding cat.

"Good, 'cause I'm beat," Brandi's father said. "Your mother thinks that I'm still a young man. She forgets that I need my rest."

"I don't forget, dear," Brandi's mother said. "I just see you as my knight . . . my hero. I haven't admitted to myself that you've aged. You're still the man I fell in love with and married all those years ago. I haven't admitted that I've aged. There's no way you can."

"That's so sweet," Brandi cooed.

"Don't be fooled by your mother's glib tongue," her father said with a happy grin. "She's just saying that to keep me at her beck and call."

"Well, whatever the reason, I hope Brandi will feel

the same after we've been married as long as you two," Sam said.

Turning to Sam, Brandi's father said seriously, "Marriage to this woman is the best thing that ever happened to me. She has pushed and pulled, encouraged and advised, and loved me every step of the way. I can't imagine the emptiness I would have felt if I hadn't met her. I hope you kids will be as happy as we've been."

Lifting his glass, Sam toasted, "To marriage, to my beloved, to eternity together."

Brandi's eyes filled with tears at Sam's uncharacteristic sentimentality. Looking at her parents, she could see their total approval and acceptance shining on their faces. She felt incredibly happy and secure.

Her parents were the first to retire for the evening, but Brandi and Sam soon followed. As they fed the cat and turned off the light, Brandi turned to him and asked, "Do you really love me that much that you'd want an eternity with me?"

"No, I love you more. There's simply no more time than that," Sam replied, studying her face.

"I love you an eternity's worth, too, Sam. Forever and ever," Brandi said gently.

"I'm a lucky man," Sam replied softly as he led her upstairs to their bedroom.

The day had started as the beginning of a new vitality and commitment for the neighborhood. For Brandi and Sam, it had marked a return to their shops and the restoration of their shops. It ended with two couples knowing that they were safe from the troubles of life because they were loved.

Chapter 27

Brandi and Sam were so busy in their shop that they only thought of their upcoming wedding in stolen moments. A reporter from a glossy magazine spent a day with them, recording the history of the neighborhood and the shops as well as their ownership of their newly restored joint venture. Business administration majors from one of the local colleges interviewed every proprietor on the block as part of their practicum about the realities of running a small business and for survival tips that might help others become as successful.

By the time Brandi and Sam returned home from their long day's work, they were very grateful that Mia was tending to the last of the wedding plans, removing the burden from their tired shoulders. They slept, exhausted but satisfied, in each other's arms.

Over a hurried breakfast, Brandi said, "Have you had any success in finding new staff?"

"No, but I will," Sam replied. "I'm even more determined now than ever that we'll find someone to run the shop on weekends so that we can have quality time together."

"It's easy to fall into the old habits of working long

hours. We can't let the shop absorb all of our time and come between us," Brandi reminded Sam.

Smiling, Sam said, "I'm touched. I never thought I'd hear Brandi Owens say that something is more important than her store."

"I didn't think there could be until I fell in love with you. You're all I need to be happy. Everything else is just a living," Brandi admitted, placing her hand on Sam's.

"Lady, you make my heart sing." Sam pulled Brandi into his arms for one last kiss before rushing to open the shop.

To celebrate the upcoming nuptials, Brandi's friends threw a lavish shower in her honor, which she managed to attend by leaving Brad in charge of the shop. They held it at Mia's house on the evening before the wedding while Doug entertained Sam and his buddies in a bachelor party at a well-known club.

Although Brandi was not one for ceremony and sentimentality, she was glad that she had agreed to the bridal shower. Now that the shop occupied its proper place in her life, she felt like a bride and wanted to enjoy the once-in-a-lifetime events.

Mia had decorated her house with pillars of silver and white balloons, sparkling white candles covered in silver glitter, and bouquets of white roses tied with silver bows to complement the sophisticated bridal theme. Each of the twelve tables held four exquisite table settings on a white tablecloth with silver stripes.

Mia had left nothing to chance as usual. Twinkling crystal stemware and sparkling silverware completed the setting. She had artistically folded the napkins that sat in the center of each plate to look like a dove. The ambiance was perfect with soft music playing in the background as the flickering candlelight reflected from the mirror at the center of each table. The wait staff wore white cummerbunds with a wide silver stripe in the middle.

The evening was perfect. Brandi's girlfriends turned out in full force and every table held four women who would leave with a silver bud vase as a memento. By the time the evening ended, Brandi would need a wheelbarrow to cart away her gifts.

Lightly tapping her perfectly manicured nail against her champagne flute, Mia stood and cleared her throat. As the ladies grew silent, she raised her glass and said, "Brandi, you've carefully surveyed the male population for the ideal mate. Having found Sam, you've sufficiently tested his devotion and affection and decided that he would make a good candidate. You are prepared to accept him, overlook his flaws, and live with him for the rest of your life. You are now ready to take the next step and join the sisterhood of married women. Now, on the eve of your wedding day, we would like to wish you every happiness. Ladies, let's raise our glasses to the bride-to-be, our dear Brandi!"

"To Brandi!"

"It's about time, girl!"

"God bless you and Sam!"

Amid much clicking of stemware and cheers of good luck, the wait staff appeared to serve the meal. As the quartet resumed its playing, the ladies sliced into succulent *tornedo de boeuf,* asparagus, French bread, potatoes, and aspic. The conversation was amiable and animated among the women who had known each other for years but saw little of each other due to the demands of their busy lives. Brandi was the last unmarried woman in the group, while the others had been married for years with many having several children. They were happy to welcome her into their exclusive wives' club.

As soon as dessert arrived, Mia positioned Brandi in the spotlight in the room's center. From a comfortable chair, she would open and display her gifts. Brandi obliged with a big but shy smile. Accepting the first present, she carefully unwrapped the box and handed the paper along with the ribbon to Susan, whose job it was to fashion the bouquet.

"What a wonderful gift, Nancy," Brandi gushed. "My old set of pots and pans are in desperate need of replacing."

"I'm sure it is," Nancy replied. "You bought it during our college senior year. That was not yesterday."

As the ladies laughed heartily, Brandi passed the heavy box around so that all could glimpse the complete set of French cast iron cookware. Surrounded by her old and dear friends, she felt extremely blessed and happy. Every part of her life had fallen into place perfectly.

"That's no lie. She's probably sleeping in those old ratty nightshirts from our college days, too. My gift will put an end to that," another of Brandi's old friends commented.

"You know our Brandi. She keeps things past the expiration date. I remember those tennis shoes she loved so much. Those maypops that no one could

convince her to trash. She probably still has them,"
yet another added a tender memory to the laughter.

"I do not," Brandi retorted happily. "I threw them
away last month."

Moving through the rest of the pile, Brandi did
the same with the heavy lace ivory tablecloth, the
stemware, china, and all the other items that had appeared on her bridal registry lists. With the help of
her friends, she now had all new items for the
kitchen and dining room. She would enter the
world of the married lady in style.

By the time the ladies left at ten o'clock, Mia had
filled several large trash bags with discarded paper
and the remains of the festivities. Susan had prepared a huge bouquet that Brandi would save as a
memento of the wonderful evening spent with dear
friends. Susan and Brandi loaded her car with the
gifts as soon as the last of her friends had departed.

Although Sam and Doug were not expected back
before midnight, Brandi did not want to take the
chance of seeing him the night before the wedding.
He had decided that he would occupy Mia's guest
room rather than ruining the thrill of seeing Brandi
enter the shop in her wedding gown. If possible,
Sam was more excited about the day than Brandi
was. He was glad that she had not agreed to elope;
he had become completely engrossed in making the
wedding arrangements.

Flopping onto the sofa, Brandi proclaimed,
"That's the last one. I'm whipped. This was the best
party ever! You outdid yourself. Thank you both."

Sitting opposite her, Mia replied, "I'm glad you
enjoyed yourself."

"And to think you didn't want a shower," Susan interjected from her perch on the ottoman.

"I'm glad you talked me into it. I would have missed one of the best experiences of my life," Brandi conceded with a smile.

"Tomorrow should top it." Mia nodded.

"Tomorrow! All of this culminates tomorrow. I've been so busy this week and today that I haven't had time to think about it," Brandi confessed.

"By tomorrow night this time, you'll be a married lady!" Susan said.

"I hope Sam's having as much fun as I had. This was a great night!" Brandi said.

"From the little bit that Doug would share with me, I think it's fair to say that he'll have a good time," Mia said with a knowing smile.

"What does that mean?" Brandi demanded.

Holding her hands wide, Mia stated, "My dear husband has arranged for beer and hard spirits to flow like the Potomac River. Not that the men will notice, but I planned a menu that would make any man happy. The pork barbecue sandwiches alone should make them ecstatic. All of that is in addition to the baseball tickets. It should be quite a night."

"I hope Sam won't be hungover tomorrow. It'll spoil the wedding pictures if he looks like a raccoon," Brandi said with a sigh.

"He wouldn't be the first bridegroom to appear in that state or worse," Mia said. "However, Doug has promised that he'll keep that from happening. He remembers that Sam saved him from a similar fate the night before our wedding."

"I hope he'll have a good time," Brandi said as she forced her tired body to stand. "I'd better get myself in gear before I fall asleep on this very comfortable sofa. That makeup artist you hired won't be able to work his magic if I don't get some sleep."

"Call me as soon as you get home," Mia instructed as Brandi and Susan reached the door.

"I'll drive," Susan said, reaching for the keys. She was spending the night at Brandi's and had the job of getting her dressed the next day and keeping her calm.

"Good idea," Brandi agreed as she kissed Mia on the cheek. Her eyelids were so heavy that she could hardly keep them open.

Susan had skillfully negotiated the silent streets and deposited Brandi at home so swiftly that Brandi had little time to think about Sam or the next day's events. When she did, she wondered if he was thinking about her. He was probably having so much fun at the game that thoughts of her were far from his mind.

Surprisingly, Brandi was remarkably calm about the wedding, knowing that Mia had organized everything perfectly. Tumbling into bed, Brandi muttered her thanks to Susan again and fell fast asleep. Not even her cat's demands for attention or the empty side of the bed could keep her awake.

Sam, however, was wide-awake as the umpire shouted his next questionable call. He had not attended a ball game in years and quickly discovered that he still loved the smell and taste of stadium hot dogs and peanuts. Even with the Orioles behind the Blue Jays three-to-two at the bottom of the ninth inning, he was having a ball.

"Great game!" Brad shouted above the roar. He had joined the celebration after closing the shop.

"Yeah, sure is. I hope I'll be able to hear the minister tomorrow," Sam replied without taking his eyes from the field.

"You'll be okay," Brad replied. "It's louder than this at concerts."

"Don't worry," Doug replied. "I'll nudge you when it's time to say I do."

"But who'll tell you? You won't be able to hear either," Sam said.

"Yes, I will. I don't want my wife mad at me. I came prepared for the noise. You'll learn self-defense skills as soon as the ink dries on the marriage certificate," Doug responded as he pulled out the earplug.

"Do you have another pair of those?" Sam asked.

Reaching into his pocket, Doug produced a little package and tossed it to Sam. Tearing it open, Sam placed the plugs into his aching ears. With a thumbs-up, he returned his attention to the Orioles best batter at the plate.

"Are you having fun?" Doug mouthed.

"Great! Mia's dinner arrangements were tops, too," Sam replied.

For a moment, the crowd grew silent. With two out, one man on base, and the lead batter at the plate, the moment had come. The Blue Jays' pitcher took his stance. He stared at the Orioles' batter as if daring him to hit the ball. *Thwack!* The crowd rose to its feet. The ball soared toward the center field wall. The runner ran to first base, keeping his eyes on the pursuing outfielder. The man leaped. The ball escaped his grasp and cleared the wall. The crowd exploded. The Orioles won by one run.

Momentarily removing the earplugs, Doug said, "I promised Mia that I'd have you back to our house no later than one A.M. and sober."

"Is that some kind of rule?" Sam asked, finishing the last of his third beer.

"It is with Mia," Doug replied with a shrug. "You've got to look your best for those photos."

"Oh yeah, I remember that part from your wedding. I don't want the wrath of Mia on my neck. I remember that I did the same for you all those years ago. It's over anyway. What a night!" Sam said.

Pushing through the crowd, Sam thought about Brandi. He had just seen the best game of the season. He had enjoyed the company of his buddies, but he wished that she could have seen the Orioles beat the Blue Jays. He would have to share some of the details with her one night after their day's work was done as they lay in bed together.

By the time they arrived at Doug's house, Sam was ready for sleep. He had been careful not to drink too much, more from the desire to avoid Mia's scrutiny than for concern about the photos. Slipping into bed, Sam fell sound asleep with thoughts of the next day and his love for Brandi playing on his mind.

Chapter 28

The next morning, the sun shone brightly, making it a perfect day for a wedding. The birds sang as if part of a chorus to herald the union of Brandi and Sam. Flowers bloomed in profusion throughout the neighborhood. Summer in D.C. had arrived in all of its glory.

It was almost noon when Brandi awakened. She could not remember when she had slept so late or so soundly. She stretched and momentarily wondered why Sam did not lie in bed beside her. As the fog of sleep cleared from her mind, she remembered that he had spent the night at Mia and Doug's house. She had slept alone in keeping with the tradition of not seeing the bridegroom on the day of the wedding, although they both thought that the idea was outdated. When Mia insisted, they had given in rather than argue with a formidable force. Alone, the bed felt cold without Sam's presence. Even the cat, which usually snuggled against Sam's warm body, appeared forlorn.

Brandi could hardly wait to hold Sam in her arms again. They had planned for the big day with precise detail. With abundant assistance from Mia, every detail had been considered, and nothing had been left out. As a matter of fact, Mia had done most of the work and arranged components of the wedding about which Brandi knew nothing. Mia wanted her best friend to have a few surprises to remember over the years.

Brandi and Sam had waited so long and survived so many disasters since they first realized the love they felt for each other. Now the event had finally arrived. The entire neighborhood would attend as well as old friends and family. Brandi and Sam's wedding would definitely prove to be an event to remember.

"Don't worry. He'll be here tonight and every night for the rest of our lives . . . all ten of them," Brandi said consolingly, pulling the cat closer.

An understanding meow escaped from the cat's mouth. Easing itself from Brandi's arms, the furry friend stretched and jumped from the bed. If it could not find Sam's warmth, the cat would go in search of sustenance.

Brandi stretched, rose, and made the king-sized bed, an easy task since she had slept on only one side of it. She tightly clutched her robe against her body as she plodded down the stairs to the kitchen. The house was painfully quiet with Sam away. The silence had not seemed oppressive before he filled it with his size and laughter. Before Sam entered her life, Brandi had found the house cozy and welcoming. Now, however, it was empty and very lonely without him.

Even the warm, sunny kitchen appeared changed. Missing was the delicious aroma of coffee that greeted Brandi every morning. Sam always woke a little earlier and made coffee and cocoa for them.

Sometimes, he would bring up a cup to the bedroom so that they could sip and talk before starting their day.

With Sam at Mia's, Brandi decided to revert to instant coffee instead of making an entire pot for herself. Seeing an almost full pot of coffee would make her feel incredibly lonely. Tasting the watery brew, Brandi scrunched her face at the thought that, not too long ago, she had actually lived on it but not anymore.

Carrying the steaming cup upstairs, Brandi stopped on the landing to look down into the living room. She felt strange and cold not finding Sam sitting in his favorite chair by the window. He liked to read the paper in the sunbeam that shined through the panes. Shaking off the feeling, Brandi smiled at the thought that the chair and the room would never feel empty again. Sam and a life of joy and laughter were only hours away.

Entering the bathroom, Brandi again listened to the silence of the house. No one sang in a fabulous baritone behind the shower door or filled the room with enough steam to lift the wallpaper off the walls. Brandi was alone in the house, and she did not like it. Filling the tub with tepid water, she wondered if Sam was missing her as much as she longed for him. Chuckling to herself, Brandi mused that he was probably fighting a hangover that was more consuming than his loneliness for her.

Just as Brandi slipped into her robe, the doorbell rang. For a moment, she ignored its insistent pinging, thinking that Sam would answer it. Realizing that she was alone, Brandi sprinted down the steps as the caller began to knock furiously.

"It's about time!" Mia scolded as she entered the house carrying an oversized garment bag in both arms accompanied by a pair of female photographers hired to record the day. "These gowns are not lightweight, you know."

"Sorry," Brandi replied, helping her friend unload her burden onto the sofa. "I forgot that Sam wasn't here to open the door. How is he, by the way?"

"When I left home, he was pacing and muttering something about eloping. He doesn't do waiting well," Mia said, flexing her arms.

"Neither do I," Brandi said. "This day is passing so slowly. I'm anxious for today to be over."

"Why? This is your special day. You should enjoy every minute of it. Pamper yourself. Take it easy. Have a slow day. Isn't there a saying about a woman never being prettier than on her wedding day?"

"Or more bored or lonely. I miss Sam," Brandi whined as the cat rubbed against her ankles.

"You'll have more than enough time to look at Sam once you've said the I-dos. You'll even get tired of seeing him twenty-four-seven, 365,'" Mia said calmly.

"You don't get tired of being with Doug."

"We're not together as much as you and Sam will be. We share the same office, but we're with customers almost all the time. I might not see him again until dinner. It'll be different for you. All you have to do is look across the room."

"True, and I'll never get tired of seeing him either," Brandi insisted, planting her feet stubbornly.

"I'm sure you won't, but if you don't start getting ready, you'll never know. It takes time for Serge to

make even a natural beauty like you look stunning."
Mia led Brandi to the stairs.

"It's too early to get dressed," Brandi protested,
nibbling nervously at the bagel that Mia had pressed
into her hands.

"No, it's not. It's after two. The photographers are
ready to shoot the candids. Let's go upstairs and get
started," Mia urged, pushing Brandi slightly.

At that moment, the doorbell rang again. This
time, Susan entered, using the extra key that Brandi
had given her. Her hair was still in curlers and her
face devoid of makeup. Behind her stood Brandi's
parents.

"Your father insisted on coming here with his
camera. It's not enough that the photographers are
recording everything. He wants a personal video of
his own. I tried to tell him that we'd get a copy of the
official one, but he wouldn't listen. Just kick him out
if he gets in the way or on your nerves," Mrs. Owens
quipped.

"I want to remember this day for the rest of my
life. My little girl is getting married," Mr. Owens said
mistily, looking especially dashing in his tuxedo.

"You'd think he gave birth to this child himself.
He kept me awake all night with his tossing and
turning. I look a wreck. Even my bags have bags,"
Mrs. Owens said with a sigh.

"Don't worry, Mrs. Owens, the makeup artist will
do your makeup, too. You'll look so lovely that
everyone will mistake you for the bride," Susan said,
leading Brandi's mother into the guest bedroom on
the second floor.

"Wait for me!" Mr. Owens called. "I want movies
of everything."

Brandi rolled her eyes and Mia giggled as Mr. Owens fumbled with the newly purchased video camera as the photographer recorded every misstep. They both wondered if he would capture images of anything other than his shoes and fingers. Despite his bungling, Brandi felt incredibly loved by his determination to capture her big day.

While Mia converted the guest bedroom into a makeup studio under the watchful eye of her father's camera, Brandi slipped from her robe into her undergarments. She had purchased a cream silk bra and panty set that slid over her body effortlessly, hugging and accentuating every curve. Sheer panty hose, decorated with the prerequisite blue and white garters, glistened on her shapely legs. Slipping her feet into heels elegantly embroidered with pearls and sequins, Brandi immediately started to feel like Cinderella dressing for the ball.

Taking her place at the makeup table, she carefully prepared her skin to receive the makeup that would transform her from beautiful to stunning, if it kept its promise. She would have preferred to wear nothing more than mascara, a touch of blush, and lip gloss, but Mia had insisted that the camera would make her look washed out if she did not apply more makeup than usual.

"Decent?" Mia called from the hall. "Your father wants to video your makeover, too. Your mom looks great, by the way."

Brandi replied, "I'm all yours."

Like an advancing storm, Serge immediately filled the bedroom with energy as he dabbed and patted, lined and accentuated Brandi's features until the reflection in the mirror was indeed breathtaking but foreign. Discarded cotton balls and powder flew everywhere. Even Brandi's father was speechless by the transformation.

"Finished!" Serge proclaimed, looking pleased and tossing the brush onto the table. "You look ravishing. Your bridegroom won't recognize you. He'll think that you've hired a model to stand in for you."

"Sam won't recognize me? I don't recognize me. Am I really under all that powder and paint?" Brandi asked, afraid to move her forehead for fear of breaking the cast that she felt covered her face.

"You look lovely. I've highlighted your positive features to perfection and minimized the little lines on your forehead," Serge replied, studying his handiwork.

"You look wonderful. You'll have the best photo album ever," Mia proclaimed.

"You are gorgeous," Mr. Owens said proudly from behind his camera. "I don't think I've ever seen a lovelier bride."

Studying her reflection, Brandi replied, laughing happily, "Look at me! I'm the girl in the Fashion Fair haze."

"Mia's right. You are the most beautiful bride I've ever seen, although you'd be beautiful with a freshly washed face. If you're uncomfortable with the makeup, remove it," Mrs. Owens gushed as she gazed lovingly at her daughter.

"Over my dead body!" Mia protested, as Serge packed the cosmetics bag.

Feeling loved and supported, Brandi replied, "Thanks, Mom, but I'll wear it. Mia's right about needing it for the camera. It's more than I usually wear, but I'll get used to it. It's only for a few hours."

Rising, Brandi walked toward her closet door on which hung the exquisite gown that would complete her transformation into a storybook princess. Not being someone who liked frills, she had selected the satin gown accentuated with hand-applied Austrian crystals and pearls for its elegant simplicity. She would wear a matching cap to which the elbow-length beaded veil was attached.

"Daddy, you'll have to leave now," Brandi said softly.

"What? Oh yeah. Mother, the camera's all yours," Mr. Owens replied as he scurried from the room.

Laughing, Mia commented, "I bet your father just set a new record for leaving a woman's bedroom without the assistance of a shotgun at his back."

The mother and daughter laughed as Brandi ducked under the gown's full skirt assisted by Mia and Susan. As the material fluttered to the floor, she turned toward the mirror on her closet door and gasped. She had become every little girl's dream . . . a princess ready to meet her prince.

Holding the camera steady, Mrs. Owens dabbed at the tears that glistened on her lashes as Mia and Susan fixed the satin cap upon Brandi's head. She had always dreamed that her daughter would meet a man whom she could love and who would love her in return. Now the day had arrived, and she could not have been happier.

After adjusting the veil, Mia smiled at the transformation. All of her plans and arrangements would soon culminate in a glorious day for her best friend. Willing tears not to flow and ruin her makeup, Mia hugged Brandi and walked to the door. Opening it, she ushered in Brandi's father so that he could see the beautiful bride that he would escort down the shop's aisle and give away.

"Oh, Brandi!" Mr. Owens said as his eyes misted.

"I'm so happy, Daddy. I didn't want all this hoopla, but all of you insisted. And I'm so glad you did," Brandi cried, looking from her parents to Mia and then Susan.

"I'm glad you did, too, baby," Mr. Owens said softly through his tear-choked throat. "I thought your mother was the most beautiful woman I'd ever seen until this moment."

"She is; I'm a distant second," Brandi replied, squeezing her parents' hands.

"I hate to break this up, but the photographer is waiting downstairs," Mia said, dabbing at the tears on her lashes.

Turning away, Mia walked to the window and waved. Immediately the sound of violins floated up to greet them. Looking confused, Brandi turned to Mia, who had swooped up the train of her gown and tossed it over her arm. Susan only smiled as she juggled the three huge bouquets of white roses.

"Violins?" Brandi asked.

"You'll see," Mia replied with a wink.

"I can hardly wait. I hope you haven't done anything to turn this extravaganza into a spectacle," Brandi whispered as she eased through her bedroom door.

Mia giggled. "Never! I've simply provided my best friend with a day that she'll never forget."

"That's exactly what I'm afraid of," Brandi retorted with a happy smile.

As soon as Brandi opened the front door, a cheer rose from the gathered crowd of friends and neighbors. Each adult held a bouquet of balloons and a noisemaker. To the right, a string quartet composed of familiar faces stood on the lawn under her living room window and played valiantly despite the noise that drowned out their efforts. Something resembling snow fluttered in every tree. Gazing uncertainly at the happily smiling faces, Brandi turned to look at her parents, Mia, and Susan, all of whom wore expressions of supreme contentment and satisfaction. Even the photographers smiled at the show.

Hugging Brandi's shoulders, Mia explained, "I thought we'd really make this wedding a community affair. Everyone offered to help with the planning, the food, and the entertainment, and I've used their talents as often as possible. One of your neighbors makes to-die-for cakes, so I hired her to create yours. You should see it; it's a masterpiece. Those gentlemen wanted to provide the music. Did you know that they performed at the White House last Christmas? As you can hear, they're top shelf. Just wait until you see the shop. The neighbor around the corner is a florist, and she outdid herself for you. You're part of the life of this community, and they simply wouldn't be content until they could do something to make this day special."

"The musicians are a wonderful touch, but I don't understand why people are standing on the sidewalk rather than waiting from us at the shop. Where's the limo? Did you forget to order a car?" Brandi whispered as her father held his arm out for her to take.

Before Mia could answer, Susan said, "They're your escort. Think of your neighborhood as a village. The residents want to escort you to your wedding as you walk along the flower-strewn path."

Looking from one smiling face to the other, Brandi saw that Susan was not kidding. The neighborhood girls, who only days ago had been her students, wore Sunday school dresses and carried baskets of flower petals. The boys, looking uncomfortable in dress shoes and ties, had already woven streamers and ribbons into the branches of the shrubs that lined the sidewalk.

"They must have gotten up at the crack of dawn," Brandi exclaimed.

Susan smiled and said, "Mia certainly thought of everything."

"Let's go!" Mia ordered. "Your bridegroom awaits."

"This is so romantic!" Susan said with tears in her eyes.

"I don't know about romantic, but it's definitely over the top." Brandi took her place behind the flower girls.

For the first time in years, Brandi allowed herself to relax and go with the flow. She was the center of attention on her day. Rather than fight it, she allowed the festive mood to take possession of her and lift her along the sidewalk. A day like this one would never happen again.

Chapter 29

As the procession wove its way through the streets, Brandi felt her embarrassment at being the center of attention fade away. The great outpouring of love from her neighbors and friends was overwhelming as she allowed herself to float toward the shop on a pleasing mixture of musical medleys and laughing voices.

Brandi felt incredibly loved and blessed as the fragrance of crushed red rose petals wafted in the warm air. With each step, she fought back the tears that would have ruined her makeup. Her father had relinquished the camera to Brad so that he could join his wife in walking with their daughter. Periodically, he would discreetly touch his finger to his moist eyes while his wife openly dabbed at happy tears. Mia and Susan, dressed in identical mauve gowns, carried her train in one hand and their bouquets in the other.

Holding her bouquet of white roses and matching ribbons while her parents' hands lightly grasped her elbows, Brandi smiled and called greetings to neighbors and friends who had lined the sidewalks to watch her processional. Their streamers and balloons bobbed in the breeze as they joined the end of the procession. Mia and Susan were right, this would be a day that she would remember forever.

As she approached the shop, Brandi saw that someone had decorated the entire strip of stores in white bunting, sparkling glass bells, and delicate red crystal hearts. All who had not joined the procession now waited impatiently on the sidewalk for the bridal party to arrive. Children stood on tiptoe and adults peered over each others' shoulders as they watched first the boys, then the girls, and finally Brandi and her parents come into view. A deafening roar rose to greet her as they opened a path on the flower-strewn sidewalk.

At the shop's door, Mrs. Owens kissed her daughter lightly on the cheek and allowed Brad to escort her inside. She disappeared into the shop decorated with sprays of flowers and bunting that hung from the bookshelves and the glittering chandeliers. Brandi's eyes once again misted, knowing that she would soon join the ranks of married ladies like her mother. No longer would she be exclusively a daughter, but also the wife of a wonderful man.

Adjusting Brandi's veil, Mia smiled through her tears at her best friend and took her place behind Susan and the flower girls, who already stood in the doorway waiting for the music to begin again. In the shop cleared of its display tables, everyone in the waiting crowd craned their necks to see past them to catch a glimpse of Brandi.

As the musicians struck the first chords of the wedding march, the little flower girls and the boys, one of whom served as the ring bearer, stepped into the shop. Brandi could hear her guests' reaction to the cute way in which the girls distributed the flowers and the boys dropped streamers on their way to the arch under which the ceremony would take place. Brandi watched as their bobbing heads vanished into the flickering candlelight that had transformed her shop into a chapel.

Next, Susan and then Mia left the sunlight for the glow of the shop's interior. They smiled brightly as they prepared the way for Brandi's arrival. They processed steadily, knowing that they were only the preamble for the long-awaited event.

All eyes now focused on the empty doorway. Brandi gazed misty-eyed at her father, who beamed with tearful pride at his beloved daughter. He kissed her lightly, adjusted her veil, and linked her arm through his. The moment about which he had dreamed and dreaded since the day of her birth had finally arrived.

Nervously, Brandi smiled into the faces of her friends and neighbors as she walked down the narrow aisle that led into the shop's depths. She could not have asked for a more perfect, storybook day or setting. The shop had never looked more elegant as the book spines added a dash of color against the richness of the shelving. The aroma of spicy potpourri, rose petals, and perfume combined magically with that of freshly polished wood. The chandeliers set on low and the flickering candles created the illusion of starlight. Mia had not missed a beat in the preparations.

Brandi knew that if she could see Sam her nervousness at being the center of attention would vanish. He made her feel secure and happy. He added warmth and unbounded energy to her life. Sam had been her rock during tough times and her playmate during moments of relaxation. She wanted to make him happy more than she had ever desired anything else in the world . . . and she would.

Barely hearing the mellow sound of the string quartet, Brandi continued the procession from the front door of her store to the imaginary dividing line that connected her world to Sam's. On that spot, Mia had supervised the building of a platform and an arch, both of which were now covered in white satin bunting and ribbons artistically dotted with tea roses and greenery. Although the distance was not great, Brandi's face felt as if she had been smiling forever behind the veil that fluttered with each breath. Following the path of the red carpet runner covered in streamers and flower petals, Brandi and her father made steady progress through the throng of well-wishers.

Walking past the counter that she could not see for the crush of people, Brandi and her father made a sharp right turn. Suddenly, instead of a wall of people, she could see a clearing containing the platform and the arch surrounded by their friends and neighbors. However, Sam did not occupy the spot to the right. Instinctively, she slowed her step to a crawl. Maybe he had changed his mind. Perhaps he had experienced misgivings. It might even be possible that a final night of carousing with the boys had rendered him incapable of attending his wedding. Whatever the reason for his absence, Brandi had no intention of reaching the platform before her bridegroom.

"Slow down," Brandi whispered to her father.

"Where are Sam and the minister?" her father asked through barely parted lips.

"Beats me, but I won't be the one waiting at the altar," Brandi replied. "Do you think he developed cold feet?"

"Not unless he's totally crazy. No man would stand up my daughter," Mr. Owens stated loyally.

Brandi and her father were now making slow progress. To walk more languidly would have meant that they were standing still. Everyone's eyes mechanically moved from the bride's lovely face to the vacant platform. Brandi could almost see the same question play across their faces as they realized that Sam was not waiting for Brandi under the arch.

Moving at a snail's pace, Brandi overheard one of her guests ask the person standing near her the question that burned on everyone's mind, including hers. The woman had carefully covered her mouth to muffle the sound, but the other guests could still hear her above the violins and the impatient shuffling of shoes. Besides, everyone had wanted to ask the same question but was too kind to put the dreadful thought into words.

Speaking in a tone that could best be described as a stage whisper, the woman demanded, "Where's Sam? Do you think he'll be a no-show? How embarrassing! This has certainly not been the year for Brandi . . . the audit and the fire and now this. You don't think he'd do that, do you?"

"Of course not. Sam's not that kind of man," the person beside her replied.

"Don't let that bother you," Mr. Owens said, seeing the expression of concern that creased Brandi's brows.

"Where is he? Why hasn't he appeared?" Brandi demanded with a mixture of irritation and concern.

"I'm sure he'll have a good explanation," her father replied, continuing to creep toward the platform surrounded by guests but missing the two most important elements of the ceremony . . . Sam and the minister.

Even Mia and Susan looked concerned as they stood to the left of the empty platform. They tried not to fidget with their flowers although they continually cast glances in the direction of Sam's side of the shop. Mia more than once stood on tiptoe to peer around the platform.

Suddenly, the crowd starting moving, almost imperceptibly at first but gradually forming a distinct aisle from Sam's side of the shop to the platform. At first, Brandi could only hear a soft murmur of excitement as the space widened until the voices became more urgent. Finally, she could recognize the familiar baritone.

"Excuse me! Let me through, please. Excuse me!" the voice demanded with a mixture of confidence and urgency.

"Coming through!" Doug's tenor voice stated firmly.

"Here he comes. Move over. He's here," a woman's voice announced, followed by a chorus that repeated the instructions.

With one final push, Sam burst into the opening. His jacket was open and his cummerbund twisted from the effort of making a path through the crowd in the packed shop. Behind him followed the minister, whose vestments had also suffered from the walk from the shop's door. Doug, looking almost frantic and very apologetic, emerged as the crowd closed together again.

Straightening his vestments, the minister stepped
onto the platform and assumed the air of authority
and composure that all men of the cloth wear during wedding ceremonies. With his hands folded over
the Bible, he appeared strangely serene for a man
who had just fought his way through a crowd of people. Sam, however, did not appear as composed.

Looking worriedly at Brandi and gesturing with
open hands in a helpless manner, Sam tried to re-
arrange his clothing but only succeeded in making a
bigger mess. The bow tie that had been barely knotted now hung in two wrinkled strips down the front of
his shirt. His shirttails had escaped the waistband of
his trousers as he fought a losing battle with the cummerbund that unfastened and slipped to the floor. As
he and Doug bent to pick it up at the same instant,
they bumped heads loudly and appeared dazed and
confused. Neither could retie the bow tie or fasten the
troublesome cummerbund.

The guests who stood in front of the platform immediately burst into first embarrassed, then
full-throated laughter. Those who stood to the right
and left of the platform and had missed some of the
antics pressed closer for a better view and demanded to know the source of the entertainment.
Soon, everyone except the principals was laughing
uproariously.

Taking matters into her own hands, Mia handed
her bouquet to Susan, crossed in front of the be-
mused minister, and began reassembling the
bridegroom's attire. Her deft fingers had the bow tie
skillfully knotted and in its proper place and the
cummerbund fastened in rapid order. She quickly
adjusted the best man's clothing, too, kissed him

lightly on the cheek, and returned to her place to the left of the platform. From the lift of her eyebrows, Brandi could tell that Mia would have a few words for Doug as soon as she had him to herself. Something or someone had sabotaged her perfectly planned wedding, not something that happened often to Mia.

With the bridegroom, best man, and minister in place, the violinists, no longer shaking with laughter, began to play again. The laughter subsided to giggles and then to silence as the guests turned their attention to Brandi and Mr. Owens. Throughout the spectacle that Sam and Doug had made of themselves, the bride and her father had not moved an inch. During that time, Brandi had been hatching a little drama of her own. She did not want to be outdone by her tardy bridegroom.

Lifting her veil and motioning to the violinists for silence, Brandi turned to her father and asked in a clear voice, "Do you think I should marry this man? He arrives late, looks a mess, and can't even tie his own tie. Do I really want to marry this guy?"

Seeing the mischievous twinkle in Brandi's eyes, her father replied, "I don't know, daughter. I'm afraid that you'll have a lifetime of fixing him up if you do."

"Mother, what do you think?" Brandi asked, pulling Mrs. Owens into the action.

Knowing her daughter, Mrs. Owens replied from her position near the platform, "I can't advise you, dear. You'll have to decide for yourself if this is the life you really want."

Opening her arms to her friends and neighbors, Brandi said, "Friends, you've come to see a ceremony that will unite two people for the rest of their

lives. Considering the groom's entrance and un-
kempt appearance, I wonder if I should take this
serious step. What would you advise me to do?"

Brandi surveyed the crowd of friends that initially
looked uncertain about the role they should play.
They looked at each other, back at Brandi, and then
at Sam. A few of them smiled, but most appeared
confused.

To lighten their concern, Brandi said, "Give me a
sign. Should I marry Sam? If you don't tell me what
to do, I'll have to rebuild the wall between our
shops."

Looking from one to the other, the gathered guests
slowly started to chant. Their voices rose in unison
and volume as they made their preference known.
The poor suffering Sam, who was not able to read
Brandi's expression from that distance, felt lost and
helpless as the intensity increased.

"Marry him! Marry him! We came for a wedding!
It's too late to turn back now!" they sang.

"I guess that settles it. We might as well have a
wedding. I'll get to the bottom of this later. Let the
music play on!" Brandi called for all to hear, smiling
broadly and tugging her veil into position.

With that, the violinist again started to play the
wedding march. This time, Brandi and her father
did not stop but continued the trip toward the platform without a hitch. Beaming both love and
appreciation, Sam walked a few steps to meet them.
Dramatically, he bowed low and kissed her hand.
Without taking his eyes from Brandi's veiled face,
Sam backed to the platform and took his place beside Doug, who smiled broadly at the sight of his

friend humbling himself before his future bride. A murmur of satisfaction filled the shop.

Smiling sweetly, Brandi listened as the minister intoned the ancient rite of marriage. The warmth of Sam at her side was comforting as her father lovingly lifted her veil briefly to kiss her cheek, and placed her hand in Sam's. Handing her bouquet to Mia, Brandi allowed Sam to lead her up the steps and onto the platform.

Standing under the arch of fragrant flowers, Brandi felt overwhelmingly happy. Life looked so promising with Sam at her side. No obstacle that came her way could cause her to be unhappy now that she would forever have him as a companion and helpmate.

As the minister proclaimed them man and wife, the crowd erupted and a jazz band began to play over the cheering throng. Magically, waiters appeared from everywhere carrying trays of champagne flutes, cookies, shrimp, and little sandwiches. While Brandi, Sam, and the wedding party posed for photos on the platform, the caterer's staff set up tables complete with white damask tablecloths, twinkling stemware, crystal bowls containing long-stemmed white roses, and sparkling silverware. The transformation from chapel to reception hall occurred so seamlessly that no one was in the slightest bit inconvenienced as the setup took place around the celebrating guests.

By the time Brandi, Sam, and the wedding party had posed for an abundance of photographs, both professional and family, the guests had found their name cards and were awaiting the reception dinner. Mia, as always, had selected a menu that would appeal to everyone regardless, even the most

discriminating palate. Delicately sweet cream of
broccoli soup opened the meal, followed by spinach
salad with mushrooms, a selection of filet mignon or
roasted capon, heavenly baked potatoes, green
beans with pearl onions. Breads of every description
overflowed the baskets, accompanied by soft butter
in the shape of flowers.

In addition to wedding cake for dessert, Mia had
ordered an ice cream confection in the shape of a
book. It featured coffee as its main ingredient yet
was delicately laced with chocolate and raspberry.
Naturally, Sam's special blend, a favorite with all of
his customers, would flow constantly from the shining coffee urns that sat on discreetly placed serving
tables.

The laughter changed to the soft murmurs of appreciation and the clicking of silverware as the
guests relished every bite of the feast. At the head
table, Brandi and Sam exchanged happy smiles and
held animated conversation that neither would remember. The shiny gold bands on their left hands
signaled that they were new members of a very old
club.

Leaning her shoulder against Sam's, Brandi asked
playfully, "Now, exactly why were you late to our wedding?"

"You really had me worried. I was afraid you
wouldn't marry me because I was late. I'll explain
later. I'm really sorry. You know it's not like me to be
late for anything. I've never opened the shop late or
picked you up late. It was just one of those bizarre
happenings," Sam said, kissing Brandi lightly on the
lips.

Studying Sam with suspicion in her eyes, Brandi

said, "You know I can't stand not being in the loop. I'm a big girl. You can tell me."

Looking embarrassed and frustrated, Sam replied, "I must have gained weight since I ordered this tux. Living with you is a fattening proposition. I dropped my boutonniere. When I bent over to pick it up, my pants split. The seam just let go. I don't keep thread in the shop. Even if I did, I wouldn't have been able to find it with all of this stuff in the way. I had to go home to fix them."

"I didn't see you," Brandi said, struggling to keep her composure.

"I know." Sam sounded exasperated. "I waited until you had left and then I snuck behind the procession. I had to go blocks out of the way to keep you from seeing me. By the time I finished stitching the seam, you were standing at the shop's front door. I had to sneak into the back through all of that junk in the storeroom. I was fighting my way past the latest shipment of coffee when the music started."

"Were Doug and the minister with you?" Brandi asked, biting the inside of her cheek to stifle a laugh.

"No. I ran out of here so fast that I closed the door behind me. They were locked out. Rather than follow me through the streets and risk being seen, they waited in the alley."

"What a story!"

Looking offended, Sam stated, "If you don't believe me, you can ask Doug or the minister, but every word is true."

"Oh, sweetheart, I believe you." Tears of laughter sparkled on Brandi's lashes. "You'll have to tell this one at our fiftieth anniversary party."

"It's your fault, you know. You're a good cook, and

I've been eating too much since we've been together. When we return from our honeymoon, I'm
going to start working out again."

"I'll just have to fill that 'honey-do' jar to keep you
busy. By the way, you still haven't told me where
we're going on our honeymoon." Brandi dabbed at
the last of the tears.

"No. You laughed at my suffering. You'll just have
to wait," Sam teased as he turned his attention to the
sumptuous meal.

"Oh, but Sam . . ." Brandi begged.

"Begging and pleading will have no affect on me,
Mrs. Carlson. I'm a hardened man," Sam teased.

"Mrs. Carlson. I like the sound of that." Brandi
sighed, resting her hand on his.

"I do, too. Even if I did look like a flasher with my
white underwear showing through the rip in my
pants, I would do it again to be with you." Sam held
the offered hand tightly and kissed her lightly.

"Ahem! There'll be plenty of time for that later,"
Mia interrupted. "It's time to cut the cake."

Armed with the knowledge that nothing could
top Sam's adventure, the bride and groom rose to
the challenge of feeding each other slices of a wedding cake that was truly too beautiful to cut.
Ribbons, butterflies, and hummingbirds fluttered
among the marzipan roses that cascaded from the
groom's cake at the top tier.

Leaning toward her new husband, Brandi com-
manded, "Open wide!"

Sam, despite his resolution to lose weight, obliged
but not wide enough. Fragments of the rich rum-
laced cake tumbled onto the floor at his feet. His
effort to feed Brandi was even more entertaining as

he succeeded in adding icing to the makeup that covered her cheeks.

"Oops!" Sam laughed, licking the icing from his finger and handing Brandi a napkin.

"What a mess!" Brandi laughed. "You missed worse than I did. We definitely don't look like the perfect wedding couple."

"We have a lifetime to gain perfection," Sam said.

In front of their friends, Sam held Brandi close and kissed her gently. Strangely, Brandi did not care who saw them. She belonged in Sam's arms forever.

"Break it up, you two. Everyone's watching," Doug whispered.

Reluctantly releasing his bride, Sam said, "If I must, but only for a short time."

Their guests laughed happily and then turned their attention to the rich desserts as wine and coffee flowed freely, bringing the feast to a fitting close. With the exception of Sam's tardiness, the wedding had progressed just as Mia had planned. Besides, a few hitches only made for more perfect memories.

Ringing a little dinner bell that Mia considered more refined than tapping a knife on a crystal wineglass, Doug stood and called everyone to attention. The meal had been excellent, and now it was time for the toast that would lead to the first dance. Mia had made him practice the speech so many times that he could deliver it in his sleep.

Raising his glass, Doug said, "Ladies and gentlemen, we have gathered here today to witness the marriage of our friends, Brandi and Sam. We've watched their growing affection over six slow years during which we knew the outcome but they didn't. We've waited with bated breath as Sam summoned

the courage to do more than buy a copy of the
paper and fill her order for hot chocolate. We observed his painstakingly slow courtship of the
woman for whom he has been pining for years. And
we painfully watched his repeated attempts at breaking the ice and wished that we could give him a push
or at least a kick in the pants.

"Despite his slow start, we saw their commitment
to each other grow even in the face of competition,
both financial and personal. We observed their
steadfast love as they rebuilt the businesses that had
brought them together. We watched them take their
vows and spill cake on each other.

"Now it is time to wish them happiness, health,
and wealth. They truly prove that there is a pot of
gold over the rainbow where people from different
worlds can meet and fall in love. So, let's raise our
glasses and toast the happy couple. To Brandi and
Sam, may your life together be filled with all the
happiness that the rainbow has to offer."

Following the loud chorus of cheers, Mia stood
and raised her glass. Clearing her throat, she began
by saying, "Dear friends, I have known Brandi for a
lifetime. We have shared laughter and tears, dreams,
and ambitions. However, until she practically fell
over Sam, I had not been able to interest her in mat-
rimony, despite having introduced her to an
overwhelming collection of single, handsome, black
men. She turned down attorneys, physicians, sur-
geons, and elected officials. She refused to date
athletes and celebrities, choosing instead to nurture
her shop while waiting for the right man to come
her way.

"However, when she discovered Sam on the other

side of her cup of cocoa, Brandi dedicated herself to landing him with the same energy that she applied to making Over the Rainbow a smashing success. Sam never stood a chance.

"Just as she inventoried every book and scrap of paper that entered the shop, Brandi catalogued everything about Sam, every smile, every laugh, and every word spoken between them. She applied every lesson in the mantrap book, and he willingly allowed her to reel him in.

"Well, today Brandi and Sam have become husband and wife. Their love has survived many obstacles, making me know that it's the real deal. So, let's toast their marriage and wish them a long life filled with happiness and laughter."

As the cheering ended, the jazz band struck up a waltz. Without hesitation, Sam took his bride by the hand and led Brandi onto the small clearing that would serve as a dance floor. Pulling her into his arms, he gracefully executed the ancient dance steps as everyone watched and applauded.

"You're a man of many talents, Sam Carlson. I had no idea that you could dance, and so well," Brandi said as she kissed his chin and lips.

"Don't talk to me; I'm counting," Sam ordered. "I only learned to do this last week."

"Oh, Sam, that's so sweet!" Brandi gushed, kissing him on the cheek. "You learned to dance for our wedding."

Looking at the nearby dancers and replying sternly, Sam said, "Hush! I don't want everyone to know! I did it out of love for you. I wouldn't have done it for any other reason. Dancing's not my thing. Besides, if you keep doing that, I won't be able to dance or walk either. You don't want everyone here to know the thoughts that are on my mind at this moment, do you?"

"No," Brandi replied slowly as she ran her fingers along the tender skin above his collar, "but I'm reading you loud and clear."

Chuckling thickly, Sam said, "I hope all this frontal pressure won't make my pants rip again. I didn't sew them that well."

"If they do, we'll have to go home immediately. I wouldn't mind if you took them off," Brandi cooed. "Ouch! You stepped on my toe!"

"Sorry, but I told you not to say things like that; you distracted me. I'm not very good at this," Sam apologized as they stood together on the dance floor.

She held his serious face in both of her hands. "You're terrific at everything that really matters. I've never been happier in my life. Not even the success of my shop made me feel this good inside. I love you, Sam, forever and always."

"That's a long time. Do you really think you'll be able to stand me for that long?" Sam asked, pulling her close.

"Oh yes. I can't think of anyone I'd rather stand up or lie down with," Brandi replied with a wink.

Dancing near them, Mia said, "Sorry to break up this little picture, but it's time for you to leave. You don't want to miss your flight."

"I don't? I don't even know where I'm going." Brandi grinned.

"And you'll never get there if you don't leave now," Doug insisted.

"Gather around, everyone. Brandi's going to

throw her bouquet," Mia announced, motioning to the band.

Laughing, Brandi and Sam eased toward the door followed by all the unmarried women in the room. A dramatic drumroll signaled the momentous event. Lofting the flowers high, Brandi momentarily watched as it fell earthward into Susan's hands. She did not have to wonder who Susan might marry. . . . Neither did Brad, who hugged her close.

Instead of rice, the guests threw rose petals as Brandi and Sam rushed into the sweet night air. This time, no violins or crowds greeted them as they trotted through the silent streets. They were a married couple needing no fanfare.

Reaching the house, they stopped on the sidewalk as two figures walked from the porch to greet them. Instinctively concerned for his wife's safety, Sam stepped in front of Brandi. Their breathing quickened in the dark night. They breathed a sigh of relief when they heard a familiar voice call a greeting.

"Best wishes, guys. I hope your life together will be filled with happiness and laughter," Kevin shouted.

"Best wishes," the shorter person echoed.

"Why didn't you come to the wedding?" Brandi demanded, studying Kevin's face.

"He didn't think that I'd be welcome," Ally answered, stepping from the shadow.

Shaking her head, Brandi stated, "No, it would have been just fine. That's the past; it's behind us now. I'm sure there's plenty of food left if you'd like to take a plate home. At the very least, you should get some cake."

"Then you've forgiven me?" Ally asked tearfully.

Taking her outstretched hands, Brandi said, "Ally, I was hurt, angry, and disappointed, but I'm over it now. Look at the good that came of it. Your intrusion into my life forced two people to stop hiding in their shops. I'm married to the most wonderful man. I can't hold a grudge when everything turned out so well."

Ally sobbed softly in the dark night as Kevin held her close. Looking over the top of her head, he said, "Thanks, Brandi. It means a lot to me as your neighbor and friend that you've forgiven my wife."

"Your wife!" Sam exclaimed.

"We were married this morning," Kevin stated. "I guess I've always loved her, but I was confused for a while by the glow of a very warm star. At any rate, I offered her comfort when the neighborhood turned on her. One thing led to the other, and we decided to make our relationship permanent this time."

Sniffling, Ally added, "Kevin saved me from a very lonely life. I owe him so much and love him even more."

"That's great!" Brandi said. "I hope you two will be forever happy."

"We will," Ally and Kevin said together as he added, "I'll see you guys after we all return from our honeymoons."

Looking at Ally in the darkness, Brandi asked, "Did Kevin tell you where you're going?"

"No, I couldn't even get a hint from him," Ally replied.

"Me either. I guess we'll both have to wait," Brandi said.

"If we don't get changed and on the road, we'll miss our flight. You won't need to wonder where we're going. See you two in a couple of weeks," Sam said, pulling Brandi toward the front steps.

The house, so lonely when Brandi had left it that afternoon, now felt full to bursting with Sam's return. Stopping only long enough to feed the cat, they rushed upstairs and undressed. If they hurried, they would still make the required check-in time at the airport.

"Need help?" Sam offered suggestively.

"No, thanks. Your kind of help only slows down the progress." Brandi laughed as her head popped through the neck of her T-shirt.

"I'll help you take it off in the hotel. Off is more fun than on anyway." Sam chuckled, grabbing the bags.

"You still haven't told me where we're going," Brandi reminded him as she grabbed her purse.

Sam laughed. "I thought you told me that you'd follow me anywhere?"

"I will, but I want to know where I'm going!" Brandi insisted as Sam steered the car into the quiet street.

"We're going over the rainbow where worlds meet," Sam replied, chuckling.

"Where?" Brandi turned to study his face in the streetlight.

"You heard me." Sam laughed again.

Leaning back, Brandi said, "Since I know we're not spending our honeymoon in the shop, that wasn't much of a clue."

"You'll have to wait until we arrive at the airport for more," Sam said as they sped up on the highway.

Brandi sighed and relaxed. She still did not know where they would spend their honeymoon, and she really did not care. She was with Sam, and they were happy. As far as Brandi was concerned, she had already found the pot of gold at the end of the rainbow in Sam's love.

About the Author

Born in Washington, D.C., Courtni Wright graduated from Trinity College (D.C.) in 1972 with a major in English and a minor in History. In 1980, she earned a Master of Education degree from Johns Hopkins University in Baltimore, Maryland. She was a Council for Basic Education National Endowment for the Humanities Fellow in 1990. She has served as consultant on National Geographic Society educational films on the practice and history of Kwanzaa, the history of the black cowboys, the story of Harriet Tubman, and the African American heritage in the West.

Ms. Wright's writing career covers multiple genres. Her first romance novel entitled BLUSH was published under the Arabesque imprint in September of 1997. Since then, eleven other titles have followed. Holiday House published her children's books, JUMPING THE BROOM, selected for the Society of School Librarians International list of "Best Books of 1994"; JOURNEY TO FREEDOM, named a "Teacher's Choice" book by the International Reading Association; and WAGON TRAIN, an acclaimed favorite. Her venture into Shakespearean analysis entitled THE WOMEN OF SHAKESPEARE'S PLAYS was published by University Press of America.

She lives in Maryland with her husband, two Pomeranians, and a cat. She is the proud mother of a naval officer stationed aboard a submarine.

The Arabesque At Your Service Series

Four superb romances with engaging characters and dynamic story lines featuring heroes whose destiny is intertwined with women of equal courage who confront their passionate—and unpredictable—futures.

__TOP-SECRET RENDEZVOUS – *Air Force*

by Linda Hudson-Smith   1-58314-397-1 $6.99US/$9.99CAN

Sparks fly when officer Hailey Douglas meets Air Force Major Zurich Kingdom. Military code forbids fraternization between an officer and an NCO, so the pair find themselves involved in a top-secret rendezvous.

__COURAGE UNDER FIRE – *Army*

by Candice Poarch   1-58314-350-5 $6.99US/$9.99CAN

Nurse Arlene Taft is assigned to care for the seriously injured Colonel Neal Allen. She remembers him as an obnoxious young neighbor at her father's military base, but now he looks nothing like she remembers. Will time give them courage under fire?

__THE GLORY OF LOVE – *Navy*

by Kim Louise   1-58314-411-0 $6.99US/$9.99CAN

When pilot Roxanne Allgood is kidnapped, Navy Seal Col. Haughton Storm sets out on a mission to find the only person who has ever mattered to him—a lost love he hasn't seen in ten years.

__FLYING HIGH – *Marines*

by Gwynne Forster   1-58314-427-7 $6.99US/$9.99CAN

Colonel Nelson Wainwright must recover from his injuries if he is to attain his goal of becoming a four-star general. Audrey Powers, a specialist in sports medicine, enters his world to get him back on track. Will their love find a way to endure his rise to the top?

Now Available in Bookstores!

Visit our website at **www.arabesquebooks.com.**

Arabesque Romances
by *Roberta Gayle*